T0196848

Buried by the Sea

Mysteries by Kathleen Bridge

The By the Sea Mysteries
Death by the Sea
A Killing by the Sea
Murder by the Sea
Evil by the Sea
Buried by the Sea

The Hamptons Home and Garden Mysteries
Better Home and Corpses
Hearse and Gardens
Ghostal Living
Manor of Dying
A Design to Die For

Buried by the Sea

A By the Sea Mystery

Kathleen Bridge

LYRICAL UNDERGROUND
Kensington Publishing Corp.
www.kensingtonbooks.com

LYRICAL UNDERGROUND BOOKS are published by

Kensington Publishing Corp.
119 West 40th Street
New York, NY 10018

All Kensington titles, imprints, and distributed lines are available at special quantity discounts for bulk purchases for sales promotion, premiums, fund-raising, educational, or institutional use.

Special book excerpts or customized printings can also be created to fit specific needs. For details, write or phone the office of the Kensington Sales Manager: Kensington Publishing Corp., 119 West 40th Street, New York, NY 10018. Attn. Sales Department. Phone: 1-800-221-2647.

Lyrical Underground and Lyrical Underground logo Reg. US Pat. & TM Off.

First Electronic Edition: April 2021
eISBN-13: 978-1-5161-1002-5
eISBN-10: 1-5161-1002-1

First Print Edition: April 2021
ISBN-13: 978-1-5161-1004-9
ISBN-10: 1-5161-1004-8

Printed in the United States of America

I dedicate this book to Debra "Debbie" Barry, my childhood best friend. Thank you for all the magical times we spent together as children: sleepovers; playing Barbies, Kick the Can, and board games; reading Nancy Drews side by side and watching many of the television shows mentioned in my By the Sea series, including Dark Shadows. *(And, yes, I'm still traumatized by the Emmett Kelly clown picture with the moving eyes that hung on the wall in your basement when we had seances and worked the Ouija board!) Thanks, Deb, for the memories...XO, Kathy*

Acknowledgments

I would like to thank John de Bry, PhD, FAC, who is the director of Florida's Center for Historical Archeology in Melbourne Beach (www. historicalarchaeology.org), for taking the time to answer my questions about archeology as it relates to the Treasure and Space Coasts of Florida, along with specific questions about Juan Ponce de León's landing in Melbourne Beach. As always, I am forever grateful to my wonderful agent, Dawn Dowdle at Blue Ridge Literary Agency, and to my editor Liz May and everyone at Kensington/Lyrical Press. And to my family and friends who are so understanding when I must disappear into my writing cave—your support means everything. And of course, to all the bloggers and my loyal readers in the Cozy Mystery Community for your continued support—I am forever grateful.

Indialantic by the Sea regulars who live on the grounds or in the hotel

Liz (Elizabeth) Amelia Holt, writer
Aunt Amelia Eden Holt – Liz's great-aunt, 1960s television character actress
Fenton Holt – Liz's attorney father and Aunt Amelia's nephew
Ryan Stone – Liz's boyfriend, private investigator
Chef Pierre Montague – Indialantic's chef
Betty Lawson – teenage-mystery writer
Captain Clyde B. Netherton – skipper of the Indialantic's sightseeing cruiser
Susannah Shay – assistant hotel manager

Pets
Barnacle Bob – Aunt Amelia's macaw
Carmen Miranda – Aunt Amelia's new macaw rescue
Caro (Carolyn Keene) – Betty's black-and-white cat
Killer – Captain Netherton's black-and-white Great Dane
Venus – Greta's sphinx cat
Bronte – Liz's gray-and-white cat
Blackbeard – Ryan's mixed-breed rescue

Indialantic by the Sea Shopkeepers
Kate Fields – Owner of Books & Browsery by the Sea and Liz's best friend
Pops Stone – Owner of Deli-casies by the Sea and Ryan's grandfather
Minna Presley – Co-owner of Home Arts by the Sea, mixed-media artist
Francie Jenkins – Co-owner of Home Arts by the Sea, expert seamstress
Ziggy Clemens – Aunt Amelia's boyfriend and owner of the Melbourne Beach Theatre Company, former owner of Zig's Surf Shop by the Sea, which is now the home of The Amelia Eden Holt School of Acting by the Sea
Brittany Poole – Owner of Sirens by the Sea, women's clothing and jewelry shop

You take away the loose earth, and you scrape here and there with a knife until finally your object is there, all alone, ready to be drawn and photographed with no extraneous matter confusing it. That is what I have been seeking to do—clear away the extraneous matter so that we can see the truth—the naked shining truth.
—Agatha Christie

Chapter 1

Aunt Amelia tapped a long stick with a pointed rubber tip against the seventy-inch flat-screen TV. "Children, children, listen up." Using the remote in her other hand, she pressed Play. "This is especially important, and something every actor needs to pay attention to. Even though the camera is centered on Jonathan Frid, can you catch the nuanced way in which I enter the room?" Tap. Tap. Tap. "Can you see how the focus shifts immediately from him to me? That's what makes a good actor. So many clues are given in just this short scene. Like, what could possibly be in the glass I am carrying on the silver tray? Am I afraid of the person sitting in the wing chair? Everything can be answered by viewing my expression and the fluidity of my movements."

She aimed the remote and paused on a close-up of herself, a young, twentysomething Amelia Eden Holt. "On a side note," she said, grinning through fuchsia lips that glowed neon in the darkened space, "how fabulous did hair and makeup do in that shot? They made me look ten years older than I was. A lot different from when I played the sixteen-year-old cousin of Billie Jo, Bobbie Jo, and Betty Jo on *Petticoat Junction*. The hardest part of the episode was keeping track of which Jo was which." Aunt Amelia giggled. The others in the room just looked confused. One of the girls yawned. If Aunt Amelia heard her, she pretended not to, then she played the next scene in s-l-o-w-w motion. "There!" Tap, tap with her stick. "When I placed the tray with the glass of claret on the table, did anyone catch the tremor in my hand? Is that a foreshadowing of what's to come in the next frame? It just might be." She froze the screen.

Liz twirled her left hand in the air, giving her eighty-year-old great-aunt the wrap-it-up sign from the back of the room. Aunt Amelia glanced her way, then continued with her presentation.

The scene in TV's *Dark Shadows* was one Liz had watched numerous times in the Indialantic by the Sea Hotel's screening room. It ran only two minutes, but with her great-aunt's long commentary it seemed like twenty. It was a good thing the girls were ordered to leave their cell phones in the plastic bin by the studio door, giving them no choice but to pay attention. No one, not even her thespian great-aunt, could compete with that kind of distraction.

"Now," Aunt Amelia continued, excitement catching in her voice, "even though my face is offscreen and I'm standing behind Jonathan as he reaches out his pale, bony hand, sporting the Collins family crest gold ring, you can still feel my presence. I am there. Waiting for the exact right moment to deliver my line. But first, I must wait until he tastes the claret. That's a particularly important acting tip. Never rush a scene. And of course, don't overshadow your fellow actors, especially when doing live television broadcasts. We were ahead of our time, I tell you. What a long day it made. But we saw the results in our paychecks and our huge fan base." Aunt Amelia chuckled, then pointed her stick at the screen. All that could be seen peeking out from behind a wing chair was a headless figure wearing a black cotton dress and white French maid's pinafore, a pair of shapely legs, and black-laced shoes. "Okay, get ready for it," Aunt Amelia said, pressing the remote. "Jonathan is tasting the claret. There! He just put down the glass. Now, listen carefully to my line. *Will there be anything else, Mr. Collins?*" Aunt Amelia leaned the stick against the podium, placed the TV remote on top, then clapped her hands. Looking expectantly at her audience, which consisted of eight tween-aged females, she asked, "Did you catch it, ladies? The tremble in my voice?"

A ponytailed brunette wearing glasses and braces asked, "Miss Amelia, why are his teeth so pointy? And what is that gooey stuff that looks like Hershey's chocolate syrup dribbling down his chin and onto his girly lace blouse? Is he sick?"

"Oh, he's not ill, dear Melissa. Since this early episode was filmed in black and white, I think our director wanted to make our viewers imagine that the ruby-red claret might have been blood. Because that's what—"

"He's a vampire?" one of the girls in the front row asked excitedly.

"Oh yes! Barnabas Collins was a wonderful vampire. The part of a lifetime. Our show, *Dark Shadows*, set the bar for what a well-layered vampire should be. We had werewolves and witches too. Very avant-garde for our time."

Sitting next to the brunette, a tall, skinny blonde with perfect posture said, "I think the guy's creepy looking. Nothing like Edward from the *Twilight* movies. So-o-o old school. I think this prehistoric soap opera is what my old acting coach would call *campy*." She got up dramatically and headed for the door. Looking down at the large, square-faced watch on her thin wrist, she addressed the girls, not Aunt Amelia. "Just got a text from my agency about another commercial. Catch ya later." Obviously, the young prima donna hadn't needed a cell phone to connect to cyberspace. She grabbed her cell from the bucket, and as she passed Liz, the girl pointed to the four-inch scar on Liz's cheek. "Is that for a part? Needs to look more realistic if it is."

Before Liz could answer that the scar was indeed the real thing, the girl breezed out the door. It seemed Aunt Amelia had met her match. Not that Liz was complaining. This might be one venture that would truly keep her great-aunt out of harm's way, especially after the last disastrous event she'd spearheaded to keep the Holt family-run hotel and emporium financially solvent: a wedding gone wrong—dead wrong. The Amelia Eden Holt School of Acting seemed a safer bet. Another plus: between the acting school and her great-aunt's time at the Melbourne Beach Theatre Company, she would be too busy to interfere with the guests staying at the hotel.

With her father and Charlotte off on their European wedding and honeymoon, and assistant hotel manager Susannah Shay away at a two-week family reunion, Liz had promised to take care of her great-aunt and help with the running of the Indialantic by the Sea Hotel and Emporium. Fortunately, Liz was between books. Her most recent book, *An American in Cornwall*, was scheduled to come out in the fall. She had a few weeks before she had to deliver a synopsis for her next book, which would be the third in the trilogy. The first novel took place during World War I, the second during World War II, and the yet-to-be-written novel, in modern day. The only link between the three was that they all took place at the same castle in Cornwall, England.

So far, things were easy, breezy with the guests. She hoped it would stay that way. The group of archeologists who'd been staying at the hotel for the past week had been low maintenance. Breakfast and dinner were served buffet-style in the hotel's dining room. For lunch, the hotel's resident chef made bagged meals worthy of a three-star Michelin restaurant for the group to take with them to their dig site, which was located at the adjoining property to the Indialantic.

The team had come to find further proof that Spanish explorer Juan Ponce de León had first landed in Melbourne Beach, Florida, not St. Augustine, as many had thought for decades. The junglelike Bennett property next door—the only unexplored six acres on the barrier island that wasn't part of the National Park Service—had seemed the best place to start.

There had been one thing involving the group that had caused Liz a modicum of worry. This morning, she'd overheard a heated argument between Dr. Nigel Crawford and his wife Dr. Haven Smith-Crawford. Something about the Mrs. flirting with someone and an astronomical credit card bill. They'd been booked in the hotel's best suite, the Oceana Suite, and Liz knew from helping the hotel's housekeeper Greta clean the suite that the Crawfords didn't share a bed. Dr. Nigel slept on the open pullout sofa in the sitting room and Dr. Haven in the bedroom. Their voices had been heated, each berating the other. A pair of excellent marksmen with their zingers, both going for the jugular. No one was the winner because they seemed evenly matched—like the couple in the movie *The War of the Roses*—only on steroids. Then, half an hour later when Liz passed them in the hallway, their frowns had turned upside down and they'd acted like a couple of lovebirds.

Based on all the past troubles, including a few murder investigations that the Holt family had gone through since Liz moved back from Manhattan, she couldn't help but be overly cautious when it came to the Indialantic's guests. But she was determined to mind her own business, and thanked her lucky stars that she and Ryan were in a deep, loving relationship. He was definitely *the one*. The relationship she'd had before Ryan had been a colossal mistake. At the thought of Travis, she instinctively traced the scar on her cheek. It had taken time, but she'd forgiven him for his part in the accident. Travis had been drunk and out of his mind. It was amazing the feeling of peace she had now. All thanks to a good therapist and twelve-step meetings aimed at helping people impacted by the alcohol and drug problems of others. She'd learned you can't change anyone, only yourself. Who knew forgiving could bring such peace. *Too bad Travis had never found any*, she thought.

Aunt Amelia tapped her stick at the screen, which now showed a close-up of actress Barbara Eden, the star of the sixties sitcom *I Dream of Jeannie*. She was telling the girls about how it felt to be on set with the actor Larry Hagman, who played Major Anthony Nelson and later went on to star in *Dallas*. "Who shot J.R.?" Aunt Amelia said, adding a belly laugh.

A roomful of blank faces looked back at her. Maybe her great-aunt should have enrolled only baby boomers, instead of babies. But she didn't give up. "Now, let's move on to this scene of mine on the musical television show *The Monkees*. And no, girls, they aren't the Beatles, but in my opinion, a close second."

That was stretching it, Liz thought.

More yawns from the girls. Liz tried to think of a way to keep the kids' parents from asking for their money back. She raised her hand and said, "Miss Amelia, didn't they do a *Dark Shadows* movie starring Johnny Depp?"

That was the ticket. The conversation did a one-eighty back to vampires and other creatures of the night.

Liz exhaled in relief when Betty walked into the acting studio. Not only was she happy to see Betty because of the distraction, but she knew of all of them, Betty was best at wrangling midcentury television character actress Amelia Eden Holt into the twenty-first century.

Out of breath, Betty slid into the chair next to Liz and whispered, "How's the first class going? And where are all the boys?"

"Girls only. I thought she'd lost them, but once the words 'vampire' and 'werewolf' were mentioned, they seemed to perk up."

"I'm sure at the end of the session Amelia will be able to give out a trophy to the student who's able to name every sixties television show she starred in."

"Don't forget all the commercials," Liz added. "Thank God Barnacle Bob's not here. He'd be singing all of Auntie's midcentury jingles."

"Where's the bratty macaw?"

"Taking a time-out in the elevator. Apparently, he's not getting along with Aunt Amelia's flamboyant new rescue macaw, Carmen Miranda. Or I should say, she wants nothing to do with him."

"Thought macaws mated for life," Betty said.

"I have a feeling Carmen might have already mated for life. We know nothing of her past. She was just another macaw left at the doorstep of the Melbourne Avian Rescue Shelter. BB might be out of luck in the romance department. Not that he doesn't keep trying."

Betty unwound a turquoise silk scarf from around her neck, draped it on the chair next to her, then reached into her handbag and took out a bottle of water. After removing the cap, she chugged the whole thing. Beads of sweat bubbled near her hairline. Liz had never seen eighty-three-year-old Betty Lawson, teenage-mystery writer and year-round Indialantic Hotel resident, sweat. Then again, it was sunny and ninety-five outside. Not unusual island weather for the end of August. "You okay? I don't think in all the years I've known you that I've seen you perspire."

Betty laughed. "That's because I'm usually smart enough to stay inside in the middle of the day, only going out in the early morning or evening. I was at the dig site. It's getting quite exciting over there."

Betty's cheeks pinked, and Liz didn't think it was from the heat. Glancing at Betty's sleeveless white sheath dress, she said, "Well, I'll be, Betty Lawson. You're all dressed up. Is this to impress your old archeologist boyfriend?"

"Walter is not an old boyfriend. Well, he was. Kind of. But we only dated for a short time. After he introduced me to my future husband there was no going back. Best decision I ever made."

"From what you've told me about your happy marriage, I'm sure it was. But maybe it's time to rekindle things with Professor Talbot. After all, it was you who suggested that the group stay at the Indialantic."

"As a favor to Amelia after he called me. No. That ship has sailed. Walter and I have barely kept in touch over the past fifty-some years."

"Plus, you have our illustrious Captain Clyde B. Netherton at your beck and call," Liz added. "I think he's jealous of Professor Talbot; I saw him staring at the two of you at dinner last night."

"It'll be good for him," Betty said with a twinkle in her alert gray eyes. "Plus, Clyde is the biggest flirt on the Atlantic coast."

"Used to be. Until you finally reeled him in."

"I did no such thing!"

Liz couldn't read her. Betty had the best poker face on the planet. She'd known Betty most of her life, and Betty still refused to disclose which five Nancy Drew books she'd ghostwritten in the 1960s under the pseudonym of Carolyn Keene.

"Quiet in the back," Aunt Amelia called out.

"Sorry. My bad," Liz said. She wasn't that frightened of the woman at the front of the room even if she was carrying a big stick. Her great-aunt had been like a mother to her, taking the place of her own mother who'd passed away when Liz was five.

"Oh, Betty, is that you?" Aunt Amelia cooed, stepping toward them. "I'm so glad you stopped by. Please stand up. I'd love the girls to meet you. Ms. Lawson's new Sherlock Holmes London Chimney Sweep Mysteries has been optioned to become a prime-channel television series, and Ms. Lawson deserves a round of applause." Aunt Amelia clapped her hands and the seven girls joined in. "Bravo, Betty. Bravo!" Aunt Amelia cheered.

Before standing up, Betty whispered to Liz, "I live at the Indialantic. I didn't stop by. I was more like ordered to make an appearance by Dame Holt."

"Please, Betty," Aunt Amelia cajoled, reaching out her bejeweled fingers, which sported long acrylic nails in her signature shade of dragon red and were adorned with an assortment of oversize rings. Instead of wearing her fiery orange hair on the top of her head in large soup-can curls, her great-aunt had tried for a stern schoolteacher's bun. Which would have been fine if she'd toned down her pearlescent baby-blue eye shadow, black winged eyeliner, and oversize stenciled eyebrows. Aunt Amelia usually wore jewel-toned, diaphanous boho-style caftans, but today she had on a black leotard, a transparent black organza side-tie skirt, and black tap shoes. She looked ready to perform a dance scene from Bob Fosse's *All That Jazz*. Who was Liz fooling; she was sure her great-aunt would break out in song and dance at some point. It was just a matter of time.

"Betty, I mean Ms. Lawson, I'd like you to meet my class." Aunt Amelia grabbed Betty's wrist and pulled her to the front of the studio. Putting her arm around Betty's thin shoulders, she said, "Ms. Lawson, if these young ladies work real-ly, real-ly hard at their craft, maybe in the near future they might win a role on your series." Aunt Amelia was no dummy, dangling the fame-and-fortune carrot in front of her teenage protégées. "As part of your tuition, girls, Ms. Lawson has kindly offered to give each of you a copy of *The Insensible Equation*, the first in her series."

Betty fielded questions from the girls: like who was going to play the lead character in the series, and how wonderful it would be if the girl chimney-sweep character, who dressed like a boy and helped Sherlock Holmes solve small cases, could be an unknown like one of them.

"It's not beyond the realm of possibility. Right, Ms. Lawson?" Aunt Amelia elbowed Betty.

Betty elbowed her back and said, "Just because my books have been optioned for the screen doesn't mean they'll make it past the pilot episode. And I don't think I'll have a say when it comes to casting. Plus, they'll be filming in England."

"Pshaw!" Aunt Amelia said, shaking her head. "You're being too modest. I'm sure you'll have full control. After all, it is your work. From your own very own imagination, right, girls? I think it's *very* safe to say that if one of these young ladies plays their cards right, they might have a chance to be at least a street urchin with a few key lines. Don't you think, Ms. Lawson?" Again, she elbowed Betty, only this time in the ribs.

"Oh, just think, Miss Amelia!" Melissa said, her eyes as big as her adoration. "Maybe I'll be discovered, just like you were!"

"Yes. I was lucky, and you might be too." Aunt Amelia winked at Betty, and a section of her false eyelashes on her right eye came unglued and took flight, then landed. In a deft motion, Aunt Amelia peeled it off her cheek and stuck it back in place. No one but Liz was the wiser. Then, not missing a beat, Aunt Amelia took a few steps away from Betty and threw her arms out theatrically. "There are so many stories about famous actors who started out as nobodies. John Wayne was one. Did you know his real name was Marion Morrison? Why, he—"

Betty interrupted Aunt Amelia, no doubt reading the girls' clueless faces. "And Stefani Germanotta is Lady Gaga's real name." Leave it to Betty to keep up with the times. Maybe it had something to do with her expertise in cybersleuthing and knowledge of anything of an IT nature. Aunt Amelia was still learning how to text.

Liz decided now would be the perfect time to sneak out and check on things at the hotel. If everything was status quo, she planned to investigate how the archeologists were doing at the dig site. She grabbed her handbag and headed to the door, swiped her cell from the bucket, and stepped into the emporium's hallway.

She was afraid to look back, knowing Betty would probably be shooting her the evil eye for abandoning her.

Every woman for herself.

Especially when it came to her great-aunt.

Chapter 2

Everything was quiet at the hotel. Liz breathed a sigh of relief, grabbed her hat, and hurried out the lobby's revolving door, wanting to see if there were any new developments at the dig site. With the rich history attributed to their barrier island, anything was possible. The team had the potential to unearth something from sixteenth-century Spanish explorers like Ponce de León, or maybe they would find a shard of pottery or canoe from the Native American Ais tribe, like a member of the historical society had found last fall.

There was also the possibility of finding an artifact, or better yet, treasure from the Spanish fleet that had sunk nearby. Liz and every other child who'd grown up in Melbourne Beach and Vero Beach knew the story. In 1715, an entire fleet of Spanish ships carrying gold, silver, and decorative pottery sank in a storm off the Sebastian Inlet. Then, in the mid-1950s, a hurricane hit the area, exposing the remains of a survivors' camp. Soon after, a large cache of treasure was discovered. To this day, usually after a hurricane or storm, salvagers could be seen foraging for odd pieces on the barrier island's beaches, items washed ashore from *El Capitana* and other lost-at-sea ships. Treasure hunting on the beach was one of Liz's and her great-aunt's favorite pastimes. Finders keepers if they found a gold or silver Spanish coin onshore. If something was found offshore, it would be a fifty-fifty split between the state of Florida and the salvage crew who'd secured the license to excavate the shipwreck.

Dr. Nigel Crawford told Liz his first night at the hotel that the team of archeologists wasn't here to uncover any treasure from the 1715 fleet (although she was sure it would be an added perk if they did find some), they'd come to find unequivocal proof that Juan Ponce de León had landed on the shores of Melbourne Beach, not St. Augustine, as many scientists had thought for decades; he told her of a Colonel Douglas T. Peck, who'd done a reenactment of Ponce de León's voyage. Peck used modern-day technical equipment, wind and current charts, and detailed notes from Ponce de León's ship's log to determine that Ponce de León had landed in Melbourne Beach. Soon after, a large statue was forged of Ponce de León, which now stood a few miles up the road at the public beach aptly named Ponce de Leon Landing Park.

Liz took the hotel's southern shell-and-gravel path leading to the only landlocked entrance to the Bennett property. She was thankful she'd grabbed her straw hat to protect her scar from the blistering sun, but wished she'd also brought an insulated water bottle. With the temperature in the low nineties, adding ten degrees for the heat index put it at over a hundred. Typical for August. Seeing she'd lived on the island almost seventeen of her twenty-eight years, she shouldn't have been surprised. But she had to hand it to the archeologists to be working all day in these conditions. Then she remembered the team had just returned from the tropical rain forest in Brazil—another steamy environment—so they were probably acclimated to the excessive heat.

Liz quickened her pace, remembering Betty's words earlier that things were heating up at the dig site. The archeologists had put in long hours during their first week on the island, but so far, no great discoveries relating to Ponce de León's landing. The professor had told her that a piece of metal from a Spanish conquistador's helmet or breastplate would the their best find, but they would even settle for a sixteenth-century shard of pottery, a button from a conquistador's uniform, or even an arrow point from a forged Spanish spear.

Last week, Aunt Amelia and Liz had come to visit Birdman, the owner of the property. On their way to his cottage, Liz had asked, "What's the story again about the Bennetts?"

That's all it took; Aunt Amelia was off to the races. "From what my mother told me about the old house," she said softly, looking in the distance like it was another decade, "Birdy's grandfather originally planned to use this land and more acres to the south to start pineapple groves. Back in the 1880s, there weren't any bridges from the mainland. Each day Birdy's grandfather and his workers would have to take a boat across the Indian River Lagoon and dock at Snaggy Harbor. Deciding it would be easier if they stayed on the land to oversee the fields, they built the mansion. He probably should have waited until after his first crop of pineapples came in before building such a monstrosity. Swarms of mosquitos, sand flies, no-see-ums, and chiggers were too much for the workers, not to mention the pineapple's sharp spines, which caused open puncture wounds on their hands that would then fester and become infected in the muggy, damp, insect-ridden environment. After the second crop failed, the Bennett family abandoned the main house and moved to the gulf coast of Florida for a spell.

"Fast-forward to the late 1940s. This is when things get a bit shady. After Birdy's grandfather passed, Birdy's father, Rory, inherited and moved into the mansion with his wife and son. Rory started to hold parties. Raucous parties. The people who attended the parties weren't like the guests who came to the Indialantic by the Sea Hotel At least that's what I was told. They were *rough types*. Birdy's father was only invited to the Indialantic once, for my mother's thirtieth birthday party. Actually, it was more like a ball than a party. I remember being allowed to come into the ballroom for the first half hour. Father had a full orchestra and a few celebrity guests. You know the portrait of your great-grandmother in the library?"

"Of course I know that painting." And Liz knew the story she was now telling; it was part of the Indialantic by the Sea folklore.

"Mother is wearing the emerald-and-diamond necklace and earrings…."

"And matching ring," Liz had added.

"Well, there was also a bracelet. The set had been passed down to your great-grandmother. The entire set was said to have once belonged to Mary, Queen of Scots, if you can believe that."

"It's feasible; after all, she came from England," Liz had said.

"Well, my mother, unbeknownst to my father, had invited the Bennetts, only Birdy's mother was too ill at the time to attend, so 'rough' Rory, as my father called him, came alone. Rory was a terrible womanizer, and that night apparently lost money at cards, got drunk, and they found him in the billiards room after everyone had left. Father wasn't too happy to discover him, especially because earlier he'd been flirting with my mother and every other married woman in the ballroom. Father kicked him out and told him never to come back. The next day, the emerald bracelet, which Mother had taken off before the ball and had left on her dressing table because the clasp was broken, was missing. Not only that," she said excitedly, "so were other pieces of fine jewelry from four other guests' suites. Father naturally blamed Birdy's father. The police searched the Bennett mansion, but the jewelry wasn't there. My mother told me the theft and the accusation against Rory was in all the papers. She said it was a shame because Birdy's mother, Millie, was the sweetest woman she'd ever met."

After wiping away a rivulet of sweat that made a white line in the center of the neon-pink blush on her right cheek, Aunt Amelia had continued.

"Soon after, Birdy's father ended up in jail, I think it was for racketeering, not theft. After being released from prison, he came back and tried to make amends with Millie, but Mother told me she never forgave him. While Rory had been in jail, Millie couldn't afford the upkeep on the mansion and it fell into disrepair."

"And none of the jewels ever showed up, right?" Liz had asked as Birdman's cottage had come into view. "And what about the 1715 fleet treasure Birdy's father stole from the Pieces of Eight Company?"

Aunt Amelia had stopped, then continued her story in a whisper. "After returning from prison in the late 1950s, Rory signed on with a treasure hunting company that had permission to salvage near the 1715 Plate Fleet survivors' camp. Rory was accused of stealing a cache of gold and silver coins, but before he could be arrested he disappeared, leaving behind his wife and child. They found his body in the waters near the survivors' camp the day after a hurricane slammed the island. Everyone thought Rory had left with the treasure, but it appeared his greed got the best of him and he was looking for more. The story even made the national papers."

"How heartbreaking, especially for Birdman."

"Very," Aunt Amelia had said. "Sadly, Birdy's mother got TB soon after his father's death, and Birdy stayed home to help her."

"Wow, that's depressing about the tuberculosis. I don't remember you telling me that last part when I was younger."

"I only tell you age-appropriate stories, my dear," she had said, then they moved on to more cheery subjects.

After passing the summerhouse, Liz continued until she saw a small hole in the dense greenery heralding the entrance to the neighboring property. She ducked, then entered. Perhaps she should have brought a machete *and* a water bottle. The good news was that the temperature seemed to drop once she entered the junglelike terrain, the canopy of trees over her head acting like a huge umbrella. The scent of a flower she didn't recognize hung on the moist air. She sniffed around until she spied a small cluster of white flowers on a green bush, then inhaled the citrus scent, which reminded her of her father's aftershave and how much she missed him.

Knowing the team was working beachside, she continued south. As she got closer to the old mansion, or she should say, the *shell* of the mansion, she looked ahead. The roof was gone, and a huge lime tree still bearing fruit jutted up from where the center courtyard of the mansion used to be. Next to the lime tree was a marble statue of an ethereal-looking woman. On the statue's arm, her only arm, was a basket of pineapples. If it weren't for the three golf carts parked in front of the mansion's sloping veranda, which was held up by six Grecian columns that looked ready to topple like a stack of dominoes, Liz could almost imagine she'd stepped back in time.

At the trail leading to the turnoff to the archeologists' beach site, Liz recalled her first interaction with Birdman Bennett, at age seven. Aunt Amelia had sent her to the Bennett property toting a basket containing a wounded brown pelican. Her great-aunt found the poor guy limping along the hotel's dock. Wordlessly, Birdman had taken the basket from Liz, then disappeared into his junglelike yard. A week later, they saw the same brown pelican sitting on a piling with a bandaged right knee. After that, Liz took it upon herself to bring another basket to Birdman as a thank-you. Only this time it was filled with a half dozen of Chef Pierre's French pastries. Soon after, she and Birdman became good friends, and even though she and Aunt Amelia invited Birdman to the Indialantic each time they visited his property, Liz didn't remember him ever coming over to borrow a cup of sugar, or anything else for that matter. Once, during a Category 4 hurricane while Liz was away at college, Aunt Amelia and Liz's father convinced Birdman to spend the night with them in the Indialantic's basement. Her great-aunt told Liz that Birdman's sleeping bag had been positioned underneath Barnacle Bob's cage, saying, "I think Barnacle Bob is the only bird on this planet Birdman doesn't get along with. Especially after one of BB's midmorning screeching sessions. You know BB. When he gets frightened, he tends to spout midcentury commercial jingles or TV theme songs. In this case, it was 'A horse is a horse, of course of course...'" When she'd told Liz the story, Aunt Amelia had continued with the rest of the song and Barnacle Bob had joined in from the butler's pantry to verify the tale.

Liz knew the ditty from watching and rewatching with her great-aunt the episode where Mr. Ed falls in love with a pretty little filly that just happened to be voiced by a young Aunt Amelia, whose line was "Hey, stranger. What's shaking...besides your tail." As her great-aunt liked to tell Liz, "No part is too small for a real actress. You get to rub elbows with someone who just might do you a big favor somewhere down the line." Liz wondered how far she'd gotten rubbing hooves with the horse playing Mr. Ed. She wasn't one to criticize her great-aunt's early career in television, as it had made her what she was today: a sweet, if out-of-the-box, flamboyant, loving, wacky character, whose heart was always in the right place.

A mosquito the size of a Cadillac landed on Liz's arm. She swatted it away but of course missed, then turned to the east. Halfway to the beach dig site, she stopped. Cupping her hand to her ear, she thought she heard the loud call of a sandhill crane. It got louder and louder with each step she took. When she felt warm breath on the back of her neck, she couldn't help but break out in a grin. "Okay, Birdman, I know it's you. Remember, you tried to teach me the sandhill crane's distinctive mating call, or should I say honk, and I never got it right."

"But you've learned others, my little hatchling." Out from the dense thicket of palmettos stepped a barefoot, reed thin, darkly tanned, elderly man dressed in tattered shorts and a worn SAVE THE SEA TURTLES T-shirt. His white hair hung to well below his shoulders. A navy bandana was tied around his head *Rambo*-style. Birdman hadn't changed much in the ten years Liz had been away in Manhattan pursuing her writing career. Like dogs are said to resemble their owners, Birdman Bennett, with his skinny legs, long, narrow nose, and white hair, resembled one of the barrier island's snowy egrets.

Smiling, she said, "I've come to see how the dig is progressing."

"No strawberries this time of year, Berry Girl," he said as he glanced away, avoiding eye contact.

"I know that," she said, "you've taught me well. Am I a hatchling or Berry Girl?" He'd christened her with the name Berry Girl because of her strawberry-blond hair and love of strawberries. When she was young, they would go on treasure hunts. Not searching for gold and jewels from the 1715 fleet, but instead exploring Birdman's six acres in order to discover new nests, baby animals, turtle eggs, and ripe wild strawberries. Birdman's strawberries tasted sweeter than any from a grocery store.

"Both," he answered.

"How are things going?" she asked, noticing the dark circles under his eyes. "Hope the team of archeologists is being respectful of your property."

He sighed, then joined her on the path, giving her shoulders an affectionate squeeze. It was the most demonstrative he'd ever been with her, but she could tell by the furrowing of his brow that something was bothering him. Finally, he said, "They need to leave. Disturbing my birds. I've been watching them. Sneaking where they shouldn't. Disturbing the lagoon and shoreline. They need to leave," he repeated. There was a catch in his voice, as if he were pleading with her.

And here she thought everything had been going smoothly during the past week while the archeologists had been digging on his property.

Chapter 3

They walked in silence for a few minutes until Birdman finally spoke. "Need you to see."

He was a man of few words. She gazed up at his pale blue eyes, paler than her own cornflower blue, and thought she saw tears welling.

He gently took her hand. "Come."

Birdman led her through a series of twisting paths. Instead of taking her to one of the two dig sites, the Indian River Lagoon or the Atlantic Ocean, he stopped at a clearing near his small cottage and pointed to his large garden. Someone had dug deep holes, leaving mounds of soil along with uprooted corn, field peas, bell peppers, green beans, sweet potatoes, collard greens, and even some sugar cane.

"What the heck? Who did this?" she asked, incensed at the destruction of what amounted to most of Birdman's vegetable garden. Birdman lived mostly off the land and ocean. "Do you think one of the archeologists did this? And what is that sticking up from the ground? A trident? Some kind of garden tool?"

Before Birdman could answer, Jameson Royce appeared through the thicket, a collapsible shovel sticking out from the knapsack on his back. "Hello, birdy boy. I really think you should reconsider letting us take those golf carts to the dig site. It's gotta be a hundred degrees on the beach." He took a silk pocket square from his back pocket and wiped his forehead.

Birdman didn't answer. In fact, based on the look on his face, Liz was worried he might punch Jameson in his chiseled jaw. Did he suspect Jameson, who Betty said was the moneyman bankrolling the team, of destroying his garden?

To dispel the awkward silence, she turned to Jameson and chirped, "It's pretty hot. You might want to move to the lagoon location for a couple of days. The temperature's supposed to cool down by ten degrees on Wednesday."

Still, Birdman remained silent.

Jameson's cold, pewter-gray eyes looked Liz over from head to toe, reminding her to take a shower as soon as she got back to her beach house. Always willing to give people a second chance, she realized in that moment that Jameson Royce had just used up his second chance. And there wouldn't be a third. Last evening, when she brought in the food for the dinner buffet, he'd actually pinched her rear end, saying, "You must work out. Am I right, gorgeous? You would think that scar would make you not so attractive, but it adds an air of mystery. Makes me want to get to know you better." She'd slapped his hand away, delivered the food to the sideboard, then hurried to the kitchen, where she explained to Greta, the hotel's housekeeper, why her face was so flushed. She was happy Ryan hadn't been there. He'd probably try to defend her honor, even knowing that she could handle herself. Jameson tried anything like it again and she'd deliver one of Aunt Amelia's jujitsu kicks.

Liz had to admit Jameson was good-looking, even though he was sweating enough to fill a bathtub. He had short, layered, brown-black hair, a clean-shaven face, high cheekbones, and broad, muscular shoulders. His face was taut. Too taut. The first time she'd met him, she'd guessed he was in his early forties. But as she'd watched him in conversation last night at dinner she noticed his forehead never wrinkled and there weren't any laugh lines when he broke into raucous laughter after telling one of his politically incorrect jokes. He'd obviously had a procedure or two, or three, so she upped his age to at least fifty.

"No golf carts," Birdman said. "I allowed that excavator on my property to dig your pit. That's enough desecrating for a lifetime." Birdman clenched and unclenched his fists, and glanced her way. Softening his tone, he said, "I have work." He nodded his head toward the mounds of earth in front of them. "Before it rains."

"Rains, birdy boy," Jameson said, opening his eyes wide, *trying* to raise his eyebrows. "I don't think so. My weather app says no rain for two weeks. Reason we came last week."

Liz didn't speak up. But if there was one thing she'd learned from spending time with Birdman, if he said it was going to rain, it would rain.

Jameson glanced toward the dug-up land in front of Birdman's modest three-room cottage. "Hope you're not accusing us of doing something so childish, Birdy, my boy. And don't blame the excavator for those rabbit holes in your garden; we only had the machine for one day. You can check it out with the rental company."

"Who else would do it?" Birdman asked, taking a step toward Jameson.

"Chill out. You're on thin ice already. I would think after that talk we had last night you'd understand the importance of us being here. Of me being here. Don't forget you signed those papers. Notarized papers. Time to relax your rules about things around the old decaying homestead."

Liz almost expected Jameson to add, *or else.*

Jameson sneered at Birdman, his eyes narrowing, then he focused his stare on Birdman's bare feet. His expression reminded her of a character from Aunt Amelia's arsenal of vintage Saturday morning cartoon shows—Snidely Whiplash. "Isn't he the most perfect villain, Lizzy dear?" Aunt Amelia had asked six-year-old Liz when they were in the Indialantic's screening room. "Snidely's a perfect foil for Canadian Mountie Dudley Do-Right. That's an important recipe in any storyline—the battle between good and evil." Snidely had a blue-tinted complexion, curled black mustache, and wore a tall black Abe Lincoln hat. The cartoon hadn't been one of Liz's favorites, but she knew the antifeminist message was apropos for the time period. Snidely liked to tie women to railroad tracks, then a Canadian Mountie called Dudley Do-Right would ride in at the last second on his horse named Horse and save the poor defenseless female from an oncoming train. Most times, the woman tied to the tracks was Dudley's girlfriend, Nell. And instead of dunderhead Dudley, nine times out of ten it was Horse that was the true rescuer.

If Liz had to pick a cartoon character from the sixties that she could relate to on a feminist level it would be Wilma Flintstone. Wilma was a strong female who wore the dress in the family, even though her caveman hubby Fred wore one also. Wilma didn't put up with Fred's antics. Aunt Amelia had told her that Wilma was based on the character Alice from the old show *The Honeymooners.* The one time Liz watched *The Honeymooners,* she'd been appalled by the boisterous Ralph character shouting, "To the moon, Alice. To the moon," while sending threatening fist pumps into the air. Her great-aunt had assured her that Ralph was all bluster and no action. Even so, she'd thought about how far women had come; then Liz glanced over at Jameson Royce and thought, *maybe not.*

"If it does rain, we'll be extending our stay," Jameson said, moving toward the path leading to the golf carts. He addressed Birdman, not Liz. "No questions asked. Right, Birdy?"

Liz didn't like the way Jameson was talking to Birdman. He was a guest on the property, and she couldn't understand how he could be giving Birdman ultimatums.

"We will see," Birdman answered.

"You're a strange bird," Jameson said, "and a stubborn fool."

What was that supposed to mean? Why was Jameson threatening Birdman? Placing her hands on her hips, she said, "Before you go, Mr. Royce, how about helping Mr. Bennett clean up this mess? Think of it as a thank-you for being able to use his land. You have a shovel on hand, I see." She glanced at the one in his backpack. "And—"

"Don't want *his* help," Birdman answered, just as Evan Watkins came toward them dragging a metal cart filled with all kinds of paraphernalia, including a sleek metal detector, nothing like the one Liz got from her father on her tenth birthday so she could search for treasure on the Indialantic's beach. "Birdman," he called out, "I can help. Where do we start?" Dr. Haven Smith-Crawford's college intern was the youngest on the team. He was in his early twenties and had told her that this was his last internship before graduating from the University of Florida in Gainesville.

"Thank you," Birdman answered.

Evan walked over to where the spear with the three razor-sharp tines was and pulled it out of the ground. "What the hell, Birdman. Why is there a Hawaiian sling diving spear here? You using it to catch a fish an osprey drops when he's flying overhead?"

So that's what it was. She should have known; it hadn't looked old enough to have belonged to a Spanish conquistador like Ponce de León or even a member of the extinct Ais tribe, or for that matter, Neptune. The pole was about five feet long, and the part that had come out of the ground had a thick yellow rubber band–type handle.

Birdman went over to Evan and put his arm around the intern's shoulder. They seemed to be pals, surprising seeing they'd only known each other for a week. "It's mine, but I didn't put it there. I keep it in the shed. Haven't used it in decades. I don't go diving anymore." Birdman narrowed his eyes at Jameson. "But I have my suspicions of who did put it there."

Jameson strode up to them. "Hope you're not accusing me. And Mr. Watkins, your job isn't to help out our recluse hermit here. I have plenty for you to do. Like sending out those soil samples I gave you. FedEx comes in an hour. Now scoot."

Evan looked from Birdman to Jameson, then eventually shrugged his shoulders in defeat. Evan always had a smile on his face, his white teeth shining fluorescent in his tanned face, but he wasn't wearing one now as he looked at Jameson. From what she'd witnessed in the past week, Evan did all the gopher work—go for this, go for that. "Sorry, Birdman. I'll come back after dinner and help you." Then he glanced at Jameson defiantly. "On my own time. I'll be back, you can count on it." Then he followed Jameson out of the clearing toward where the golf carts were parked.

She waited until they were out of sight before saying to Birdman, "I don't like that Mr. Royce. If he gives you any problems let me know. I'll give Auntie your message that you want them to leave. Do you think he's the one who did this? Is that why?"

"Not for you to worry. Leave it be. Changed my mind. Don't tell Miss Amelia. Probably some kids trying to scare a crazy old hermit." He pointed to himself.

"You're not crazy, far from it," she answered. But he was old. And he looked tired and frail. Liz promised herself to have a talk with Aunt Amelia about what should be done. Then she changed her mind; why get her great-aunt involved? She would take care of things herself.

"Come by in the morning," Birdman said, giving her hand an affectionate squeeze. "Something exciting to show you."

She smiled. "What time, Birdman? The crack of dawn?"

"No," he answered. "Before that."

She laughed. "I could help you right now."

"Evan will do."

"You sure?"

He nodded his head yes, then grabbed the diving spear and walked to the path that led to the small shed behind his cottage.

Something was going on between Jameson Royce and Birdman. It was as if the jerk was holding something over Birdman's head. And who was digging on his property? And what was the deal with the diving spear? A warning of some kind?

Maybe she was over evaluating things. She'd be sure to ask Birdman what was going on when she met him in the morning.

For now, she would let it go.

Which turned out to be a big mistake.

Chapter 4

Usually, the full-time residents at the Indialantic opted for meals in the hotel's cozy kitchen; after all, they were considered part of the Holt family. But with the arrival of the archaeological team, Aunt Amelia had decided that everyone should have cocktails in the library, followed by dinner in the hotel's dining room.

Liz glanced around the library. The furniture was similar to the lobby's—lots of rattan settees and chairs with cushioned seats and bamboo side tables set up in conversational groups. A huge rattan glass-topped desk stood in front of French doors that opened to the south patio, which had a view of the ocean and summerhouse. Naturally, there were books. Tons of books. Carved mahogany shelves overflowing with books, some of the volumes dating all the way back to the late 1700s. Liz's great-grandfather, William Holt, had commissioned a ship to bring every book from her great-grandmother's library at Isle Tor in Cornwall to America. After the death of her mother, the library had been an oasis to Liz. And still was. The hours spent there as a youth fostered her desire to become a writer.

As Liz surveyed the room, she noticed the hotel's guests seemed happy enough, speaking in low conversational tones, a couple of laughs here and there. Nothing like she'd just witnessed on the Bennett property between Birdman and Jameson Royce. So far, so good. Aunt Amelia sat on the sofa between the Crawfords and was waving her hands wildly in the air, probably telling them how well her first day of acting school had gone. A few minutes earlier, when Liz had asked Dr. Haven Smith-Crawford if she would like more wine, she'd answered, "Please call me Haven, and can I call you Liz?"

Evan the intern and Jameson were nibbling from one of Chef Pierre's magnificent charcuterie boards. When Liz had brought it in and placed it on the library table behind the sofa, she'd felt compelled to take a photo with her phone; the arrangement on the large teak board would make the perfect cover shot for a gourmet magazine or one of the brochures for Indialantic by the Sea.

Betty was standing by the rectory table chatting with Professor Talbot, looking lovely as usual. When she caught Liz's eye, she motioned for Liz to come over.

"The supposed Fountain of Youth Ponce de León was apparently looking for when he landed on your shores has turned out, as far as the scientific community is concerned, to be pure bunk," Professor Talbot said as Liz joined them. "However, Betty, I can see by your ageless beauty that you just might prove those scientists wrong. Tell me the truth, is the fountain hiding somewhere on the Indialantic by the Sea's grounds? You haven't changed a bit from when I met you sixty years ago."

Betty blushed. "Now, Walter, we both know that's not true."

Moss-green eyes sparked with admiration in the professor's tanned, leathery face. Most of his wrinkles were concentrated at the outer corner of his eyes, as if he spent a lot of time squinting in the sun or laughing. Probably both. He was about eight inches taller than Betty and had a neatly trimmed mustache. His hair was white, and he had tons of it. Liz knew Professor Talbot was Betty's age, around eighty, and she could see how in his day he must have been attractive. Obviously not attractive enough for Betty to choose him over her late husband. As if Betty would ever be that superficial. Plus, she had Captain Netherton as a companion, a handsome man in his own right.

Last Wednesday, Professor Talbot, at Aunt Amelia's insistence, had given a short presentation to the Barrier Island Historical Society in the Indialantic's screening room. Liz had helped Aunt Amelia set up and had stayed to hear the distinguished professor's lecture about conquistador Juan Ponce de León, who had landed in the spring of 1513 on Melbourne Beach's shores to become the first European to set foot in Florida. The professor liked to wax poetic, capturing the imagination of everyone in the room when he told of Ponce de León's first steps on land, making it seem like he'd been standing right beside him all those centuries ago. "There is a documented letter from Ponce de León to the king of Spain in which he promised to ship gold and silver cast into coin from the Americas to Spain three times a year. Mining gold and silver was Spain's primary reason for wanting to colonize. Eighteen months after his letter, Ponce de León left on his first journey to what would become known as Florida. When he landed, he admired the area's lush landscape and promptly named his discovery *Pascua Florida*. It was Eastertime, and *Pascua Florida*, translated to English, means 'Festival of Flowers.' Can you imagine the beauty of this island when it was unspoiled and natural?" the professor asked.

Dr. Nigel Crawford had called out, "You're forgetting about all the mosquitos, Walter. That's why at one time, this area of Florida was called the Mosquito Coast. In the 1600s the Ais tribe survived by surrounding themselves in clouds of smoke, then at night, burying themselves in the sand for protection. One of the reasons they left this barrier island was that in the 1700s there were mosquito-borne epidemics of dengue and yellow fever."

Not happy that Dr. Crawford had commandeered the discussion away from the subject of Ponce de León, the professor had immediately put a kibosh on any more interruptions. "You're right, Nigel. But I think it's sad to say that once the mosquito population had been annihilated, early twentieth-century developers arrived and caused their own type of destruction. Acres and acres of forests and mangroves were destroyed to build homes. Not to mention important wildlife ripped from their natural habitats. Luckily for you who live here, Teddy Roosevelt set up the first national wildlife refuge at Pelican Island." In a condescending tone the professor had added, "However, Dr. Crawford, we're here to talk about Ponce de León, not the Ais tribe or mosquitoes." Then the professor went on to talk about Ponce de León's voyage with Christopher Columbus on Columbus's second trip to America in 1493, telling them that Ponce de Leon had boarded the ship as a *gentleman volunteer*. That was one fact Liz hadn't known. The professor tied things up to a round of applause, the loudest clapping coming from Aunt Amelia. She'd added a two-fingered whistle.

Now, watching the professor flirting with Betty, Liz asked something she had meant to ask him after that lecture. "Professor Talbot, do you have any idea why old history books mention that Ponce de León was looking for the Fountain of Youth? Is the explanation in your book *Tales from the Pits*? Betty loaned me her copy. I've just started it, and so far it's fascinating."

The professor grinned. "No, the Fountain of Youth isn't mentioned in my book. By the way, stop by my rooms and I'll give you a signed copy. However, I think I know where the legend came from."

"Do tell," Betty said.

Nothing like a mystery to get mystery writer Betty interested, Liz thought.

"Some scholars believe that the Fountain of Youth was a metaphor for the brew made from the Bahamian love vine. The islands of the Bahamas were one of the stops on Ponce de León's tour from Spain. It is possible that our adventurous conquistador partook of a special brew that the natives said was an aphrodisiac. It's been theorized that Ponce de León mistook the native word *vid*, 'vine,' for *vida*, the word for 'life.' Hence the mix-up on terminology: fountain of life, instead of fountain vine. Some even say Ponce de León, who was at one time the mayor of Puerto Rico, tried to re-create the brown tea elixir, calling it the Fountain of Youth."

Evan overheard the professor speaking and called out, "Good story, Professor. I'll have you know the leaves of the love vine are still used today to make bush tea in the Bahamas. They tout it as a cure for sex weakness." For some reason he was staring at Haven when he added, "Not that it's something I need to partake in."

Haven looked away, and her husband said, "Cassytha filiformis is a parasite vine that grows wild. It's also used as a soothing bath for prickly heat and itching."

"Well, well," the professor said, clicking his tongue, "enough talk about such delicate matters. There are ladies in the room." He addressed Betty. "Can I refill your wineglass, my dear?"

"No, I'm good."

Liz looked over at the bar cart and saw she needed to restock the red wine. Not only restock it, but add it to Jameson Royce's tab. He'd told Aunt Amelia that he would be the one responsible for paying for the archaeologists' food and lodging. So far, they hadn't seen a cent. Aunt Amelia told Liz the agreement was that he would pay weekly. The week was up. If assistant manager Susannah Shay had been on duty and not at a Vanderbilt family reunion, she would tie Mr. Royce to a chair and pistol-whip him until he settled his bill. Knowing what she'd seen of the obnoxious man, he would probably enjoy it.

Liz excused herself from the library, went to the butler's pantry, and grabbed a bottle of merlot. It wasn't as good a vintage as the other three bottles she'd put on the bar cart earlier, but until Jameson paid up, she would save the good stuff for later.

She glanced over at Barnacle Bob, who was uncharacteristically quiet in his cage, his beady little eyes downcast. Was he depressed? If he was, it must have had something to do with Carmen Miranda. "Hey, BB, don't you worry, she'll come around."

Instead of appreciating her concern, he waited until she stepped under the threshold and into the kitchen, then cackled, "Keep your mitts off the booze, you lush!"

She should have known. "Put a muzzle on it, BB. Or I'll tell Carmen Miranda you've sworn off female birds of a feather."

That shut him up.

She returned to the library, opened the bottle of wine, poured herself a small glass, then went to stand on the south side of the room, leaning her back against the marble fireplace mantel so she could observe the group. After what she'd witnessed at the Bennett property between Birdman and Jameson, she wanted to take Jameson aside and have a little talk with him. But first she would discuss it with Ryan. She had a habit of rushing into things before thinking them out. *Where was Ryan, anyway?* Evan the intern walked over to her, then looked above her head at the portrait of Liz's great-grandmother. "Wow. Look at those emeralds and diamonds. I heard she was some kind of royalty."

Liz laughed. "Not royalty, but my great-grandmother was born in a castle in Cornwall, England. You're right about the necklace, earrings, and ring, though. They are rumored to be handed down from royalty. Who told you about Great-Grandma Maeve?" *Probably Aunt Amelia,* she thought. Her great-aunt loved reciting Holt history to anyone who would listen, sometimes taking people on tours of the Indialantic and pointing out what famous people had stayed in the rambling hotel when it was considered the jewel of the Treasure Coast. No longer a jewel, but not too bad for being around for almost a hundred years.

"Miss Amelia told me. The lady in the portrait looks like you," Evan said, his eyes darting back and forth between the portrait and Liz's face.

Someone called out Evan's name, and he turned. It was Haven. Without saying "excuse me," a millisecond later he was at her side.

Liz went back to perusing the hundreds of leather-bound books to her right, looking for one she might have missed reading. Doubtful. But possible. It was strange to be in the library without her father. Last week he'd given Liz and Aunt Amelia an hour's notice about his upcoming nuptials, then whisked his fiancée Charlotte, Brevard County's lead homicide detective, across "the pond" and into the sunset. She smiled thinking of the party she was planning for when they returned from their honeymoon, and reached for a book on Florida history. Her hand stopped in midair when she heard, "Talbot, you are a doddering old fool."

Surprise, surprise. The person causing the elderly professor so much strife was none other than Jameson Royce.

The tension was palpable. Maybe it was just the August heat; whatever it was, she felt that familiar prickle at the back of her neck forecasting rough seas ahead. As she glanced around the room, she was particularly concerned about the professor, worried that the raised purple vein at his temple and the wineglass he held in his hand might explode at the same time.

Betty's mouth flew open at Jameson's name-calling.

"I beg your pardon," the professor said, addressing Jameson. His hand trembled as he placed his wineglass on the table.

"I told you to cool your jets, Talbot," Jameson said. "Have I upset your delicate puritan sensibilities? Get with the times."

The professor ignored him, stabbed a piece of truffle cheese with a toothpick, and offered it to Betty.

Go Professor, Liz thought.

"You can ignore me all you want, Professor Dumb-as-a-door." Jameson glanced around to see if anyone else noticed the Harry Potter reference. The professor kept his back to Jameson, but that didn't stop Jameson from continuing. "I've had a little chat with the research foundation, and guess what? They need more money for this little project. Good thing we won't need it."

Liz could tell by the way the professor stood up taller that he was interested.

Jameson shook his head and laughed him off. "Not talking, are you. Remember something—you wouldn't be here if not for me and my money."

Liz pondered why Jameson was so interested in digging up Spanish relics. Wouldn't he be better off on some mega-yacht, cruising the Mediterranean? She'd googled him after coming back from Birdman's, and learned his net worth was up there with the best of them. He lived in Palm Beach, but had made his fortune by building an exclusive development on nearby Orchid Island called Leon de Mar, which in Spanish translates to Lion of the Sea. More than likely, Jameson liked the play on words of using Ponce de León's surname. Leon de Mar was an exclusive development that had its own post office, restaurant, beach club, gourmet store, church, and clubhouse. Liz wasn't jealous of her mega-wealthy neighbors down A1A and their utopian lifestyle, because the Indialantic's emporium had a coffee shop/deli, women's jewelry and clothing boutique, used book and vintage shop, women's arts-and-crafts collective, and most recently, Aunt Amelia's acting studio. Add a hotel to the mix, an eco-sightseeing tour boat, a lawyer (her father), and a private detective (her boyfriend), and Liz thought the Indialantic had more to offer than any ritzy gated community. Plus, the Indialantic served the public, not just the elite.

Liz put down her glass and walked over to Professor Talbot and Jameson Royce, now nose to nose and glaring at each other. She was ready to break things up if need be.

Where is Ryan? He'd promised to join them for dinner. She could use his calm reserve before things got out of hand. In his previous life, Ryan had been an arson investigator for the FDNY in Brooklyn. Liz was pretty sure—no, absolutely sure—Ryan's decision to rent the caretaker's cottage from Aunt Amelia and move permanently to Melbourne Beach had a lot to do with their budding, now flowering, relationship. Ryan was her lawyer father's private-investigator investigator-on-call, and he also helped his grandfather, who everyone called Pops, with his gourmet coffeehouse/deli/ bistro, Deli-casies by the Sea, in the Indialantic's emporium.

In case she had to physically separate them, Liz sidled up to Jameson and the professor. By the expression on Betty's face, she knew she had backup. Betty might come across all demure and ladylike, but from what she'd seen of the eighty-three-year-old in the past, she was a force to be reckoned with.

"What were you thinking, Professor, coming out of retirement at this late date?" Jameson chided. "Nigel, back me up. Don't you think Grandpa here should have stayed in his pasture instead of chewing his cud and gnawing the end of one of his stinky non-Cuban cigars? Have some spine for a change, Nigel. Speak your mind. Weren't you the one who was slated to be the head of the team, not this octogenarian?" Jameson raised his palm to the professor's chest to keep him from speaking. Then he turned to the sofa and addressed Dr. Crawford. "Although, you aren't that much younger, are you, Nigel, old boy?" Jameson glanced at Haven and smiled his Snidely Whiplash evil grin. "How'd you ever catch such a young beauty?"

"You're crossing a line, Jameson." Dr. Crawford stood up from the sofa. Haven followed suit. Leaving Aunt Amelia alone, looking very uneasy. Aunt Amelia started tracing a repetitive circle on the top of her right knee with the pointer and middle finger on her right hand. Liz knew that when stressed, it was Aunt Amelia's tell. Liz also knew what would come next if she didn't calm down the situation. Her great-aunt might start belting out show tunes from her repertoire of past musical productions. On second thought, that might be better than Liz dumping the contents of her wineglass onto Jameson's white linen shirt. Especially seeing he hadn't paid a cent toward the bill yet.

The Crawfords walked up to where Jameson, the professor, Betty, and Evan were standing. Dr. Crawford didn't have Jameson's looks or his height. His nerdy black-framed glasses, short-sleeved woven plaid shirt, and pocket protector overflowing with pens and pencils screamed nerd. Dr. Crawford's shoes were scuffed. Liz almost felt sorry for him. If his wife was involved with Jameson based on his looks, Dr. Crawford didn't stand a chance.

"S-s-sorry, Jameson," Dr. Crawford stuttered, trying to keep his voice under control, "I guess my wife didn't marry me for my money, unlike your past four wives. Haven married me for my brain, the same reason I married her. And I'm not vain enough to risk injecting botulism into my face."

Score one for Dr. Crawford.

But when Dr. Crawford turned to look at his wife, a section of his thinning black hair, which had been swept into a comb-over to hide a shiny patch of sunburned scalp, fell over his right eye. Haven deftly put the section of hair back in place.

Liz couldn't tell if Haven was embarrassed by her husband's looks in comparison to Jameson's or embarrassed about the focus being on herself. "Jameson, you're such a charmer," she said.

He is? Score one for Jameson.

Haven was attractive, probably in her early forties, the same age as Charlotte, Liz's father's fiancée, or she should say, her father's new bride. Haven had hazel, catlike eyes, shoulder-length blond hair, flawless skin, high cheekbones, full lips, and white teeth with a slight overbite that made her look slightly vulnerable. Liz could tell she had exquisite taste in clothing and jewelry, and if she wasn't mistaken, the Hermès Kelly handbag she'd had on her arm was the real deal. Liz had seen enough of them at the parties her ex-boyfriend Travis dragged her to when she'd lived in Manhattan. Haven's husband looked like he bought his clothes from Goodwill, not that there was anything wrong with that; it was where her bestie Kate found some of her prized items to put in her vintage shop, Books & Browsery by the Sea. Liz also remembered the Crawfords' argument this morning and the mention of Haven's huge credit card bill.

Dr. Crawford grabbed his wife's elbow. "Stay away from Haven, Jameson. I know what you're up to. She's taken."

"I'm no one's property!" Haven growled at her husband in the same tone Liz had heard this morning during their argument.

Score one for Haven.

"Be honest, Nige," Jameson said, adding a laugh. "You can't afford Botox on your piddly salary at the museum. And it's obvious your wife doesn't need any. She's perfect the way she is."

"That's it!" Dr. Crawford said, taking a step closer to Jameson.

Professor Talbot finally found his voice. He raised a shaky arm and pointed a trembling finger at Jameson. "You've been nothing but a troublemaker since we decided to do this dig. We all got along in South America under much worse conditions. Why can't we do that here?"

"You make it sound like this dig was your idea," Jameson said. "It would be fine if this was the beginning of the twentieth century, but how in blazes do you expect to uncover anything using a dental pick, sieve, and a hand trowel? Do you know how much money I've sunk into those 'newfangled tools,' as you call them? Well, it's a good thing I did. Do you even know anything about noninvasive geophysical equipment? Resistivity meters, magnetometers, ground-penetrating radar, global positioning systems? Well, speak up, Professor." Jameson reached over and popped a garlic-stuffed olive in his mouth, mumbling as he chewed. "Doesn't matter, anyway. Tomorrow I plan to show you and the press the fruits of my labor. I will soon make my mark in the pages of Florida's history forevermore."

Game. Set. Match. Jameson.

"Don't you mean *our* place in history?" Professor Talbot said. "Most people in academia would concur that the meticulous methods used for recovering archeological remains haven't changed in centuries. I am sure the Crawfords would agree." Needing backup, he looked first to Dr. Crawford, then Haven. None came. "And what's this about the press? No press is allowed at the site until I verify whatever it is you think will put you in the pages of history. You're not an accredited archeologist and you don't hold a PhD, so you better come up to my suite before you retire, and we'll coordinate things using the *proper* channels. And you know as well as I that the possibility of finding anything extraordinary relating to Ponce de León is slim at best. So, before you go showing off your findings, you need to take time to get whatever it is verified in the scientific community. There's rigorous protocol associated with archeological finds. But I suppose because you're not an academic, only a layman, you wouldn't know these things." The professor got out a small spiral notebook and a pen from his shirt pocket and started writing down something. Because of his memory loss, Liz had given Grand-Pierre a similar notebook to jot down things he might forget. Did Professor Talbot also have memory problems?

"Oh, ye of little faith," Jameson spat. "Didn't you hear about the skeletal remains of dozens of mammoths at an airport construction site in Mexico? Human remains also. And you, Professor, should be an expert on how long ago mammoths roamed North America, because you were probably there. If those old bones in Mexico can be found, then it's not a long shot that I've found something dating from the early sixteenth century."

"He's right, Professor," Evan said, putting down his drink. "How about Vero Man? Back in 1915, some human bones from the Ice Age were found about twenty miles from here, where the Vero Beach airport now stands."

"That's true, young man," Professor Talbot said. "There is photographic proof, though the bones were misplaced somewhere traveling between museums. Unfortunately, this happened before carbon dating, so they never were correctly analyzed."

Not about to give up, Evan looked directly at Dr. Haven and said in a voice louder than necessary, "How about the fossil hunter who found the etching on bone of a mammoth in the same area where they found Vero Man? That was only about eight years ago. It was originally thought to be one the oldest pieces of art from this area."

The professor raised a white bushy eyebrow and said, "The person who found the engraved bone, or the fossil hunter as you call him, sold it to a private collector instead of donating it to the Smithsonian to be analyzed and dated. We might never know if it was authentic or not."

"There's photos."

"You know better than I, son, that a photo is worthless. There's no doubt the bones were old, we just don't know how old."

"The area is still being studied today, so maybe they will find something," Evan added.

"Enough of this chitchat, you're boring the ladies," Jameson said.

"I'm not bored, I'm interested," Betty said, sending him a dirty look.

"And Walter, what's with you and that notebook? Are you writing down things so you can report me to the archeology police, or aren't you tech savvy enough to use your phone or a laptop?"

"None of your business, Jameson. Are you paranoid that your find will be debunked as a fraud?"

Before Jameson could offer a rebuttal, Ryan came sailing through the door.

Haven asked, "Who's this?"

My savior, that's who, Liz thought, just as Aunt Amelia started humming "Ya Got Trouble" from the Broadway show *The Music Man.*

Chapter 5

In its heyday, the Indialantic by the Sea's dining room had been twice the size it was now. That being said, it could still seat sixty people. Liz sat with Aunt Amelia, Captain Netherton, Betty, and Ryan at a round table in the center of the room, under the hotel's original Lalique chandelier, installed when the Indialantic first opened its doors in 1926. The hotel's five guests sat at two tables near the French doors that opened to an interior courtyard at whose center was a twenty-foot palm tree. The doors were closed because of the sweltering heat. Haven, her husband, and Professor Talbot sat at one table. Jameson and intern Evan sat at another. There was room for six at each table, but they had chosen to sit separately. After what she'd seen in the library between Jameson, Professor Talbot, and Dr. Crawford, Liz thought it was for the best they were separated.

For dinner, Pierre Montague, the chef de cuisine at their family-run hotel for over thirty years, had made one of his signature dishes, pink Key West shrimps over orange grits covered in his famous champagne sauce. Before sending out the dish, Liz had done a taste test and was glad to note that the chef hadn't forgotten one ingredient. Recently, there'd been a slight memory improvement in the man she called Grand-Pierre, a play on the French word for grandfather. The chef was under the care of both an MD and a homeopathic doctor, and Liz was thrilled that the times he got confused seemed less severe than when she'd first arrived home after being away for ten years. Grand-Pierre had passed on to Liz everything he'd learned as a young man in Paris, and even though she didn't hold accreditation from Le Cordon Bleu like Chef Pierre, she felt she'd be able to hold her own if she ever went on a television cooking competition. Not that she didn't worry about Grand-Pierre. When it came to the people she loved, she always worried.

"Oh, Lizzy," Aunt Amelia said, clapping her hands together. "So, what did you think about my first class?" Not waiting for Liz to answer, she continued, "Ryan, you should have seen it. I will have those little female thespians eating out of my hand in no time. Ziggy thinks I should open a talent agency. I told him, one thing at a time, love. You wouldn't believe what he's doing right now. Remodeling *my* dressing room at the theater—I mean, the lead actor's dressing room," she added, not too coyly.

She called her boyfriend and owner of the Melbourne Beach Theatre "love"? Liz supposed that even when you were in your eighties it wasn't too late to fall in love. Not that you'd ever know Ziggy and Aunt Amelia were of a "certain age." Especially if you watched them surf the swells at the Sebastian Inlet. "Always a bridesmaid, never a bride," Aunt Amelia liked to recite, but from what her great-aunt had told her about her love life, Aunt Amelia wasn't deficient in close relationships. Her great-aunt had confided to Liz that when she'd lived in Burbank during her 1960s television years, she'd been engaged five times. Twice to the same actor, who Aunt Amelia refused to name. Liz had a feeling whoever it was had to be more a movie star than a television star. "Never settle for less than you deserve," she always told Liz. "And if it's not a hell yes! it's a hell no!" Her great-aunt had high standards; too bad Liz couldn't have had those same standards when it had come to her ex, Travis Osterman.

Speaking of relationships, she glanced over at Ryan, who was chatting with Betty. She took a moment to admire him, not only for his handsome profile but also for the way he gave his full attention to the person he was speaking to. Liz thought of the way he smiled at her each time their eyes met. Which was often, because he lived behind the Indialantic, near the lagoon in the caretaker's cottage, only a half mile away from the hotel's converted beach pavilion that Liz now called home. Between visiting her father in his apartment and law office at the rear of the hotel, hanging out with her best friend Kate, helping the chef with meals, putting out Aunt Amelia's fires, or bringing Bronte and her laptop up to the hotel's bell tower to work on her current novel while trying not to get distracted by the panoramic views of the ocean and lagoon, Liz barely spent time in her beach house.

Liz glanced around the table and realized she was happy. Truly happy. Much happier than when she'd lived in Manhattan and had been on the literary merry-go-round of fame and fortune. Barring a few recent murders at the Indialantic, including one that had hit too close to home, Liz was finally living the life she'd always imagined. Her agent had called just this morning to say that the early beta-reader reviews of *An American in Cornwall* were coming in at five stars across the board. All this good news, including her father's marriage, made her determined to make sure things went smoothly with the unruly archeologists. Speaking of which...

"Evan," Jameson demanded, wiping his mouth with a white linen napkin embroidered with a capital I, "help me move our table closer to theirs." It was obvious what his motive was for rearranging the dining room's furniture. He wanted to sit closer to Haven. All through dinner, he'd been leaning over and chatting with the beautiful woman. Oddly enough, Haven hadn't seemed to mind.

Liz had had enough of Jameson to last a lifetime. She turned her attention back to the conversation at her table.

"So, Francie is excited for the fashion show. You should see her sketches," Aunt Amelia said, her emerald-green eyes bright with excitement. "And I got a sneak peek of your two outfits, Lizzy."

"A fashion show?" Ryan raised a dark eyebrow and pretended to be upset. "Liz, how come I don't know anything about this?"

"Oh, don't you worry, we wouldn't leave you out, would we, Auntie?" Liz laughed at the surprise in his eyes. "Can't wait to see what Francie comes up with for you to wear."

Francie Jenkins was part owner of the Indialantic's emporium shop Home Arts by the Sea. She was an expert seamstress and sewing instructor who made her own retro clothing patterns, then sold them to fabric stores worldwide. If the show was successful, Francie planned to partner with a manufacturer and produce her own line of vintage-inspired clothing.

Ryan raised his arms and put both palms in front of him. "Whoa, back up. I'm not a fashion show type of guy."

Liz smiled. "Oh yeah? What about that fashion show and calendar you did with the guys from your old fire station? Shirtless, I might add, Mr. February."

"That was for a good cause, and it was *Mr. March*," Ryan said, grinning. "I knew I shouldn't have shown you that calendar."

"Our fashion show is for a good cause too, Ryan," Aunt Amelia said. "The money is going to the children's hospital. It will be magnificent. Ziggy's allowed us to have it at the Melbourne Beach Theatre. Francie has her students coming into Home Arts after hours just to make sure we get things done by Labor Day. There's a rumor that Tom Dun from *Operation Runway* might come in from New York."

"Why don't you tell Ryan what type of fashion show it is, Amelia?" Betty said with a mischievous grin.

Aunt Amelia returned her grin. "Betty, I didn't tell you the good news! You and Captain Netherton will also be in the show. Francie hasn't decided yet on what the two of you will wear. Don't worry, Betty, I've volunteered to have you sit with Francie and me to go over who will wear what, seeing the sixties fashions are in my wheelhouse. We're going to lay out all the dolls and outfits on the long table in Home Arts and go through them together for ideas."

"A good idea," Betty said. "Not that I don't trust your taste, Amelia, it's just that you tend to dress a little more...what should I say...flamboyantly than I do."

She was right. This evening, instead of Aunt Amelia's prim schoolteacher bun she'd worn for her acting students, her fiery, carrot-red hair was coifed into an elaborate updo with not one but two fake hairpieces, one on top of another, making her look like the cartoon character Marge Simpson, only with red hair instead of blue. Liz counted ten, no twelve strands of iridescent glass bead necklaces hanging from her great-aunt's neck, all in electric peacock colors. Liz was surprised her great-aunt could keep her head upright against the weight of them all.

"Dolls? Okay, you've lost me, Aunt Amelia," Ryan said, throwing his hands in the air.

"How silly of me, Ryan. In our show, everyone will be modeling life-size interpretations of the sixties' fashions made for Barbie and her friends. How fun. Of course, Ryan, you'll be wearing something of Ken's, right, Lizzy?" She clapped her hands then added, "You have no idea how many commercial spots I did for Mattel. In fact, this is a secret between us, but I believe one of Barbie's ensembles may have been copied from the gown and accessories I wore to the 1964 premiere of the James Bond movie *Goldfinger* at Grauman's Chinese Theater in Hollywood. If I told you who my escort was, you wouldn't believe it." Under Aunt Amelia's blush, her cheeks reddened to a deeper shade of fuchsia—if that was possible. "And you wouldn't believe who sat next to us at the premiere. Honor Blackman herself." Aunt Amelia looked around the table at their vacant faces. "You know? Pussy Galore!"

Those sitting at the other two tables turned their heads at Aunt Amelia's last statement. She waved. "All's good. Dessert will be served shortly."

Captain Netherton laughed and tugged at his goatee. Aunt Amelia thought the captain of the hotel's sightseeing boat and live-in resident was the spitting image of Edward Mulhare, who played the captain and ghost in the old television series *The Ghost & Mrs. Muir*, with his Vandyke beard, distinguished gray hair, and nautical attire. Just as Betty's black-and-white tuxedo cat (with an adorable milk mustache) was attracted to Captain Netherton's huge black-and-white Great Dane, it also seemed in recent months were Captain Netherton and Betty. "The only ones here who know who Pussy Galore is would be us oldsters, right, Betty?" the captain said with a wink.

Betty put her napkin on her plate and smiled. "Oldsters? I'm sure Fenton would know who Honor was. Liz, isn't your father a big James Bond fan?"

"He sure is."

"Every guy's a James Bond fan," Ryan added.

Liz thought it was a long shot that the clothing her great-aunt wore to the premiere had been copied by the Mattel Toy Company for a 1960s Barbie, but on the other hand, it could be true. For all of Aunt Amelia's theatrics, Liz never heard her tell a lie. A little embellishment now and then, sure. But that was all.

It was obvious that Aunt Amelia would have been too old to have played with Barbie when the doll was introduced. But that didn't stop her, forty years later, from allowing Liz and her best friend Kate to play with the dolls and accessories given to Aunt Amelia as a perk for starring as a young mom in a few midsixties Mattel commercials. Liz remembered that it had felt like Christmas in July, opening all the vintage mint-in-box Barbie items, including a cardboard Dream House and the Fashion Salon, that had been stored in a trunk in the Indialantic's luggage room. Liz and Kate, and truth be told, Aunt Amelia, would play Barbies for hours. When Liz was older, she'd looked up the value of the Barbie items and realized that if they'd left the dolls and accessories in their original packaging, they would have been worth thousands of dollars or more today. Who knew? Maybe Aunt Amelia would have been able to afford to refurbish the hotel's original brass Otis accordion-gate elevator in the lobby. The same elevator it was rumored Al Capone rode up in with one of his cronies, then came down in alone. Liz didn't believe the guy had been whacked, but she knew for sure that Al Capone had been a guest of the Indialantic by the Sea Hotel because his signature was in the hotel's old guest register.

"Let me guess," Betty said after taking a sip of her wine. "Sean Connery was your date to *Goldfinger*?"

"I will never tell." Aunt Amelia pretended to put a lock on her lips, then throw away the key. "Of course, Francie is all for making a copy of the Enchanted Evening outfit for me to model in the show. Lizzy, I hope you don't mind, I loaned your doll cases to Francie. She promised to keep things neat and organized, just like you left them, waiting for your future daughter to play with." She turned to Ryan when she said the word "daughter." Thankfully, Ryan was looking in the other direction. Aunt Amelia giggled. "I can't say I'm as slim and trim as a Barbie doll, but I sure was back then. Francie will have her seamstress's work cut out for her, trying to make things to fit this old body."

"You're not old!" everyone at the table shouted—as they'd done a million times before.

Chapter 6

After helping Greta clear the dinner dishes, Liz brought dessert into the dining room. Grabbing the decaf and regular coffee decanters from the sideboard, she went over to the two guest tables, straining to overhear what Haven and Jameson were talking about. Whatever it was, it caused Nigel's face to turn as red as Barnacle Bob's head feathers, what few there were left—poor BB had lost a few more since Carmen Miranda flew onto the scene.

Liz saw Haven lean in even closer to Jameson and Evan's table. "Come on, just give us a little hint," she cajoled.

"No can do," Jameson said, wearing a Cheshire-cat grin, "not even for you, my beauty. You'll have to wait and see."

Liz was also curious about the thing or things Jameson had found that would put him in Florida history books. "Would anyone like coffee?" she asked. "And please help yourself to dessert."

"Decaf for me," Dr. Crawford said. "My wife will have leaded. Even though her tossing and turning in the middle of the night keeps me awake. I can't seem to convince her that it's all her late-night coffee-drinking. Can't tell the woman anything." Dr. Crawford's cheeks were pink, not from embarrassment, but sunburn. His nose had started to peel in thick layers and his high forehead looked redder than the maraschino cherries in the Manhattan he was holding like a lifeline in his right hand. Instead of worrying about caffeine, he should have been worried about sunscreen.

Haven looked ready to answer him, but instead she said to Liz, "As the *doctor* stated, I'll have regular. Although I don't think a PhD in anthropology is the right credential to be making dietary suggestions regarding stimulants and their relationship to my sleeping patterns."

Dr. Crawford opened his thin-lipped mouth to reply, but Liz cut him off. "Chef Pierre's kiwi-lime soufflé is one of his specialties. And if you're in a chocolate mood, there's a chocolate-raspberry clafouti, Chef's twist on Julia Child's famous recipe."

Haven put her napkin on the table and stood. "You don't have to twist my arm. Would you like anything, darling?" Liz couldn't tell if she was being sincere or sarcastic. Probably the latter.

Haven's beauty was understated. There was something about her that made you want to be encircled in her light. Her face was unwrinkled, except for a few laugh lines around her mouth. It wasn't just her physical looks that made her so appealing, it was also about the way she carried herself. If there was a crowded room, Liz was sure she'd be in the center of it. Her tall, erect figure would stand out in any gathering, and her easygoing manner was a quality Liz admired. Even though Liz modeled during college, won a PEN/Faulkner Award, and at one time had been half of a high-profile Manhattan power couple, she'd never liked the spotlight. Probably the reason she became a writer and not an actress like her great-aunt. And then there was her scar. The stares never bothered her, but she always felt like she needed to give an explanation if someone's gaze lingered too long on her right cheek.

Evan jumped up and said, "Dr. Haven, I'll get dessert for you."

Liz had noticed earlier the way Evan's adoring green eyes never left Haven's face. Yesterday, at the Indialantic's swimming pool, Evan had challenged Liz to a ten-lap race. He'd won, then sheepishly admitted he'd been a Brevard County lifeguard on his summers off from the University of Florida in Gainesville. When she'd asked how he came to be part of the dig, he'd explained, "I was Dr. Haven's teaching assistant when she was doing an eight-week lecture series on Florida's sixteenth-century Spanish explorers." By the way his eyes lit up when talking about Haven, it was clear he was her biggest fan. When Liz had asked Evan what had made him want to get into the field of archeology, she wasn't surprised when he'd told her that he'd never thought of it until he sat in on a lecture series with Dr. Haven. "She makes everything so exciting; she's not dry and stuffy like her husband. It's an honor to be in her company." He had certainly seemed enamored by his mentor and didn't try to hide it. The opposite was true when he talked about her husband. Was it jealousy or something more?

Could Evan be who Dr. Crawford accused his wife of having an affair with, not Jameson?

Not that Liz cared, promising herself to keep clear of any of the hotel guests' personal business. Aunt Amelia had already christened Evan with the moniker Sandy, referring to the older brother in the 1960s television series *Flipper*, about a friendly dolphin who liked to save people by getting up on his tail and sending out high-pitched, squeaky warning whistles, much like Lassie did in barks. There was a resemblance between Evan and the actor Luke Halpin; both had dirty-blond, tousled hair, green eyes, and a lean, sinewy surfer's physique. After her great-aunt assigned Evan his nickname, she'd gone on to tell Liz about the episode where she played the love interest of the actor Brian Kelly, who played Porter Ricks, Sandy and Bud's father on the show, the park ranger who was in charge of all the sea life (including Flipper) in Coral Key Park, Florida.

Usually when Barnacle Bob heard Aunt Amelia mention the name Flipper, he'd break into the show's theme song, "They call him Flipper, Flipper, faster than..." repeating the same stanza over and over again. But that hadn't been the case last Tuesday. Barnacle Bob hadn't even noticed when the word "Flipper" was mentioned. He'd been too distracted by the Indialantic's new macaw Carmen Miranda to think of anything else. So far, he'd crashed and burned after each attempt to woo her. But that didn't stop him from trying. Maybe if he'd learned his manners at a young age, he and Carmen would be sharing a cage and thinking about starting a family. The only thing Carmen Miranda wanted was Aunt Amelia's shoulder. So, not only were Barnacle Bob's advances pooh-poohed, he had to play second fiddle to his adoptive mother. Liz *almost* felt sorry for him, but when she offered her own shoulder for him to ride on, he'd shaken his tail feathers at her, saying in an Italian accent, "Mama Mia, that's a spicy meatball," then added loud passing-gas noises. *Lesson learned*, Liz had thought.

After dessert, Liz noticed Jameson reaching over and grabbing Haven's hand. He said something amusing that caused them both to laugh. Dr. Crawford jumped up. His chair went flying backward, smashing against the Spanish tile. He focused his anger on Jameson, who looked up at him in mock surprise. "I'll see you dead before I let you bribe my wife over to your dark side!"

"Relax, Nige," Jameson said, obviously not frightened by Nigel's thin, short form. "I think we should all make it an early night." He looked from Nigel, then to Professor Talbot. "It seems a few of us might have a case of sunstroke. I'm going up to my suite to make a few phone calls. See you all in the morning when I make my big, no, I mean my *humongous* announcement."

"Oh, no you don't," Professor Talbot said in a shaky voice. "I'm the head of the team, and I want to know what's going on. I'll see you in your suite after I finish my coffee." He brought his cup up to his lips and took a drink, refusing to meet Jameson's eyes.

"Whatever. But you won't get anything out of me. And at this point, seeing I financed this whole slipshod operation, I don't have to share anything with any of you."

Dr. Crawford stepped closer to Jameson. "I'm afraid you're wrong with that flawed premise. You need an accredited professional to document whatever you *think* you've found. Or you might as well take your trinket and sell it on eBay."

"We'll see about that. And if I do need someone to verify my discovery, it won't be you, Nige, or the ancient professor." Jameson stood and focused on Haven. "You know who that leaves, don't you?"

At first Haven looked flustered, then she brushed it off, saying with a smile, "Boys, boys. Let's play nice. We're a team, remember? Think about our time in the rain forest. There weren't any problems."

"That's what you think," Dr. Crawford said, narrowing his already narrow eyes on his wife.

Jameson pushed back his chair and headed for the open door to the hallway that led to the hotel's lobby.

"Wait, Jameson," Haven called out, then placed her napkin on her plate and stood.

As she took a step away from the table, her husband, who was still standing, grabbed her wrist. "You go after him, and that's the end of our marriage."

"Don't be so dramatic," she answered, shaking off his hand. Then she followed Jameson out the door, with Dr. Crawford running after them.

Evan, apparently not wanting to be left out, thanked Aunt Amelia for dinner, then followed in their wake.

After a couple of moments of silence, Betty whispered to Liz, "I better go check on the professor, make sure he's okay. I know he has heart problems, a pacemaker, I think."

Liz looked over at the professor, who didn't seem upset in the least. In fact, he looked pretty darn happy. He had his phone to his ear and was writing something down on his little notepad, talking in a very calm manner. When he hung up there was a small Mona Lisa smile on his lips that turned into a full grin as Betty approached his table. "Care to join me in my suite for a nightcap?" he asked, standing up and holding out his hand.

"Sounds wonderful," Betty answered. Instead of taking his hand, she slipped her arm through his, then looked over at Captain Netherton, whose mouth was wide open. "You coming, Clyde?"

Relief flashed across the captain's attractive face, the opposite of the expression on the professor's. Captain Netherton said, "You betcha, my dear."

Aunt Amelia got up to get seconds of dessert. "Just a tiny slice, for my tiny waistline," she said with a chuckle before walking away.

After she'd gone, Liz pulled Ryan closer to her and whispered, "Before something else happens, let's follow Jameson, Evan, and the Crawfords."

"That doesn't sound good. What about dessert?"

"We'll raid the fridge later, like we always do," Liz said. "Mr. Stone, we need to nip this in the bud before—"

"No need to finish," he said, standing. "I know the drill."

Aunt Amelia sat back down at the table and looked at them. "What is it? What are you two up to? No good, I bet. Count me in!"

Liz innocently batted her eyelashes. "No, Auntie, we were just talking about going for a romantic walk in the moonlight." She elbowed Ryan.

"Yep. Yes. What she said." He feigned embarrassment and added one of his roguish grins.

"Oh, how wonderful! Should I start looking for a photographer?"

Ryan turned his head, like his dog Blackbeard did when he heard the word "treat." "Photographer?"

"For the engagement photos," Aunt Amelia answered.

Now his embarrassment was real.

"Auntie! Stop."

"Just joking, darling. You run ahead for your romantic rendezvous. Greta and I will clean up. Just sayin'. Life is short."

Liz stood and put her hands on her hips. "This coming from the woman who has been engaged five times."

"Exactly. I'm an expert at knowing when it's *not* the real thing. And that's what you two have—the real thing. I'm sure of it. So there."

Liz glanced at Ryan's flushed face. He put his hand on the table, like his legs were shaky and he needed the support. "Come on, Ryan, let's go for our walk. And Auntie, you worry about your own love life. I'm pretty sure if you look closely enough, you'll see Ziggy is the one." Liz grabbed Ryan's hand and pulled him toward the exit leading into the hallway.

"Wait. Lizzy," Aunt Amelia called after them, "I just remembered something. I got terrible news in the mail today."

Liz stopped dead in her tracks and turned. "What is it, Auntie? I hope nothing's happened to Father or Charlotte."

"No, darling. But it is a disaster. The building inspector wants to set up an appointment, and without your father here I'm worried they might shut us down."

"Whyever would they do that?"

"There was something I was supposed to do after the last time they were here looking around the basement. It just slipped my mind. I kept putting off what they wanted, because at the time we didn't have the funds or manpower to do it. Oh dear."

"What exactly needs to be done?" Liz asked, trying to extract the information as quickly as possible so she and Ryan could escape and she could fill him in on the day.

"Apparently, there was a problem with a crumbling wall. I mean, I told them we never go down there, which probably wasn't the right thing to say. They said if the wall isn't repaired, we'll have to close off the basement and fill it with sand and rock. I meant to take care of it, but time sure flies, doesn't it?" she said, adding a nervous laugh.

"Don't worry, Aunt Amelia," Ryan said. "I'll take a look at it. Repairing the wall will be a lot less costly than the other thing. When are they coming?"

"Next Friday," Aunt Amelia said. "Oh, I'm such a ninny."

Liz grabbed Ryan's arm and pulled him through the open doorway, then called back over her shoulder. "You're no such thing, Auntie. We'll meet tomorrow and make a plan, right, Ryan?"

"Right."

"I'm sure everything will work out."

*Un*truer words were never spoken, because like some kind of bad omen, when Liz looked toward the French doors that opened to the oceanfront terrace, she could have sworn she saw Birdman sprint by.

Birdman, who never left his property except the one time there was a Category 4 hurricane.

She grabbed Ryan's arm and whispered, "I think I just saw Birdman run by the window. He never leaves his property. What the heck. I have a bad feeling about all this."

Truer words were never spoken....

Chapter 7

When they stepped under the ten-foot archway that opened into the lobby, Ryan said, "The hotel has a basement? I didn't know that. Thought they didn't exist in Florida, especially on an island."

"It's never used. In fact, I've only been down there once. It tends to flood when we have hurricanes."

"Not a surprise," he said.

"My great-grandfather built the hotel in the late twenties. There's rumors the basement stored bootleg booze."

"Also not a surprise."

"Hopefully, Auntie can hold off the inspectors until we fix whatever needs fixing."

He grabbed her hand and led her over to one of the rattan love seats near the lobby's revolving door. Looking down at the floor, he said, "That rug looks like it needs replacing. It's a lawsuit waiting to happen."

He was referring to the huge handwoven Persian rug in the center of the lobby that covered the terra-cotta floor. "Yes, it's worn in a few spots and has frayed edges, but with its soft muted colors and its age and pedigree, it would sell for a bundle at an antiques auction."

"There you go," pragmatic Ryan said as they both sat down. "Sell the rug, then pay for the basement repairs."

"I've already tried to get Auntie to sell it. I wanted her to bring it to auction last year; then maybe she would have had enough from the sale to fix the elevator cab. Aunt Amelia would never part with anything in the lobby—the guest suites, yes. The lobby, no. I can understand, because the lobby was once the heart of this place."

"I know the Fred Astaire story from about fifty different versions," he said.

The lobby looked almost the same as it had when the Indialantic first opened its doors to much celebration and fanfare in 1926. Except for a few nasty hurricanes, the Indialantic by the Sea flourished from September to June for almost fifty years. To Liz, whenever she stepped into the lobby with its vaulted ceiling and stucco walls, it was like stepping into another era. Laid out in conversational groupings, the spacious lobby was filled with six-foot potted palms, rattan tables, and chairs with tropical print cushions. The rattan hat rack in the corner, near the revolving door, displayed forgotten bamboo canes, a vintage umbrella, and a man's hat dating from the forties. Aunt Amelia said the hat rack was the same one Fred Astaire had chosen as a dancing partner when he burst through the lobby's revolving door upon his arrival, then entertained the hotel employees with one of his dance routines. He was greeted from behind the mahogany reception desk by Liz's great-grandmother, his room key removed from the wood cubbies behind the reception desk along with a telegram that supposedly had just come in from Paramount Pictures. Was the story true? Liz didn't know, but she liked to believe it.

Ryan pointed to the elevator. "With all the deaths and alleged accidents in the hotel, I don't think fixing the old elevator would be a good idea. Everyone uses the service elevator off the kitchen, anyway. Plus, where would Aunt Amelia send Barnacle Bob when he needed a time-out?"

All of a sudden a projectile sailed across the room and hit Liz on her bare upper arm. "Ouch," she screeched.

"What's wrong?" Ryan asked, jumping up in protective-boyfriend mode.

They turned toward the elevator to see Barnacle Bob inside the accordion-gate cab. He was cracking Brazil nuts, then shooting pieces of the shell toward them from between the bars of his cage. Ten feet away from the elevator was Carmen Miranda, inside her elegant white Victorian birdcage. Was this Aunt Amelia's idea of macaw speed dating? If so, it didn't seem to be working too well, because Carmen's rear end and tail feathers were facing BB.

"Brat!" Liz called over to BB.

Barnacle Bob ignored Liz and started to belt out a song in Spanish. Where he'd learned Spanish, Liz had no clue. "Shush, BB!" she said. "Can't you see you're upsetting Carmen?"

Carmen Miranda was on her perch with her head down, looking at the bottom of her cage. She was a beautiful bird, with her banana-yellow front and teal-blue back. Ziggy had adopted her last January as a gift for

Aunt Amelia. So far Carmen hadn't said a word. She didn't even partake in the morning screeching sessions that most macaws were known for, including Barnacle Bob.

Aunt Amelia had a theory that Carmen was depressed. It was possible. There had to be a reason she was abandoned on the doorstep of the bird rescue center. Macaws can live for fifty years or more. Maybe Carmen had outlived her owner? Sadly, that happened all too often.

"Hey," Ryan asked, "where's the rest of Aunt Amelia's zoo? I haven't seen them underfoot."

"Auntie doesn't want the felines anywhere near Carmen Miranda, for obvious reasons, and you know wherever feline Carolyn Keene goes, so does her canine buddy, Killer. And with this heat the Indialantic's pets can't lounge on the second-floor veranda. I think if you take a peek in the Enlightenment Parlor, you'll find Auntie's menagerie lounging on velveteen pillows under the AC vent."

"Then I guess I shouldn't bring Blackbeard over."

Liz smiled. "No, not a good idea. He and Barnacle Bob need a little more time to become friends. I didn't bring Bronte over this morning, either. You know that whole Tweety Bird–Sylvester thing. Once Carmen starts talking, we can introduce her one at a time to the rest of Indialantic's pets. Maybe save Killer for last, only because of his size, not his disposition."

"Just like Killer, Blackbeard's size can only be compared to his big heart. He'd never hurt a fly—or a macaw."

"Aww, Mr. Stone, you softy. I'm so happy Aunt Amelia forced you into adopting Blackbeard. At least he and Bronte get along. Surprising, seeing she's so small and he's so..."

"Big?" Ryan answered.

"I was gonna say clumsy."

"Well, whatever it is, the Indialantic's the only place I've ever seen dogs and cats getting along." He grabbed her hand. "Okay, enough subterfuge. What's going on in that beautiful brain of yours? How are you planning to keep things on an even keel?"

Liz opened her mouth to speak, just as Barnacle Bob starting singing "Feliz Navidad."

"Shush, BB!" she scolded. "And what's with the Christmas song?"

Barnacle Bob ignored her and upped the volume.

Ryan walked up to his cage. "I think he's trying to communicate with Carmen in her own language. Barnacle Bob must think she's from Mexico or Spain." He stopped a couple of feet from the cage. "Hey, Barnacle Bob, you might be onto something with those nuts. Maybe Carmen Miranda is from Brazil, where they speak Portuguese."

BB looked over at Liz, seeming confused.

Liz alliterated, "You know, BB, Brazil, like the nut you almost maimed me with a minute ago."

BB switched gears and repeated an old candy bar jingle.

"There's no question, you're a nut," she said, laughing.

The macaw was not in the mood to be laughed at, so he reverted back to another song from his television memory-vault, "Babalu" from the *I Love Lucy* show. Aunt Amelia had been too young to have been on *I Love Lucy*, but it was one of her favorite old-time shows, and Liz had no problem watching reruns with her great-aunt in her screening room, especially the candy factory episode.

"Liz, look!" Ryan said, pointing to Carmen Miranda, who was nodding her head to Barnacle Bob's beat. "I think we just figured out that Carmen Miranda might be Cuban."

"Either that," Liz said, "or an *I Love Lucy* fan." Turning to BB, she said, "Keep it up, I think you're finally getting through to her."

BB stuck out his scarlet chest and did an imitation of a bongo drum by tapping his beak against his cage.

"We have more important things to think about," Liz said to Ryan. "We need a plan. Whaddya say, Mr. March?" She lightly punched his muscular arm. "You up for the challenge?"

"We?" he asked, raising his lip Elvis Presley—style. "First, let's see what you have in mind. What's your plan? Or a better yet, why do we need a plan? For a change, as far as I know, there's no dead bodies on the property."

"Funny. Our plan is this. To try to keep the archeologists from killing each other. And praying that if they do, it will happen before my dad comes back from his honeymoon and not on the Indialantic's property."

Ryan rubbed the light stubble on his chin, his luminous, deep brown eyes taking her in. "You're kidding, right?"

"I wish I was. We should leave these lovebirds alone," she said. "Leave Ricky to his Lucy, and you and I go out to the summerhouse. I'll fill you in on the day just in case we need to stage an intervention with our hotel guests. You have a way of grounding me, Mr. Stone."

He grinned, then moved toward the lobby's revolving door, ushering Liz inside. "After you. But, am I sure I want to hear about your day?"

Liz pulled him into the partition with her, wrapped her arms around his neck, then gave him a big kiss. They fell back against the glass and were spit out onto the green carpeting under the hotel's striped awning.

Laughing, she said, "We're a team, right? I'm looking forward to your perspective. You're the yin to my yang, or is it the other way around?"

"Stop talking, Elizabeth Amelia Holt, and look at that moon."

She did.

The full moon reflected on the calm ocean waves like threads of spun gold. An owl hooted in the distance and the scent of jasmine and salty air filled her nostrils. She turned and he grabbed her hand, and they ran down the crushed shell-and-gravel path toward the summerhouse like two lovesick teenagers.

A few feet away from the summerhouse, Liz stopped in her tracks, then pulled Ryan with her under the canopy of a huge palm. "Look," she pointed, "Birdman just streaked by."

"He was naked?" Ryan asked breathlessly, trying but not succeeding in bringing levity to the situation.

She made a fist and gently punched his muscled abs. Maybe she was making a big deal out of nothing. "No, silly."

"Come. Let's go inside. You can tell me everything."

When they reached the glass house, Ryan pulled her up the stone steps, and they took a seat on the cushioned bench that followed all four sides of the space. Aunt Amelia had copied the summerhouse's design from the gazebo scene in *The Sound of Music* where Liesl sang "Sixteen Going on Seventeen." Her great-aunt's version of the gazebo turned out to be much larger than the one pictured in the movie, so they all called it the summerhouse. A bit oxymoronic, seeing the best time to visit it was in every season *but* the summer.

Liz felt her hair springing into curls from the humidity, so she removed the elastic from her wrist and corralled the mess into a ponytail.

"Hey, I like that wild look," Ryan said with a pout.

"And I like to keep cool. It feels like a hundred degrees in here." She glanced around the space. "I have such great memories of being in here. The most recent ones are of you and me," she said, smiling. "When I was small, I would write plays for Aunt Amelia, Grand-Pierre, Betty, and Kate to star in."

"Did your Aunt Amelia steal the show like she always does when she's doing a performance at the Melbourne Beach Theatre Company?"

"What do you think?" she answered with a grin.

"What about Fenton? Was he in your plays?"

"Oh, my father was our one-man audience," she said, laughing.

"Okay, back to reality, Ms. Holt. What's going on? Shouldn't we be inside, keeping an eye on the three archeologists and intern, while Betty tackles the professor?"

"Yes, but first I want to give you the 911."

"Don't you mean the 411?"

"Not in this case." She told him about the argument between the Crawfords, her time at Birdman's, and what had gone on in the library before he showed up. "And you were there to witness dinner," she added.

"I know Mr. Royce's type. There was a captain at the FDNY who acted just like him. He ended up getting fired for sexual harassment after he went too far with one of our dispatchers. Just ignore him."

"What about tomorrow when he makes his big announcement? I want to be there."

"Whoa, I wouldn't get involved. For a change you don't have a personal attachment to the players involved. Sit back and pretend you're watching one of Aunt Amelia's old movies. Use this Jameson guy as a character study."

"Hmm, which movie, *Psycho*?"

"I was thinking *Raiders of the Lost Ark*."

"Certainly not Harrison Ford's part. More like the SS officer. And *Raiders of the Lost Ark* isn't one of Auntie's old movies. Too modern. When did it come out? Sometime in the eighties?"

"A classic, nonetheless," he said.

"Oh, I almost forgot." She told him about how someone had dug up Birdman's garden and planted a gruesome-looking diving spear pointing up in the air like some kind of macabre warning.

"Probably some kids."

"I guess…. But no. I think it was Jameson or one of others. And I do have a reason to stick my nose into the situation."

"Cute nose," Ryan said.

She smiled. "Birdman has been Aunt Amelia's, my father's, and my friend for years. I don't want to see him taken advantage of, especially by the likes of that bully and name-caller Jameson Royce."

"You said Birdman asked you to tell the archeologists to vacate his property; then he immediately changed his mind. Don't you think that's strange?" He used his index finger to clear away a curl that had fallen in front of Liz's right eye. "How about we just go back and check on your guests. If everything's fine, which I'm sure it will be, we can invite Betty to join us on my boat. She can debrief us on Professor Talbot. I'll even drink that pink stuff of yours," he said with a mischievous glint in his eyes. He kept pretending he didn't like rosé when she knew he did. Just like she'd grown accustomed to some of his favorite local craft beers.

"That sounds heavenly, Mr. Stone."

He gave her a quick peck on the cheek.

"That won't do," she whispered, pulling him to her, wanting something deeper to soothe her anxiety....

The kiss worked for the time it took them to walk from the summerhouse back to the hotel, but as soon as they walked into the lobby, there came a screech so loud from the top of the stairs that Liz had an urge to turn tail and run to her cozy beach house and hide under her bed with Bronte—of course, dragging Ryan along behind her.

But it was too late. Ryan was already halfway up the staircase, taking the steps two at a time. Once a first responder, always a first responder.

Pulling up her big girl pants, she followed behind him.

Chapter 8

It wasn't as bad as Liz had imagined. She and Ryan stood in the sitting room of the Swaying Palms Suite where they had a full view of the bedroom. Jameson, dressed only in his boxers, was standing on the king-size bed. Well, not really standing, more like bouncing from one foot to the other and shouting in a high-pitched voice, "Get it out! Get it out! That bird guy's gonna pay for this!"

Liz followed the direction of Jameson's gaze and saw a two-foot red, yellow, and black snake nestled in the open bottom drawer of the armoire. *What a sissy.* Could this be the same Indiana Jones–type explorer who'd just returned from the Amazon? Then again, Indiana Jones had also feared snakes. But it was surprising that Jameson didn't know the nursery rhyme every island child learned about how to tell a poisonous coral snake from a nonpoisonous:

Red touches yellow, kills a fellow.
Red touches black, venom lack.
Yellow touches red, soon you'll be dead.
Red touches black, a friend of Jack.

She looked down the hallway. Three doors opened. Dr. Crawford stepped out of the Oceana Suite. Professor Talbot and Betty came out of Betty's rooms, and Evan Watkins charged out of the Sea Breeze, shouting, "Haven, Dr. Haven, are you okay?" They all bottlenecked next to Ryan and Liz.

Haven, who was leaning against the doorframe to the bedroom, called back with an amused grin on her face, "I'm fine, Evan. It's Mr. Royce who seems to be in a pickle."

Liz entered the sitting room, brushed by Haven, and went straight to the armoire in the bedroom. She reached down, then gently picked up the frightened creature. After a few flicks of its black forked tongue, it wrapped itself comfortably around her arm like one of Cleopatra's bracelets.

"I was just about to do that," Haven said.

Then why didn't she?, Liz thought, noticing the smirk on Haven's face as she glanced toward Jameson, who was crouching on the bed in terror.

"It was just too much fun to watch," she added.

Was Haven the snake charmer? Liz looked over at Jameson and had to agree his facial expression was priceless.

"Fun!" Jameson shrieked. "You know I'm terrified of snakes! Which one of you told Birdman? I saw him out my window. And you, Haven, of all people. Just because I didn't share my discovery with you, you turn on me like this!"

"We both know it was much more than that," Haven said, adding a laugh. "I guess what goes around, comes around, Jameson."

A voice from the now-packed sitting room said, "Outta my way."

Liz turned and watched Dr. Crawford stride over to his wife. "You were just about to do what, dear? Rescue scaredy-pants here from a harmless scarlet king snake? Or, had he made more untoward advances that you rightfully shunned?"

Dr. Crawford went to a chair by the bed, grabbed a pair of shorts, and in an angry motion, whipped them at Jameson.

Jameson slid off the bed, then stood on shaky legs and quickly put on the shorts. "Maybe it wasn't Birdman who left that little present," he said, pointing at Liz's right arm. "But I would say it's someone who knows I hate snakes. Venomous or not." He looked first at Dr. Crawford, then turned his head toward the sitting room, which now held Professor Talbot, Ryan, Aunt Amelia, Captain Netherton, Chef Pierre, Greta, and Betty. Then he turned back to the Crawfords, finally resting his gaze on Liz.

"I didn't know you were afraid of snakes," Evan said with a slight smile on his lips.

"Well, now you do. Ms. Holt, do you mind leaving with that wretched thing? This isn't what I'm paying for. Or do you want to torture me a little further?"

"Of course not," Liz answered, stepping out of the bedroom and into the sitting room, happy to leave.

"Come Lizzy," Aunt Amelia said softly, "give the poor little thing to me. I'll release it into my cutting garden."

"You'll do no such thing. It should be eradicated. This is an outrage!" Jameson called from the bedroom.

Uh oh. He didn't know who he was dealing with.

"Mr. Royce, I'll have you know that the reason these king snakes are becoming harder and harder to find is because of ignorant—" Aunt Amelia covered her mouth with her hand. "Uneducated people like yourself who mistake this poor defenseless creature for a coral snake. Would you like me to get you a list of all the benefits to nature that snakes provide? Perhaps Captain Netherton can fill you in. Or maybe you could go on an eco-tour with him on *Queen of the Seas*."

A bad idea, Liz thought, seeing what had transpired last June aboard the sightseeing cruiser.

"I'll do no such thing," Jameson spat. "We should have chosen another place to stay, but the ancient professor said this would be more convenient. How can it be convenient when there's a lunatic birdbrain running loose?"

Now, Liz was mad. "You wouldn't have an announcement to make about your great find, Mr. Royce, if it weren't for getting permission to dig on the Bennett property."

"And Jameson, if you're unhappy with the accommodations," Aunt Amelia piped up, "feel free to settle your bill. I've asked you about it more than once." She looked over at the credenza, where there was a computer printout Liz assumed was the archeologists' charges for room and board. "I see you've received it. When you calm down, please meet me in the Enlightenment Parlor. I'm sure you could use some." *Go, Auntie!* "Now, allow me to set this beautiful creature free in my garden," she said, her caftan swishing and her beads jangling as she turned toward the door to the hallway.

"I'll go with you, Auntie. No one will be eradicating anything. Right, Ryan?" As Liz passed him, she whispered under her breath, "Flex a muscle or two; show him not to mess with you."

With a mischievous twinkle in his eyes, Ryan said, "Right."

Liz couldn't blame Ryan for not taking the situation seriously. But she couldn't get rid of the feeling that something bad was about to happen. And what was Birdman doing on the grounds? Did he leave the snake? She couldn't imagine him leaving the creature as a trick, on the off chance that Jameson would kill it. If Aunt Amelia was protective of animal life, Birdman was tenfold so.

"I'll pay your bill, Miss Holt, as soon as you give me a discount for the harassment I've just endured." Then Jameson pushed Haven out of the bedroom and into the sitting room. "Everyone, get the hell out of my suite."

After everyone exited, he slammed the door.

"I hope that's not a preview of the next week," Liz said to Ryan.

"You and me both. Maybe it's time for your great-aunt to get out of the hospitality business."

Liz opened her mouth to defend Aunt Amelia but closed it.

He could be right.

Chapter 9

The next morning, hyped up on two cups of coffee, Liz knocked at Birdman's door. She waited, then knocked again. *Where is he?*

The sun was about an hour away from crowning the Atlantic. Not that they would see much of it anyway, because as Birdman had prophesied there were dense clouds, and the smell of rain hung on the thick, humid air. The weather report had another tropical depression forming in the Caribbean, apropos for August.

Following the scene with the snake last night, Aunt Amelia had uncoiled it from Liz's arm, named him Earl, then set him free in her garden as promised.

After everything had settled down, Liz and Ryan managed to corral Betty to the side in order to get the lowdown on her and Captain Netherton's time with Professor Talbot.

Sadly, the professor hadn't had much to tell, except that Jameson had refused to share what his great discovery was—only that it had to do with Ponce de León. Betty also told them that in case Jameson decided to claim the mysterious artifact or artifacts for himself, the professor had alerted Florida's Division of Historical Resources to the fact that Jameson wasn't an accredited archeologist.

Liz recalled someone had said that Jameson had been the one to choose the dig site. Did that mean whatever was found on Birdman's property would belong to the team, or be split fifty-fifty with Birdman? And what had Birdman signed that Jameson had alluded to yesterday? These were only a few of the questions she planned to ask Birdman.

If she could find him.

She opened the screen door and banged on the inside door. No answer. "Birdman, it's Liz, Berry Girl! Wake up, sleepyhead." She had a panicked thought that maybe something had happened to him. The way things were going, she wouldn't be surprised. Holding her breath, she turned the knob to the inside door, then popped her head inside the cottage and called out his name. Still no response.

The small cottage's open floor plan made it easy to view the bedroom and bathroom without stepping inside. Thankfully, the bed was made and door to the bathroom open and empty, leaving only one main room with a galley kitchen. No Birdman anywhere. Liz always loved the cottage's simplicity, with its minimal furniture but maximum books, some in bookcases and others lined up against the wall in neat stacks. Most had to do with the subject of birding, natural history, or gardening and landscaping, even some classical poetry. Birdman was organized and neat. He had no electrical appliances except for a few lamps. No television, not even a toaster.

The only thing adorning his walls were hand-sketched watercolor drawings of the island's wildlife and vegetation. Birdman made all his watercolor paints from ingredients found in nature. When Liz was twelve, Birdman showed her how to use a mortar and pestle to break down hard red clay and transform it into paint. He also used crushed shells, porous rocks, greenery, and flower petals to get his colors, much like the Ais must have done a couple of centuries ago. On the desk where he did his drawings was a stack of artist's sketchbooks. Liz had tried to get him to send them to her publisher, promising to do any of the written text on her laptop. Birdman said he would consider it. But that was right before the archeologists arrived.

She closed the door and tried to think if he'd told her where they were supposed to rendezvous. He hadn't. She'd assumed at his cottage, but he could have meant the shed in the back. However, she'd never been inside the shed and doubted it was meant to be their meeting place.

She would try it anyway.

As she passed Birdman's garden, it looked better than it had yesterday, but there was still a lot of work to be done. The diving spear was missing, and with that thought she remembered another question she had for Birdman, especially after seeing him on the Indialantic's property last night: Was he the one who'd left Earl the snake in Jameson's drawer? And if so, why?

She smiled, recalling the scene of Jameson in his boxer shorts and Haven standing in the sitting room seeming to enjoy his agitation.

The sky darkened as she stepped onto the path behind the cottage that led to the shed, then looked ahead. The tin structure appeared to be on its last legs. The next storm (there was always a next storm on the island in the month of August) would probably collapse the shed and take it away like Dorothy's farmhouse in *The Wizard of Oz*. Hopefully Birdman wouldn't be inside when it happened. She made a mental note to introduce Ryan to Birdman and offer his services to make the shed sturdier and tetanus-free.

She rubbed a spyhole into the only window with the heel of her hand, then peered in.

What looked like a human form lay on the concrete floor. It was too dark to know for sure.

Liz felt her knees quiver and her heart thump as she galloped toward the side of the building where the door was. Above the door handle was a rusty padlock, hanging on its hasp. An open padlock! She charged inside. It was almost pitch black, and the sound of thunder moved closer and closer. She took a step toward the form, praying it wasn't Birdman. From behind, she heard, "Ms. Holt! What are you doing in here!"

She turned slowly and saw Evan the intern's outline in the open doorway. It must have been too gloomy inside the shed for him to notice the panic on her face. He reached behind a metal cabinet near the doorway and flipped on the light switch. Then he stepped inside. "Looks like rain," he said.

She turned slowly around. A single low-wattage bulb dangled from a wire and highlighted what she could now see was just a rolled-up hammock. She reached down to make sure, then exhaled in relief.

"Have you seen, Birdman?" he asked, giving her a strange look.

"I was looking for him myself," she said, wondering if he could hear the thumping of her heart. "We were supposed to meet. He had something he wanted to show me."

"How'd you like the fireworks with Mr. Royce last night?" he asked, giving her a winsome smile. "Who do you think put the snake in his drawer? I'm banking on Dr. Haven. I think she's finally seeing him for who he truly is. Her marriage—"

Liz didn't want to hear about the Crawfords' marriage. Cutting him off, she said, "I was surprised Jameson was scared by a nonpoisonous snake. I would think there are plenty of snakes in the Amazon. Did you see any?"

"Oh, I wasn't there, but I do know Brazil was Mr. Royce's first dig. Mr. Royce isn't a scientist, doesn't hold a doctorate or anything. Think he's more like a contractor who happened upon some interesting relics and a gold piece or two when he built the nearby housing development, Leon de Mar. You know, he paid for the Brazilian expedition and this one."

Not yet, Liz thought.

Evan stepped closer. "Apparently, Mr. Royce contacted Tallahassee, saying he was willing to pay for the Brazilian trip on the condition we could dig here, on the central east coast. What could they say? I don't know if you realize it, but money's super tight for projects like theirs. That's one of the reasons I came aboard—couldn't pay my room and board with the student loans I owe. Dr. Haven told me that when they were in Brazil, Mr. Royce bought some expensive yurt-like tents and hired locals to set up camp. She said it was more like glamping than camping. Glad I wasn't there because setting up camp would have been my job, although I wouldn't have minded the luxury accommodations. Have to admit Mr. Royce sure knows his stuff when it comes to top-of-the-line equipment. But it seems," he said, snickering, "he isn't too knowledgeable about venomous versus nonvenomous snakes."

A huge crack of thunder made them both jump.

"So, what do you think Birdman wanted to show you?" he asked. "Wonder what it was? Did he give you a hint? I mean, I don't want to be nosey, but he's an interesting dude. I would think whatever it was, it must be exciting. Do you have any clue?"

Liz took a step back. Wow, Evan acted like instead of drinking his morning coffee, he'd mainlined it. "No clue," she said. "He told me it was a surprise. Have you been hanging out with Birdman a lot since you've been here?"

"Nah, just met the guy."

That wasn't how it looked to Liz. Birdman didn't let people into his small world easily. And yesterday, he and Evan had seemed pretty friendly. "Do you have any clue as to what Jameson's big announcement is going to be?" she asked.

"Not privy to any of that. Just the errand boy. But I know the professor knows something. I'm bunking with him in the Sea Breeze Suite. I get the sofa in the sitting room. He gets the bedroom. I caught him last night with a glass to the wall, listening to Jameson talking on the phone. Soon after, he stormed into Jameson's suite and I overheard the professor say, 'Now that I've heard what you're up to, I won't let you get away with this!'"

"What did Jameson say?"

"He just laughed at him. Then he physically pushed the professor out into the hallway."

"Did Professor Talbot tell you what the argument was about when he came back to your suite?"

"Ha! I'm just an underling. He'd never share. I guess we'll just have to find out at the big reveal. The professor said Jameson wants everyone to meet at the beach site at ten." He looked toward the window. "I wonder if he'll call it off if it's raining?"

She wanted to learn more about the argument but was worried about where Birdman had gone. "I'm going to go look for Birdman. Maybe that's where he went. The beach."

"He's probably out rescuing a bird or sketching," Evan said.

If Evan knew about Birdman's routine after only being here for a week, it sounded like he knew him better than he was letting on. Was he lying about their relationship? And if so, why?

Before exiting the shed, Liz stuck her hand behind the cabinet and felt the wall for the light switch but couldn't find it.

"It's up about five feet from the floor." Evan reached behind her and turned off the switch, then opened the door and held it so she could pass through. Before going out, she took one last glance behind her and shivered—that rolled hammock sure looked like it hid a dead body. She needed to get a grip. Not everything was sinister.

The sky had brightened with daylight. A dreary daylight. When they passed Birdman's uprooted garden, Evan said, "Wonder what happened here. Pretty crummy thing to do to the guy."

"Do you think it was one of the others?" Liz asked as they walked, feeling it start to drizzle.

"Maybe," he answered, but he didn't offer a guess on who it might have been.

When they reached the path that led to the Indialantic, Evan paused. "I guess I'll go down to the beach and secure things. If I see Birdman, I'll tell him you were looking for him. By the looks of that sky to the south, I think we're in for some sketchy weather. Might have to postpone the big reveal. When you get back to the hotel, you can tell the others not to bother coming."

Liz didn't take orders well, especially not from someone younger than herself. "No. I'll come with you. I want to find Birdman. I'm worried. It's not like him to forget we had plans."

He hesitated. Before he could voice his objections, Liz stepped around him.

"Well, in that case," he said, "I'll go tell the others not to come. Mr. Royce will get pissed if I don't give him a heads-up about the weather. And it'll save Dr. Haven from making a trip." He turned and started to walk away.

"Didn't you want to secure the site? And why were you looking for Birdman? I can give him your message." What was his deal? He wanted to go to the site alone. Why?

"Nah. That's okay. Nothing important. I'll catch up with him later."

She waited until Evan was out of sight. Something wasn't right about him, but she had no time to figure out what. She turned toward the sandy ocean path and started to walk.

Appearing from the murky green jungle, a tall figure came into view.

It was Birdman, and his hands were stained with what Liz hoped was beet juice.

She ran to his side and gave him a bone-crushing hug. "Birdman, are you okay?"

He didn't answer, his arms hanging limp by his sides.

"Birdman," she said, glancing up at his stony face, "are you hurt? What happened?"

"Go home," he mumbled. "Nothing can be done, now. It's too late."

"What? What the heck are you talking about? What's too late?"

He didn't answer, just turned his head and looked behind him, toward the ocean.

"Show me," she said.

And he did.

Chapter 10

Ryan held tight to her hand. "I'm glad you called me before 911, not that it would matter anyway from what you've told me." He looked around the wild terrain at the top of a cliff above the shoreline. "Seems like this area hasn't been touched in centuries."

The wind carried with it fine grains of sand and salt spray from the beach below, stinging her cheeks. "It hasn't," Liz answered. "These are the last acres of land on the island that are privately owned. Probably why the team chose it. Or, as I've recently learned, why Jameson Royce chose it for the dig."

"Where's your Birdman guy?" he asked, using his free hand to push back the bangs from her forehead so he could see her face.

"Birdman was almost catatonic. I told him to go wait in his cottage."

"We'd better hurry," he said. "I figure we have about eight minutes until the first responders arrive."

Reluctantly, she let go of Ryan's hand.

As she'd explained to Ryan a few minutes ago, Birdman had told her that when he'd gone to check the beach to see if the sea turtle eggs were hatching, he'd heard a phone ringing. It was coming from inside the tent the team had set up at the top of the cliff to cover the pit they'd dug. At first, Birdman had ignored the ringing. After a while, it was obvious no one was answering, so he climbed the steps from the beach and went inside. He found the phone on top of an empty wooden shipping crate, but no one was inside. Or so he'd thought, until he looked down into the pit and saw that one side of the sand and soil wall had collapsed. But that wasn't all he saw. The yellow rubber sling part at the end of his diving spear was sticking out of the dirt. He grabbed an electric lantern, climbed down the ladder, then tugged on the spear. It was stuck on something. It wouldn't budge. Birdman grabbed a nearby shovel and dug until he uncovered a body. A dead body. The spear's bloody three-pronged barbed tip hadn't been sticking in some*thing*—it had been sticking in some*one*, namely Jameson Royce.

Liz wrapped her arms around herself. Hard to believe she had the chills in August. It wasn't raining, but the sky over the Atlantic sizzled with bolts of lightning, and thunder echoed a warning about an approaching weather pattern. Liz thought it was too late for a warning. At least it was for Jameson. It would take years to erase the look she'd seen on Jameson's face when Birdman led her inside the tent and she'd peered down.

"Okay, let's go inside," Ryan said, raising his arms like a crossing guard. "But you stay behind; we don't want to compromise the crime scene. Obviously, we shouldn't even be here, or at least I shouldn't. Seeing that our in-house homicide detective connection, Agent Charlotte Pearson, your father's new bride, won't be around to feed us info, we'd better take a quick look."

"Wow! You're right. Let's make it fast. I made sure Birdman and I were careful."

It seemed surreal that there could be another murder on their tiny barrier island. Maybe she was jumping the gun. *Could it have just been a terrible accident?* But Liz knew better.

It started to rain. She scurried after Ryan, who was holding the tent's flap open, and hurried inside.

There were hand tools against the walls of the tent. The killer could have chosen one of the picks or chisels, or even the deadly looking axe-like tool the professor had called a mattock to murder Jameson Royce, but they'd chosen Birdman's diving spear. The obvious reason to Liz was to frame Birdman. Sadness enveloped her when she thought of Jameson Royce. Did he have a family: a wife, kids, a significant other? Would Haven be considered his a significant or *in*significant other?

Keeping a distance behind Ryan, she let him do his PI routine. He reminded her of his pup Blackbeard when the dog was on the scent of one of the Indialantic's cats, turning his head this way and that, his nose in the air, saving the best, or in this case the worst, for last. After peering into the pit, Ryan waved her over. "See those bare footprints? Are those from your Birdman?"

She came up next to him and quickly looked down, then away, avoiding Jameson's masklike face. It wasn't lost on either of them that it had been only last January that they found another body partially covered in dirt. "It must be; he's the only one I know who goes around barefoot," she said. "I wonder what happened to the big discovery that was going to put Jameson in the Florida history books?"

"Looks like his death, or should I say murder, might have the same result." He turned to face her. "I'm not going to get close to the body, but I want to climb down the ladder and take a few pics." He grabbed a couple of disposable gloves from a box on a nearby camp table, put his foot on the top rung of the ladder, and slowly disappear into the pit as she watched.

After he finished, he climbed back up and came toward her. "I didn't see anything unusual; I even took some video we can look over later. In the meantime, I think we better get out of the tent and wait outside. The sheriff's department should be here any minute."

"In that case..." Liz walked over to a wooden crate near the opening of the tent. She used the bottom of her T-shirt to pick up a phone with a leather case covered in a pattern of double G, the insignia for Gucci. It had to be Jameson's. The black screen was illuminated in white and flashed that there were seven missed calls, all from the same number. "Ryan, take a photo of this number."

"Yes, little grasshopper. Quick thinking," he said, snapping off a photo.

Liz tried to access the phone for any text or voice messages, but it wasn't possible to get anything, unless she climbed down and used Jameson's dead thumb to open it. That wouldn't be happening. In fact, she wondered if it would even work.

"We'd better get out of here and get ready to meet Charlotte's replacement," he said.

"Promise me something," she said. "No matter what, we won't disturb my father and Charlotte on their honeymoon. The Brevard County Sheriff's Department is more than capable. And for once this didn't happen on the Indialantic's property."

"True. But once again, all the suspects, besides Birdman, are staying in your family hotel."

Not what she wanted to hear. "Please take Birdman out of the equation. There's no way he did this." Then she remembered how angry he'd been at Jameson and the fact that she'd seen him on the Indialantic's grounds. Not to mention Jameson Royce had also seen him.

No. Birdman was a pacifist; he literally wouldn't kill a fly. "Every creature has a reason for being here," he'd once said.

"Even mosquitoes?" Liz had asked.

Birdman had laughed and said, "You've got me. But then, what would my bats eat?"

When she'd originally recounted to Ryan Birdman's story of how he had found Jameson, she'd been teary-eyed. Now, she was more worried about how guilty Birdman would look to the sheriff's department. His prints would be all over the crime scene. And it was Birdman's spear. What would be his motive to kill Jameson Royce? And how was she going to explain sending him back to his cottage?

She reached to put the phone back on the crate, her hand shaking from the impact of what Ryan had just said about the archeologists staying at the Indialantic. The phone slipped from her fingers and crashed to the ground. The case separated from the phone and a small key lay on the dirt floor.

Ryan bent over the key. "It looks like it could be from a small safe or maybe even a safety deposit box. There's some writing on the side." He took out his phone and took a photo.

"Can't we just keep it for a little while?" Liz asked. The daughter of a former defense attorney, she already knew the legal answer to her question.

"No, because if it's from a safety deposit box, only the sheriff's department can get access to what's inside." Following Liz's example, he used his T-shirt to put the key between the case and the phone, then he placed the phone back on top of the crate. "Let's go."

He was right, no time for pouting about the key. She was determined *this time* to let the sheriff's department handle things.

When they stepped outside, they were greeted with sirens and flashing lights. On the beach below, she saw four all-terrain vehicles approaching from the north. All she could think of was how upset Birdman would be if they destroyed any of the sea turtles' habitats. The hatching eggs must have been the surprise Birdman wanted to show her early this morning.

But he'd found another discovery. A gruesome one.

Liz gritted her jaw, ready to defend her old friend till the end.

So much for letting the sheriff's department handle things...

Chapter 11

Charlotte's replacement, Agent Bly, had requested that Liz tell everyone to stay put at the Indialantic until the preliminary autopsy report on Jameson came through. Bly was probably in his early to midfifties. He had a pleasant face and small, alert dark eyes that had scanned every corner of the tent. He'd been friendly, but not too friendly, not interested in anything but facts and alibis. He'd shared with them that he grew up in Melbourne Beach and was currently the lead homicide agent at the sheriff's department in Cocoa Beach. Ryan had fibbed when he told Agent Bly that he hadn't been inside the tent, not wanting to rock the boat with Charlotte's substitute. A plus for Liz and Ryan was when they'd found out that Agent Bly's daughter-in-law was a volunteer firefighter and played on Ryan's softball team. Even though Ryan wasn't considered part of the Barrier Island Fire Rescue, occasionally he was called in as a consultant on certain cases where his past expertise as a Brooklyn-based arson investigator came in useful. Plus, he was an awesome first baseman.

After he viewed Jameson's body, Liz overheard Bly suggesting to one of his officers that Jameson's death could have been an accident, saying the diving spear might have pierced Jameson's abdomen when the pit's wall collapsed. Even if that was true, it wouldn't explain what Jameson was doing with the spear in the first place. Yesterday, Evan and Jameson had been the only ones who'd seen the spear, and dead men tell no tales. She just hoped Evan would keep his mouth shut and wouldn't implicate Birdman in Jameson's death.

After the coroner had taken the body away and Liz explained her side of things, Agent Bly followed Liz and Ryan to Birdman's cottage. They found him sitting at his small kitchen table looking despondent. When they'd walked inside, Liz noticed that Birdman had washed his hands of blood, most likely a moot point seeing his fingerprints would be all over the spear and shovel. She knew from television crime shows that if there was blood near the point of entry of the spear's tip, Jameson must have been stabbed when he'd been alive. The guy had been obnoxious, but no one deserved to die that way. Accident or not.

After the three of them left Birdman's cottage, Agent Bly told them he didn't want anything leaked to the public, including the archeologists and residents at the Indialantic, about the type of weapon used until he had a chance to view the coroner's report to verify if foul play was involved. Then he'd left Liz and Ryan at the path leading to the Indialantic and headed toward the now cordoned-off beachside crime scene. Liz and Ryan walked back to the hotel slowly in order to process everything, then give everyone an update on Jameson's death.

Outside the kitchen door, Liz said, "Ryan, we agree he was murdered, right?"

"I'd give it an eighty percent chance he was."

"I'm at a hundred percent."

Ryan punched in the code next to the kitchen door and held it open for her. As she passed, she whispered, "I'm dying to call that number on Jameson's phone."

Ryan followed her in, then put his fingers to his lips to shush her, pointing to the butler's pantry, where they saw Chef Pierre sitting with his feet on his desk, his chef's toque slightly askew as usual. He'd brought back the desk from France some thirty years ago, and it was the place he wrote out each day's menu, no matter if the meals were for just Liz, Ryan, Aunt Amelia, and the Indialantic's residents, or if they had hotel guests. Old habits were hard to break, and Liz would be bereft the day the man she thought of as a grandfather wasn't in the pantry at the crack of dawn, plotting his perfect menus in his perfect handwriting on large parchment-style Crane watermarked paper, leaving at the bottom of each menu a caricature of a chef's toque and below it a curled mustache with the initials PM, for Pierre Montague.

Whether Grand-Pierre admitted it or not, he was the spitting image of how Christie described Hercule Poirot in her novels—right down to his curled and waxed mustache. It was Grand-Pierre who'd got her hooked on Agatha Christie. They were both reading *Peril at End House* for the third or fourth time, but now wasn't the time to discuss mystery novels, and she didn't see any point in upsetting the hotel's chef with the news of Jameson's death by telling him there would be one less place setting at dinner. She would have Greta tell him. Greta and the chef had become great friends, perhaps even more than friends in the past nine months. Lately, romance seemed to the order of the day at the Indialantic. Romance and murder.

She took Ryan's elbow to steer him out of the kitchen toward the back hallway that led to her father's apartment. As they quickly passed the butler's pantry, the chef was humming something that sounded like the French national anthem. Barnacle Bob, who was in his cage next to Grand-Pierre, pretended to be his accompanist but was purposely humming "When the Saints Go Marching In" off-key, just to be his old irritating self.

"Good idea to call that number," Ryan said, when they were out of hearing distance. "We need to make contact before whoever called hears he's dead."

"Let me call," Liz said. "I can always feign I'm a ditzy blonde and pretend I called the wrong number."

"Strawberry blond with not a touch of ditz anywhere," Ryan said, tapping the top of her nose. Then he held up his phone with the photo he took of the phone number from Jameson's phone.

She blew him a kiss, then punched in the number. The area code was local, which was surprising seeing Jameson lived in Palm Beach. Holding the phone to her ear, she felt like a teenager again: calling her high school crush, Jordan Reeves, just to hear his voice, then hanging up because she was too embarrassed to speak.

On the other end of the phone, Liz heard, "Hello, Suzie Malone, Sunset Realty."

While it wasn't Jordan who answered on the second ring, it was someone Liz knew from high school. Feeling tongue-tied, Liz said, "Uh, Suzie, hi, it's Liz. Liz Holt."

"OMG, Lizzy. How long has it been?" Suzie squealed. "I heard you were back on the island. Brit told me." Brit, or Brittany Poole, was the proprietor of the emporium's clothing and jewelry boutique. To this day, Liz was surprised that Aunt Amelia had rented out the space to her, especially knowing Liz and Brit's history. Suzie and Brittany might be besties, but Liz and Brittany would always remain worsties, even though her father, who believed that forgiveness was the true key to happiness, kept scolding her about it.

"You must be devastated about what happened last January with your ex in New York," Suzie said with fake concern, "and that terrible, terrible ordeal and disfigurement that was plastered all over the national papers and evening news. It even made the *Beachsider*."

Disfigurement. Liz never thought of her scar that way; apparently others did.

She heard Suzie take a deep breath. "Oh, and your *New York Times* best-seller, I haven't had a chance to read it yet. It's on my bedside table, though. Who has time to read nowadays? Especially with all the great shows on streaming networks," she added with a giggle.

Suzie hadn't changed. But Liz realized she had changed. What Suzie had just said hadn't really affected Liz like it might have a year ago; all the drama and trauma seemed so distant and dealt with. She glanced over at Ryan—plus, she had Ryan and her family, not to mention *true* friends in her life now.

"Your auntie must think I'm quite a pest," Suzie said, "but I'm so happy you've decided to put the Indialantic by the Sea on the market. You must agree, Miss Amelia is getting a little old for such a big enterprise. Does she plan to sell the hotel, land, and emporium in one package? I know Brit will be upset if that happens, but I'm sure the new owner will keep the emporium going, after all, per Brit, the rent collected from the shopkeepers is the only lucrative thing going for the Indialantic. And, as I've told Miss Amelia numerous times, I promise to get the highest price imaginable. When can I come over?" The excitement in her voice was over the top, and Liz could almost hear the calculator in Suzie's head computing what her commission might be if she sold the Indialantic by the Sea. It would never happen. Aunt Amelia would never sell.

Liz's mind went back in time to what she and her best friend Kate called "Senior Prom Gate." Liz said sweetly into the phone, "Why yes, I'd love to get together, Suzie. You free later today?" She looked toward Ryan and gave him a thumbs-up.

Suzie then filled Liz in on her adorable husband and all his numerous financial and social accomplishments; if Liz didn't cut her off soon, she was worried Suzie would tell her about how her husband's potty training had gone at age two. "Gotta go, Suze, see ya at three," then she hung up the phone. "Wow! She hasn't changed a bit," she said to Ryan.

"Who is she?" he asked.

"Suzie Malone, an old high school frenemy who now runs Sunset Realty in town."

"Why would your frenemy, as you put it, call our dead guy?"

Liz raised an eyebrow at his "dead guy" comment, then said, "We shall soon find out. And you're coming with me. If Suzie is anything like she was in high school, she'll sharpen her claws, perfect husband or not, then swipe them in your direction, drooling over fresh meat. But don't worry, darling. I'll protect you."

"Oh, Ms. Holt. Aren't you being a tad possessive?"

"Moi?" Liz said, batting her eyelashes. "We better go tell everyone what just went down. Why does all this feel like déjà vu?"

"I'm not even going to answer that one," he said as they went into the dining room on their way to search everyone out and give them the shocking news.

Within half an hour, Liz and Ryan had told everyone about Jameson's death, trying to make it sound like it had been terrible accident. When they'd told Aunt Amelia, she'd needed a cup of her chamomile Island Bliss tea laced with a shot of brandy. It was rare that Liz saw her great-aunt drink. If there was one occasion that called for it, it would be murder. Aunt Amelia had wept for a short time, dried her eyes, then gone to console the four archeologists, channeling her best Harriet Nelson from *The Adventures of Ozzie and Harriet* by going into mother-hen mode and serving tea to everyone, her cure for mending all hurts. Aunt Amelia hadn't played a mom figure on the early sixties sitcom; instead, she'd had the role of older son David's materialistic date, perfect in her bubblegum-pink lipstick, baby-blue angora twinset, and a strand of freshwater pearls at her neck.

Mystery writer Betty had been the only one to pull Liz and Ryan aside and question them. Until the coroner's report came out, she'd promised to use her cyber connections to search out anything having to do with the deceased. Betty and her trusty iPad, nicknamed Watson, were unsurpassed when it came to sniffing out a killer.

For obvious reasons, per Agent Bly, everyone was banned from Birdman's property.

At noon Chef Pierre served lunch in the Indialantic's sweltering dining room. Per Ryan, the earlier lightning storm had caused a power surge that had wiped out the motherboard on the hotel's air-conditioning system. Even though someone was on their way to fix it, Liz thought the timing couldn't have been worse. Not only was she looking around the room at four murder suspects, not believing for a second Jameson's death was an accident, she was also looking at four *hot and cranky* murder suspects. Now with Jameson out of the picture, the foursome sat together at a table near a high-powered fan that Greta had set up. Their heads were bent during the meal, discussing things in whispers and delivering sly glances toward anyone entering the room. None of them looked bereft. Not even Haven. Though she did look tired. Really tired.

Would this turn out to be one of those classic Agatha Christie murders where everyone was in on the killing?

Liz spent the next hour filling their guests' (or suspects') glasses with ice water and worrying about Birdman. The lunch menu included cold roast beef and cheddar on ciabatta bread, along with gazpacho soup topped with a dollop of sour cream.

Ryan was waiting outside for the heating-and-cooling truck, and Greta and Grand-Pierre were in the kitchen, sitting at the large farm table poring over *The Pierre Montague Cookbook* to find something cold they could serve for dinner in case the AC was still out. Aunt Amelia, Liz, and her father had compiled the chef's beautifully handwritten recipes by category, then had them copied and bound into an indie-published book for the chef's eighty-first birthday. Even though Liz knew how to prepare most of Grand-Pierre's recipes by heart, she still loved to refer to her copy of the cookbook, if only for nostalgic reasons.

Betty, Aunt Amelia, and Captain Netherton had wisely chosen to have lunch at Ryan's grandfather's gourmet deli/bistro/coffeehouse, Deli-casies by the Sea, in the Indialantic's emporium. The same place Liz planned to go for lunch after she brought out dessert to the four archeologists. Thankfully, the emporium's AC was working fine, something Liz didn't pass on to their captive guests. She figured they'd just returned from the Amazon, so it shouldn't be a problem sweating it out at the hotel for a couple of hours. If they had any complaints, let them whine to Agent Bly at the Brevard County Sheriff's Department.

"Ms. Holt, could we have something a little stronger?" Professor Talbot asked as Liz came toward them holding a fourth pitcher of ice water. "I think the occasion calls for it."

"Of course, and please call me Liz." After all, they were paying guests. At that thought, she stopped dead in her tracks, ice water splashing up from the pitcher and onto the professor's right knee. She'd just realized that Jameson Royce was supposed to foot the bill for the entire team—food and lodging. *Now what will happen?* She chided herself for such a thought and said to the professor, "Sorry about that." She grabbed a napkin from the next table and dabbed it against the professor's bony knee.

Professor Talbot laughed. "Actually, that ice water felt quite good. Maybe you should just pour it over my head." He seemed quite jovial, considering the circumstances. No love lost there. Evan had told her this morning that the professor and Jameson had fought last night. Could the kindly professor be Jameson's killer?

"Liz," Professor Talbot said, "I wonder if you could tell us more of what happened this morning?" Usually the professor appeared neat and well dressed: ironed creases in his khaki shorts and matching short-sleeve khaki shirts, his mustache and head of thick, shiny white hair always glistening with some kind of hair product. Now, he looked like a rumpled Albert Einstein after he'd stuck his finger in an open electrical socket.

Liz thought back to when Aunt Amelia had told her that Professor Talbot reminded her of the actor Lorne Greene.

"Who?" Liz had asked.

"Ben Cartwright. *Bonanza.* You remember, the father of Hoss, Adam, and Little Joe."

"Oh, yeah, *that* Lorne Greene." Liz had had no clue who she'd been referring to.

"I'm sure you recall the episode where I played Saloon Girl Number Two and tossed a mug of beer in Lorne's, I mean Ben's foxy face after he snapped my garter."

Foxy? she remembered thinking. Aunt Amelia had been right, Liz hadn't remembered the episode. But now that she thought about it, her great-aunt had been in quite a few old TV westerns as a saloon girl, dancer, or gun-toting barmaid. The only western Liz liked that Aunt Amelia had introduced her to was *Maverick.* That was because Liz was a huge James Garner fan. Not because of his role in *Maverick*, more for *The Rockford Files*, one of her father's favorite series, which she'd watched with him on DVD when she was young.

Reminiscing about the past reminded Liz of how much she missed her father, especially now that the professor was looking up at her, waiting for an explanation about what happened to Jameson Royce. Remembering what Agent Bly had told her and Ryan, she kept it short. "All I know is that someone found Mr. Royce at the bottom of the pit near your site by the beach. Part of the wall had collapsed and covered him."

Evan said, "It was Birdman who found him, I bet. Is that where he was when you were looking for him?"

"That strange man?" Dr. Crawford said. "Did he have something to do with Jameson's death?"

"We don't know that foul play was involved," Professor Talbot added. "Isn't that correct, Liz?"

Liz ignored his question, and instead asked her own. "Do any of you know why Mr. Royce was there so early? Since he's been here, I don't ever recall him getting up before nine thirty." Because they were both early birds, Liz had asked Greta and Grand-Pierre if they had seen Jameson before dawn. They hadn't.

"Not a clue what went on in that mind of his," the professor answered. "We were meant to meet him at ten." Then he glanced around the table at the others and they nodded their heads in agreement.

"What were you doing there so early, my dear?" Dr. Crawford asked Liz, looking past his long nose up at her.

Evan caught Liz's eye, then turned away. He knew Liz could ask him what he was doing there and why he'd been looking for Birdman. She didn't owe any of them an explanation. "You know what," Liz said, plastering on a smile, "I think we should just sit tight and let the sheriff's office handle things for now. I think I saw a pitcher of the chef's refreshing sangria in the fridge. Let me grab it for you."

"Nothing for me," Haven said, looking down at her plate. She hadn't touched her lunch.

Like the professor, she also looked less put together than usual. She'd skipped a button on her white linen shirtdress, and there was a beige stain on her collar. Haven's face was as pale as her dress. It was hard to reconcile the woman who looked pleased last night with Jameson's angst during the snake incident with the one who now looked ill. Maybe she had cared for Jameson?

"Is everything okay, Haven?" Liz asked. "Would you like the chef to make you something else for lunch? I'm sure he could whip up something fast. A cold calamari salad perhaps?"

"Squid? Oh, no, no. The soup looks delicious." She took a slurp of the gazpacho and started to gag. She glanced up apologetically at Liz, then jumped out of her seat. Holding her stomach, she said, "I think I caught a bug. Can you tell me where the nearest restroom is?"

"The lobby." Liz pointed to the door leading to the hallway, hoping it was a stomach thing, not something else. Liz was still shell-shocked from last June's wedding that wasn't. The one where a guest at the Indialantic had been poisoned. *If it happens again,* she thought, *Aunt Amelia might have to close the inn's doors forevermore.* Either that or hire a priest to do an exorcism.

Chapter 12

Once Haven was out of earshot, her husband said, "She hasn't been eating at all the last couple of days. Maybe it's a bug or parasite she brought back from Brazil."

Concerned about his mentor, Evan turned to Dr. Crawford and said, "I think she's just sensitive to Mr. Royce's death. It hit her hard."

"If that's the case, then explain why yesterday she was ill before bedtime? Jameson was still alive."

"Maybe it's the heat?" Evan looked at him with an accusatory stare. "And maybe you should check on her, Dr. Crawford," Evan said, a trace of anger in his voice. "I've never seen her sick. She never missed a single lecture when I was her teaching assistant. She told me it was you who she nursed in Brazil when your foot got infected from that tocoma palm tree thorn you stepped on."

"I didn't need nursing, she just gave me some antibiotics, for all the good that did. And it wasn't a tocoma palm, it was a Tucumã, astrocaryum aculeatum, to be exact. I was told by the native Brazilians that it's the same tree from which they harvest the fruit and make biodiesel fuel. Quite interesting from an environmental standpoint." He turned to Evan. "And it's none of your business, young man, to tell me what I should or shouldn't be doing with my wife. You're her little lapdog; I refuse to take on that role. Why don't you run along and find out if she's okay? She doesn't share much with me anymore. Not even a—" He caught himself before he said the word "bed."

"My pleasure." Evan stood up, threw his napkin onto his plate, and hurried out of the dining room.

Professor Talbot patted Dr. Crawford on the arm. "It will be okay, Nigel."

Dr. Crawford pulled his arm away as if he'd been burned.

The professor looked at him and shook his head, making a tsk, tsk sound. "We're all on edge, Nigel. No need to take it out on everyone. Liz, how about that sangria you mentioned earlier? Think we could all use some."

"Sure. And I'll bring dessert. Be right back."

Before the professor could ask any more questions, she hurried to the empty kitchen and opened the fridge. She removed the pitcher of sangria and a silver tray holding four bowls filled with assorted berries, each topped with Grand-Pierre's amaretto crème fraiche. After adding ice to the sangria and removing the cellophane from the bowls, she brought the pitcher and tray to the table.

Haven and Evan were still absent. She filled four wineglasses with sangria, put a bowl of berries at each place setting, then asked, "Can I get you anything else?" *Please say no.*

Professor Talbot spoke for himself and Dr. Crawford. "That's all, Liz. Have you seen Betty anywhere? I wanted to have a chat with her."

"No. But if I do, I'll pass on your message." She white-lied, because technically she hadn't seen Betty, but Liz did know where she was—dining in cool air-conditioned comfort.

"That would be aces, young lady." He dipped his spoon in the berries, scooped some of the crème fraiche from the top, and swallowed. "Delicious," he mumbled, wiping his mouth with a napkin. "Nigel, you have to try it."

Boy, he seemed chipper.

Dr. Crawford looked to have no interest in berries. "Just let us know when the AC is fixed," he said—more like demanded—then stood up. Liz didn't know if it was her imagination, but with Jameson out of the picture, Dr. Crawford seemed more assertive, almost aggressive. He handed Liz a business card from his shirt pocket. "Call me when it's fixed. I'm going to try to catch a breeze on the veranda before I succumb to heatstroke."

Liz took the card and put it in her pocket. "Will do."

Professor Talbot said to Nigel, "You'd be better off staying here in front of the fan. I think we have some things to discuss before going forward."

Dr. Crawford leaned down and lightly banged his right fist on the table. "There's nothing to discuss until we find out what happened. You do realize we have no funds to continue the expedition."

Or pay Aunt Amelia, Liz thought.

"And we'll never know what Jameson planned to announce. Unless you know something, Walter?" Dr. Crawford pushed his glasses up his nose, then looked Professor Talbot in the eye, his teeth gritted. "If we do manage to continue. I'm nominating myself to be in charge. I'm sure Haven will agree. Jameson was right about one thing; you must get with the times, old man. Whatever Jameson found, he probably wouldn't have discovered it without all the expensive high-tech equipment he brought with him."

"You know nothing of the sort, Nigel. But if you want to head up this doomed mission, be my guest. I have a feeling we won't be getting back to work anytime soon. If ever." The professor looked over at Liz and shrugged his shoulders.

Dr. Crawford strode toward the French doors that opened to the veranda and flung them open. A blast of thick, sticky air blew inside. Before stepping under the threshold, he turned and addressed the professor. "Walter, it's not like you to give up the reins so easily. If we find out foul play was involved in Jameson's demise, I will suspect you, right after that strange Birdman guy." With that, Dr. Crawford left the dining room, slamming the French doors behind him.

"Well, that was quite a show of character, don't you agree, my dear?" Professor Talbot said. "If anyone had a motive for killing Mr. Royce, I would think Dr. Crawford would take the top slot. Jealousy is a toxic substance, my dear. A quote from Lord Byron comes to mind: 'Yet he was jealous, though he did not show it, for jealousy dislikes the world to know it.'"

"Oh, I think he shows it," Liz said.

Professor Talbot took one last spoonful of dessert, wiped his mouth, and stood, then placed his napkin near his empty bowl. "I think I might go up to my suite and lounge under the Bombay ceiling fan. I remember Florida before air-conditioning. I could always handle the heat and humidity; it was the mosquitoes I couldn't tolerate. Smart neighbor you have, putting in those bat boxes. You need something to gobble up those pests. Again, if you see Betty, please ask her to come to my rooms. There's something important I want to tell her before I talk to the police."

Liz was intrigued. "Anything I can pass on?"

"No, no, dear. At this point it probably doesn't mean anything. But I remember, back in the day, our glory days, so to speak, Betty always had a good head on her lovely shoulders. And she is a mystery writer. Just want to kick something around with her."

"Sure. No problem."

"Thank you, my dear." He got up and went in the direction of the hallway to the lobby, shuffling slightly as he walked. She thought of the tall winding staircase in the lobby and called out, "Professor, there's a utility elevator in the hallway behind the kitchen, if you'd prefer that?"

"Yes, Betty mentioned it. I just want to get a copy of the local paper before I go up."

As she watched him walk away, she mused about the professor's likability factor. He always seemed to be on an even keel: steady, careful, thinking things through; but there was another factor she needed to take into account. The suspect factor.

Birdman didn't kill Jameson. That left Evan, the professor, Haven, and Dr. Crawford. Maybe it *had* been an accident? What if Jameson was the one who left the diving spear in Birdman's garden and he was planning something else with it? Maybe the spear hadn't killed him. Instead, maybe he suffocated from the sand and dirt after the wall's collapse and was buried alive? The spear hadn't been in Birdman's garden this morning. As Agent Bly suggested, could the collapse of the pit's wall have caused the spear to pierce his stomach? Maybe, if he was a contortionist. The angle seemed wrong, plus the look of surprise on his face, and, strangely, he was flat on his back on the floor of the pit, his arms by his sides as if posed. If he was buried alive, wouldn't he have been standing upright, trying to shovel out? Birdman had assured her that he hadn't disturbed the body, only checking to see if Jameson was alive.

With homicide detective Charlotte and her attorney father on their honeymoon, Liz was at an impasse on how to get important information about cause of death from Agent Bly. She wasn't about to call her father. She, Ryan, and Betty would handle things. Or at least try. Based on the past, three heads were definitely better than one.

Enough postulating, she thought. She went to the sideboard and grabbed a tray, then she piled the tray with the dirty lunch dishes. She left the berry bowls in case Haven and Evan came back, but instead of taking the tray back to the kitchen, she put it back on the sideboard. First things first. If Dr. Crawford didn't care about his wife's condition, Liz did. Especially if there was the chance Haven had been poisoned.

As she left the room, she mentally crossed her fingers she wouldn't find Dr. Haven Crawford dead. Lately, at the Indialantic by the Sea, you never knew.

When Liz stepped into the empty lobby, Evan was skipping down the stairs, wearing a huge smile. When he reached the bottom he said, "Haven's fine. In her rooms resting. Do you think you could bring her some crackers or something from the kitchen?"

Liz noticed this was the second or third time Evan had dropped the "Doctor" from Haven's name. "Of course. No problem. I was just going to check on her. I'll also bring up some of Aunt Amelia's chamomile tea. Maybe the heat got to her?"

"Maybe."

She thought she'd take advantage while he seemed in a good mood and grill him about this morning. "Evan, you never told me why you were looking for Birdman earlier."

His smile turned to a frown. "I told you. I came to help put his garden back together." No, he hadn't told her that. Evan rubbed the palm of his left hand repeatedly across the hip of his surf shorts. A nervous tic? "Gotta run. Do you see how uncaring Dr. Crawford was? What a deadbeat. Didn't even go check on his wife." He didn't wait for her to reply and went breezing out the lobby's revolving door. As he went out, heat came blowing in. She realized if the AC didn't get fixed, she might have to put up Aunt Amelia, Betty, and Greta at her beach house. Captain Netherton and Grand-Pierre could stay with Ryan in the caretaker's cottage. However, there was no way she'd let any of the archeologist murder suspects stay with her or Ryan.

Twenty minutes later, Liz was in the Oceana Suite. The suite had been remodeled after the gruesome events of a year ago. Dr. Crawford wasn't there, but Haven was under the Baccarat crystal chandelier, asleep on the sofa.

The door to the terrace was open. Storm clouds were brewing over the Atlantic; the tropical depression had turned into Tropical Storm Odette just south of Puerto Rico. The forecasters weren't sure if it would make its way up the east or west coast of Florida. *That's all we need*, she thought, looking at Haven's beautiful but pale face. Right now, storms weren't their main concern; murderers and dehydration were. With that thought, she heard the AC vent flutter and choke. Soon after, cool air flowed into the room. *Hallelujah.*

She left the tray with the crackers and tea service on the table in front of the sofa, then decided to tidy up the bathroom so Greta wouldn't have to. On her way to the bathroom she saw the sash from one of the hotel's robes jammed between the two closet doors. Liz always felt like a voyeur when she was in a guest's room, even though she'd been entering these same suites since she was age five. There were a lot of rooms you could get lost in, especially in a hotel the size of the Indialantic. The only place that had been off-limits to her had been the hotel's basement. But that didn't stop Liz and her bestie Kate from bringing a couple of local boys down there when they were sixteen. Liz had let it slip to the boys that during Prohibition, the hotel kept spirits in the basement. Not the ghost kind—although there'd always been rumors swirling that the Indialantic was haunted—the liquor kind. Before they'd had a chance to nab any old bootleg bottles of rum, her father found them, and that was the last time she was allowed in the basement. Which was fine with Liz. It was the only area of the hotel that gave her the heebie-jeebies.

She looked toward the sitting room to make sure Haven hadn't woken up, then opened one of the closet doors. She stuffed the robe to the back of the closet, then as she closed the door, she noticed a portable safe under two pairs of Haven's shoes. Maybe Jameson also had a safe in his room to keep the treasured artifact, or artifacts, he'd been boasting about. Liz had to admit she was curious as to what his great find was. Would they ever know? She thought back to the key found between Jameson's phone and its case. Could the key fit a safe like the one in front of her? Hadn't Evan told her Professor Talbot had argued with Jameson last night about the find? If there was a safe in Jameson's closet like there was in the Crawfords' suite, she was sure the sheriff's department would confiscate it. But maybe not. Jameson's death hadn't officially been ruled a homicide. Yet.

Spurred on by the idea of checking out Jameson's closet (apparently not worried about being a voyeur at the thought of being in a dead man's suite), she hurried into Haven and Dr. Crawford's bathroom, took the dirty towels off the rack, replaced them with clean, then grabbed the full garbage bag from the receptacle next to the sink and tiptoed into the sitting room.

Haven was still sleeping, and the room had cooled down considerably. Before leaving the suite, Liz took a cozy hand-knitted throw made by one of the artisans from Home Arts by the Sea and laid it on top of Haven, surprised that her husband still hadn't come to check on her.

Not my worry, she thought, closing the door softly behind her. Liz had bigger things to obsess about. Like who'd killed Jameson Royce.

Still holding the dirty towels and trash bag, she stopped in front of the door to the Swaying Palms Suite, where Jameson had been staying. The door opened and Dr. Crawford stepped out.

"Dr. Crawford, you aren't allowed in there. We still don't know what happened to Mr. Royce."

He squinted his eyes at her like he was trying to remember who she was. "That's ridiculous. You told us the wall collapsed and he was buried alive. I'm taking over the project, and I need to see where we stand."

She glanced at the laptop he was holding in his hands.

"Until I hear anything different, you need to return that to Mr. Royce's suite," she said, nodding her head at the laptop.

"You're not the police. I will do no such thing!" he said.

He moved to turn toward the Oceana Suite and Liz blocked him. "I insist you return it, or I will call Agent Bly."

"Do what she says, Nigel." Haven took a step toward them. "And thanks for checking up on me, darling," she said sarcastically. "It's so good to know how deeply concerned you are."

"As always," he answered, "you have your little protégé to help you. Evan's always by your side. Now that Jameson's gone for good, Evan will have you all to himself. And he can have at it," he said, adjusting his glasses farther up his nose, then giving his wife a once-over. "You look fine to me."

"Okay, *doctor*," Haven said softly, the fight going out of her, and looking like a gentle breeze might topple her. "Thanks for the clean bill of health. Put the laptop back, as the girl asked."

Feeling awkward but not awkward enough to leave without knowing he did as Haven asked; Liz moved toward Haven and they waited. Taking his time, Dr. Crawford went back into Jameson's suite with the laptop.

Finally, taking about five minutes longer than needed to return the laptop, Dr. Crawford opened the door and came out into the hallway empty-handed. Liz glanced inside, saw the laptop on the desk in the sitting room, reached around the door and turned the lock from the inside, then closed the door. She made a point for Dr. Crawford's benefit of jiggling the doorknob, confirming the door was locked.

Before leaving the hallway, Liz said, "Haven, I left you some of Auntie's tea and some crackers. I hope you're feeling better now that the AC is working."

"Yes, I saw. Thank you, Liz. At least someone is being considerate," she answered, giving her husband a dirty look.

"Of course. Please push the intercom if you need anything."

"I will. Thanks again, Liz."

Dr. Crawford had had enough of their chitchat. He grabbed Haven's elbow and Liz watched as she leaned into him for support, her feet dragging as they made their way toward the Oceana Suite. Where was the vibrant woman she'd met a week ago? Could she be mourning Jameson's death to the point that it made her ill? Or had she been the one to kill him? Dr. Crawford had said at dinner that his wife had also been ill last night.

Did Haven have buyer's remorse?

Or in this case, killer's remorse?

Chapter 13

"There you are!" Ryan shouted, just as Liz was about to dump the garbage from the Oceana Suite into one of the outdoor dumpsters at the rear of the hotel. Blackbeard spotted her and ran, more like galloped, toward Liz. She braced herself, happily awaiting the big smooch she knew was coming. However, she must not have been as prepared as she'd thought, because even though she was able to stand her ground when the dog jumped up on her, his nails snagged a slit in the garbage bag and trash tumbled out and onto the pavement.

Ryan walked up to them. "Blackbeard, down."

The dog listened, not his usual MO.

"Why, Ryan Stone, since when does Blackbeard listen to your commands?" She laughed, then crouched to collect a tube of mascara that had fallen out of the bag and rolled toward her.

"Since I hired a dog trainer on Aunt Amelia's recommendation. Well, she's not really a trainer per se, more like a dog whisperer."

"Can't see you believing in that malarkey, Mr. Everything's Black and White."

"I don't, but you just saw the results. Apparently, my lips have been saying *no*, but my smiling face was saying *yes*. It's all in the tone of voice and facial expression. A treat or two doesn't hurt either." He reached in his shorts pocket and gave Blackbeard a treat. "Let me help. Hand me the bag, or what's left of it."

She did.

He tied a knot where the slit was, then held the makeshift bag open.

A hot, blustery wind came off the Indian River Lagoon, causing the trash to fly toward Ryan. He moved his large sneakered foot and stomped on a tissue covered in Haven's shade of lipstick. "Ick! Is that blood?"

"No, silly. Lipstick. Don't you recognize the shade?"

"Why would I?"

"Because Dr. Haven Smith-Crawford is gorgeous. Don't pretend you haven't noticed." She bent down, he released his foot, and she picked up the tissue and put it in the bag.

"I must be blind. No one compares to you," he said with a grin.

"Aww, shucks. You'll make me blush."

Blackbeard barked. "See, my best friend agrees with me," he said.

She laughed. "I think he just wants another treat. And I thought I was your best friend." She stuck out her lower lip in a pout.

"He's my best boyfriend, you're my best girlfriend."

When Liz had first seen Blackbeard, the day Aunt Amelia had cajoled Ryan into adopting the mangy mutt from a no-kill shelter, she'd thought he was the homeliest, strangest-looking, cutest puppy she'd ever seen. His coloring was like a tortoiseshell cat's, all browns, blacks, tans, and russets. His fur had been, and still was, long and short in patches. He'd had huge paws and thick eyelashes over amber eyes. But the reason he'd been named Blackbeard was because of his black goatee, now neatly trimmed, but still there.

"We better clean this up, I'm hungry," Liz said. "Plus it's a gazillion degrees out here."

Blackbeard, thinking all the blowing trash was part of a game, fetched an empty cardboard toilet paper roll and ran over to Liz, then he presented it to her like it was a gift. "Well, thank you, boy. You know how I love it when you bring me presents." She went to reach for it, but Blackbeard pulled away and ran to Ryan. "You little scamp!" she called after him.

Blackbeard glanced from Liz to Ryan, then brought the roll back to Liz. He dropped it at her feet. Before she could pick it up, Blackbeard put it back in his mouth, then ran to Ryan. He was an equal opportunity gift giver.

"Ick. I mean, good boy, Blackbeard," Ryan said. The dog dropped it at Ryan's feet and a wad of tissue fell out from the center of the tube. Blackbeard grabbed the tissue, ran back to Liz, dropped it, and something slipped out from the tissue and onto the pavement. Blackbeard went for it. "No, Blackbeard, you don't want that thing in your mouth!" Surprisingly, he listened to her command.

Liz took a tissue from her shorts pocket and picked up the item, then glanced down at the dark plus sign at the end of the plastic wand. She held it out to Ryan and asked, "Do you know what this is?"

"A thermometer?" he guessed.

"Not exactly. A pregnancy test. A positive pregnancy test! See the plus sign in the little window? That means someone is pregnant."

"Who?"

"Like the lipstick, it came from the Oceana Suite. Haven and Nigel Crawford's suite. Looks like Haven is pregnant. That explains a lot. I'm just happy she wasn't poisoned."

"Say what!" he said, moving closer to look at the test. "Poisoned? You thought she was poisoned?"

"Haven's been ill for a few days," she said and explained about the scene at lunch.

"Well, it appears she didn't want anyone to know the results of the test," Ryan said. "If she'd been happy about the news, I don't think that doohickey—"

"Doohickey?"

He ignored her and continued, "—would have been wrapped in tissue, then stuck inside an empty toilet paper roll."

"I agree. I wonder who's the daddy? Dr. Crawford? Jameson? Heck, maybe Evan?"

"Does it matter, snoopy pants?"

"It matters if she's the one who murdered Jameson Royce. What if Haven told Jameson he was the father and he laughed at her, or threatened to tell her husband? Maybe she wanted to bump him off before anyone noticed her baby bump. Or maybe Jameson wanted to claim fatherhood, then spill the beans to Dr. Crawford, and she didn't want that."

"Baby bump? It does give her a motive in a strange way," Ryan said, "but only if Jameson is the father."

"True. Evan could also be the father."

"Wouldn't her husband be the most logical choice?"

"I don't know...."

"Why don't you know?"

"Because I know they sleep in separate rooms."

"How do you... Never mind." Ryan added the last piece of trash to the bag, then said, "Let's toss this bag, you hold on to the test, and we'll head to Deli-casies. Pops put our shrimp mango salad in the fridge. Aunt Amelia, Betty, and Kate already ate. They're in Home Arts, helping Aunt Amelia and Francie with the upcoming fashion show. You're supposed to meet them there after we eat. Oh, and another thing, I refuse to wear Ken's 'swimming trunks,' as Aunt Amelia calls them, in this wacky Barbie fashion show extravaganza that Francie is planning."

"It's not wacky. It's Francie's first foray into retailing. So, buck up and grin and bear it."

"Okay. Okay. On one condition: you wear a Barbie bathing suit and walk with me."

"It's a deal," she said, kissing his rough cheek. He looked extremely handsome today, and she thought back to when he played a pirate for one of the Indialantic's events. "I never thought I'd say this, but a fashion show starring Aunt Amelia and based on midcentury Barbie fashions will be a welcome distraction. In the meantime, what should I do with this?" She held up the pregnancy test.

"Bring it to Deli-casies; I'll give you a plastic bag to put it in. Haven being pregnant might have nothing to do with Jameson's murder. Until we know more, we need to sit tight."

"Agreed." Then she told him about the scene with Dr. Crawford and Haven, and how Dr. Crawford had tried to take Jameson's laptop from his suite. "And there's a safe in the Crawfords' suite, which might mean Jameson brought one with him that might just hold that rare find he boasted about."

"So the key we found might go to a safe," Ryan said.

"Possibly."

Ryan's phone rang. He answered, then turned his back to Liz. Blackbeard looked up at her with soulful eyes. "Sorry, bud, I only carry cat treats. You'll have to wait until your father's off the phone." She was worried about the expression on Ryan's face, but couldn't make out any of the conversation because of the gulls circling the dock and emitting loud screeches like in Hitchcock's *The Birds*. Similar to Blackbeard, it seemed the seagulls were also looking for treats—scraps left behind by Pelican Pete, the brown pelican that currently sat stoically on his favorite piling and scanned the lagoon for any leaping fish. It was probably too hot for even a fish to leave the cool water.

When the conversation ended, Ryan turned around and said, "I just got Mr. Royce's cause of death from one of my sources."

"Tell me," she said, stepping closer.

"It wasn't a puncture wound to the stomach or suffocation from the dirt wall collapsing. You weren't too far off the mark when you mentioned your concerns about Haven's health."

Liz thought back to what she'd said. "You mean Jameson was poisoned?"

"Yes, but he didn't ingest it. Something was added to tips of the tines on the diving spear."

"No-o-o."

"Yes," he answered, his tone as serious as a heart attack, or in this case, worse.

Chapter 14

"A poison dart frog!" Liz collapsed onto a bench at the end of the Indialantic's dock, her back to the Indian River Lagoon. "You've gotta be kidding."

Ryan sat down next to her and handed her a cold bottle of water. After his phone call, he'd taken Blackbeard back to his cottage and left the pooch in air-conditioned comfort. "Nope. Not kidding. My source is top notch."

"Agent Bly's sister?"

"Good try," he said.

Liz chugged the entire bottle of water, then looked over Ryan's shoulder as he typed "poison dart frog" into the search bar of his phone's browser. She bent closer and tried to make out the small print on the screen.

"I'll read it to you." Ryan glanced around to make sure they wouldn't be overheard. The only living thing visible was Pelican Pete.

"Okay, here goes. Dendrobatids, commonly known as poison dart frogs, have enough poison in them to kill ten adults. Most scientists consider them the most toxic animals on the planet." He paused and looked over at her. "And there's no antidote. Holy cow." He glanced down and continued, "When the poison, called batrachotoxin, enters your blood stream, it causes paralysis and ten minutes later or less, you're dead. Indigenous tribes in South America have used the poison for centuries, usually adding it to the tip of their blowgun darts when hunting. The poison on the dart can remain at full strength up to a year. And get this, poison dart frogs raised in captivity never develop the poison." He held his phone screen up to her. "And they're tiny. About the size of a bottle cap."

"And so colorful and cute," Liz added.

"Supposedly, the more colorful they are, the more poisonous they are, especially the golden dart frog." He continued reading. "Recently, scientists have been studying the poison and have created a synthetic version that someday may be used in small doses as a pain reliever."

"I bet the poison that killed Jameson was the real thing," Liz moaned, slapping her knee. "Brazil is in South America. Guess where the team was before coming to Melbourne Beach? Professor Talbot told Auntie and me that they flew directly from Manaus to Orlando. Hopefully, this will take Birdman out of the equation. He certainly wasn't in Brazil."

Ryan gave her a weird look.

"What? What is it?" she asked, searching his face.

"Didn't you say you saw him on the Indialantic's grounds the night before Jameson's murder? Do you think it's possible he put the scarlet king snake in Jameson's bottom drawer?"

"No. And even if he did leave the snake," she said, "it doesn't mean he poisoned Jameson with poison dart frog venom."

"Unless..."

"He found the toxin when he was in Jameson's room," she finished for him. "How would he know what it was? If Jameson did have a vial or something hanging around, I doubt he would draw a skull and crossbones on the label and mark it poison."

"It does sound far-fetched when you put it that way."

"Thank you for agreeing. We need to concentrate on the other four. Right now, I would put my money on Haven's husband. He surely didn't like the way Jameson was always hitting on his wife. What if Haven told him that she was pregnant, and he put two and two together and figured it was Jameson's?"

"Why would she hide the test if she'd already gone around and told everyone? I assume the trash is taken out daily?"

"Yes, but—"

"No buts," he said. "It's early to be narrowing our search to just one of the four."

"*Our* search?"

"Freudian slip. I think we should leave it alone."

"You're right!" she said, grinning. "I forgot about Betty. After we go to the emporium, let's hop on your boat for a clandestine meeting of the three detectiveteers. We'll come up with a plan of action."

"You know you sound like a teenager. When did you say you stopped playing with dolls and reading your Nancy Drews?"

"Funny, honey. I still say we should look first at Dr. Crawford. He seems the nerdy type. I've heard him spout off the Latin names for plants and trees; if anyone knew about frog venom, he would. That's where we'll start."

"Not so fast, Sparky. Let's see how things progress. If I were you, I would try to get everyone out of the hotel. I don't know of any law that says they have to stay."

"You know something," she said, "you're right."

"I am?"

"It sounds so simple. I'll have a talk with Aunt Amelia and give them their walking papers. Let the sheriff's department find them lodging."

"What about Betty?" he asked. "Isn't Professor Talbot her friend? Will she be willing to kick him out?"

"They were friends before she got married, like sixty years ago. Until last week, she hadn't seen him in decades."

"Good. Glad that's settled."

"So am I. None of us need the stress. And I'm still determined not to let my father know what's going on." She'd let it go for now, still reeling about the cause of death.

"You'd better pass on to Aunt Amelia and the others that Fenton and Charlotte should be kept in the dark," he said, standing up and offering his arm for assistance, which she took.

The heat and humidity felt suffocating, draining what little stamina she had left after what had transpired this morning. "I'll warn them. Now let's get out of this inferno before I need a potassium IV."

"Dehydration's the least of our worries," he said.

Liz took a step away from the bench and Ryan glanced behind her. "Aren't you forgetting something?"

She looked back at the bench and the tissue-swathed pregnancy test. "Oops."

Chapter 15

A few minutes later, as if nothing was going on except a silly ole murder, Liz and Ryan opened the double doors to the emporium and walked inside. At one time the emporium had been connected to the Indialantic, but that was before a mysterious fire had taken out the center section of the hotel. That same day, one of the hotel's maids, Cissy Bollinger, was found floating in the Indialantic's pool. Her suicide was thought to be in remorse for setting the fire. Aunt Amelia never believed it was Cissy who'd set the fire. It had happened in 1945, on V-E Day. Ever since the age of ten, when Liz discovered Cissy's small suitcase buried in the hotel's luggage room, she'd been on a mission to prove Cissy's innocence. Recruiting Nancy Drew ghostwriter Betty, who couldn't pass up a good mystery, the pair had been searching through local records, old hotel registers, and photos, hoping to find a clue to what had happened that day. Aunt Amelia had been a preschooler at the time. Her only memory had been her mother's tears when she'd found Cissy dead in the pool after the fire had been put out. Aunt Amelia said her mother hadn't cared about the fire half as much as Cissy's death. Cissy had been not only a hotel maid, but also a friend to Liz's great-grandmother. During WWII, Cissy's fiancé had been off fighting for the Allies but had gone missing in action. Cissy, and the rest of the United States Army Air Force, assumed he was dead. The same day of the fire, after Cissy was found in the pool, great-grandmother Maeve found a telegram in Cissy's room saying that her husband was alive and coming home. Another curious thing that haunted Liz was the fact that Cissy's bed hadn't been slept in the night before the fire. Just one more mystery to add to the others surrounding her death.

Liz stopped short once inside the entrance. Ryan elbowed her. "You okay?"

"I was just thinking about Cissy." Ryan knew all about the fact that Liz, Betty, and Aunt Amelia had been digging into the past to try to prove the young maid's innocence. "I just realized I was off on the count of murders that have happened at the Indialantic."

"Come along, let's get you some sustenance. One murder at a time."

She knew he was trying to make lighter a very disturbing situation, but it didn't work.

The atrium was filled with lush tropical potted plants and wrought-iron benches arranged for people to relax on while their significant others shopped till they dropped. In Sirens by the Sea, Liz saw Brittany was ringing up a sale. Brittany waved and said, "Hey there, Ryan," totally ignoring Liz. Brittany wasn't one of Liz's favorite people, but she had to admit that even though Brittany's prices were on the high side, she had good taste in her clothing and jewelry selections.

They continued toward Deli-casies, passing the entrance to Home Arts by the Sea. The space had been set up like an open workshop with three twenty-foot worktables and chairs. There were easels, sewing machines, and towering wood cubbies that held yarn, bolts of fabric, and art supplies. Natural wood bookcases displayed items for sale made by the collective's artisans: knitwear, throws, pottery, primitive-style hooked rugs, blown glass items, and handmade jewelry, just to name a few. The twenty-foot wall at the back of Home Arts featured oil, acrylic, and watercolor paintings, along with three huge mixed-media collages by co-owner and juried artist Minna Presley. Minna was currently in Miami getting an award from her last exhibition at the famed Art Basel, and Liz had to wonder if Minna knew about the vintage-Barbie-palooza her partner Francie was planning while she was away.

Aunt Amelia, Betty, Kate, and Francie sat at one of the long burnished-aluminum tables. On top of the table Liz saw her entire vintage Barbie clothing collection and accessories splayed out in a long line. Under each Barbie ensemble there were small placards with the outfit's name. One thing she had done when she packed up her collection for the last time was to match the original boxes to each outfit. At the distance they were standing, all Liz could see was Golden Glory, Fashion Luncheon, and Coffee's On. At another table, someone had set up Barbie's cardboard Dream House and Fashion Salon. Liz counted eight doll cases, and next to the doll cases was Barbie's peach-colored convertible with an aqua interior. Memories came flooding back of Liz and Kate playing Barbies in the hotel's Billiard Parlor (which had in recent years morphed into Aunt Amelia's Enlightenment Parlor). Grand-Pierre had covered the pool table with a large sheet of plywood and Liz and Kate had set up what they called Barbie World, getting lost for hours playing with Bubble Cut Barbie, Ponytail Barbie, two Midges (one a redhead, the other a brunette), Ken, Allan, and Barbie's little sister Skipper.

If only things could remain so innocent and simple, Liz thought, recalling what she and Ryan had just learned about Jameson's death by poison dart frog venom.

Francie, who Aunt Amelia and Liz both agreed looked like a young version of Sally Field, was dressed in one of her vintage clothing designs, a strapless sundress with a full skirt. The fabric had a pink-and-white-checked background with raised yellow daisies. A long yellow chiffon scarf held back her brown, shoulder-length hair; her bangs were trimmed perfectly straight, an inch above her eyebrows. She wore minimal makeup, and even though Liz knew she was in her forties, she looked the same age as Liz and Kate.

Aunt Amelia glanced over at them, waved, then put her finger to her lips for them not to interrupt Francie, who was videotaping the items on the table.

Betty locked eyes with Liz, then put her hands around her neck in a choke-hold position and mouthed, "Save me."

Wait until Betty gets a look at the outfit Francie plans on her wearing in the fashion show, Liz thought, trying to keep from laughing as they walked away.

Outside the entrance to Deli-casies, Liz said to Ryan, "As soon as we're done with lunch, I'm going to talk to Aunt Amelia, and we're going to evict our group of killer archeologists."

"You go, Tiger," Ryan said. They followed the aroma of fresh brewed coffee and entered Deli-casies.

Liz grabbed Ryan's elbow. "What are you going to tell Pops about Jameson?"

"Grandpa doesn't need to know anything for now. Tomorrow's Sunday, his day off. I'll go to his condo and tell him then."

"If it hits the news circuit, I just hope we aren't invaded like in the past. We've had our fair share of bad press, not to mention all the bad press I brought with me from Manhattan." Liz tried to keep the whine out of her voice but was unsuccessful. "Last January we were swarmed with paparazzi after you-know-what happened."

Ryan raised an eyebrow, then brought her in for a close hug. "Ancient history. Aren't you always telling me to live in the now?"

"Yes, but that was in the past," she said with smile. "Our *now,* as of this morning's murder, isn't the *now* I was talking about."

"Soon they'll be gone, and all we'll have to worry about is how many millions of copies *An American in Cornwall* will sell."

"I like your glass-overflowing attitude, Mr. Stone. You're right. Smooth sailing once we kick everyone out."

They stepped toward the back room, passing the café section and barista counter. Liz waved at Deli-casies' barista, Ashley, who probably couldn't see them from behind the burst of steam erupting from the espresso machine, nicknamed The Dragon for obvious reasons. Sadly, Ashley was leaving for college soon. She'd be missed, not only because of her coffee-making skills, but also her photography skills. Ashley had been instrumental in solving the past two murders at the Indialantic. But her services wouldn't be needed this time, because soon the archeologists would be gone, gone, gone.

After Liz and Ryan enjoyed another one of Pops's fabulous salads, served with a side of crusty bread still warm from the oven (Liz thought she would choose homemade bread slathered with butter over dessert most days—with one exception, Grand-Pierre's desserts), Ashley brought them each a demitasse of espresso to fortify them for the job ahead: spreading the news about Jameson's murder before it actually hit the news. But they didn't have to search out Aunt Amelia and Betty; after they'd put away their dolls, Betty and Aunt Amelia stepped into Deli-casies to show them a few of the fashion sketches Francie had drawn up.

"What do you think, Lizzy?" Aunt Amelia asked after plopping down on a bistro chair at the table next to them. "I even got permission for some of my girls to wear the fashions of Skipper, Barbie's little sister." She passed over an artist's portfolio case and Liz and Ryan flipped through it.

Ryan tried a few oohs and aahs, but Liz could tell he wasn't into it. Liz said, "Wow, these are fabulous."

"Aren't they?" Betty said, standing behind them, looking over Liz's shoulder. "I was apprehensive when Amelia told me about the fashion show, but now I'm on board. I never was into dolls when I was younger. My mother didn't know what to do with me. I was always off in the woods with the boys, playing army." She laughed. "They always tried to get me to play nurse, but I guess I was a tomboy. I never went in for any of those gender assignments. And when I wasn't playing army or Kick the Can I was in my tree fort reading."

"I bet all you read in your tree fort were mysteries," Ryan said.

Betty grinned. "Actually, I had a fondness for hard-boiled detective novels and pulp fiction."

"Why am I not surprised," Liz said.

Aunt Amelia reached across the table and grabbed Liz's espresso cup, downing the last few sips. After putting it back on the table, she said, "Speaking of hard-boiled detectives, did I ever tell you about the time Humphrey Bogart and Lauren—"

Liz bit the bullet. "Auntie, before you tell us, we have something to tell you. Betty, you might want to take a seat for this one."

Aunt Amelia took the news in stride and a few minutes later went to attend to her young thespians. Liz had cringed when her great-aunt had said they were going to act out a scene from Tennessee Williams's *Cat on a Hot Tin Roof*, the next play scheduled for the Melbourne Beach Theatre Company. Not that it wasn't a great play, but it was hardly relatable to a group of twelve- and thirteen-year-olds. Liz had half a mind to help her great-aunt modernize the play, like they'd done in the movies with *Clueless*, based on Jane Austen's *Emma,* and *Bridget Jones's Diary,* based on Austen's *Pride and Prejudice*. Then she thought of the situation at hand, put helping with the play on the back burner and instead moved finding Jameson's killer to the front burner.

After Aunt Amelia left Deli-casies, they filled Betty in on the poison dart frog venom.

"Wow," was all she could come up with as she reached for her bag to bring out her iPad. After a few minutes, Betty looked over at them and said, "Double wow. I didn't see that one coming."

At least they were all on the same page.

Chapter 16

Liz and Kate were sitting on the cushy sofa at the back of Kate's vintage shop, surrounded by cardboard boxes of Kate's recent estate sale finds. Books & Browsery by the Sea was set up differently than the rest of the emporium. It had the same short perimeter walls, but Kate had created a mazelike obstacle course from a dozen seven-foot-tall barrister bookcases that she'd scored at an estate sale. Scattered randomly around were chairs, wooden benches, tables, dressers, and crates filled with her "precious junk," as Kate's boyfriend Alex called it. Towering bookshelves were packed with books and vintage/antique knickknacks. Each shelf had a theme that coordinated with the books' subject matter. The shelf closest to Liz had to do with Melbourne Beach and Vero Beach. There were books on the Spanish treasure shipwreck of 1715, books on diving and fishing, along with ships in glass bottles, maps, seashells under glass cloches, a brass spyglass, and more. Kate had a good eye when arranging her shelves, and Liz was proud of her friend's success over the past year.

"That's quite a story," Kate said, lapping at the whipped cream on top of the iced caramel macchiato Liz had brought her from Deli-casies. "I'm glad Aunt Amelia took the news of another murder in stride."

"She probably thinks some miscreant walking the public beach has done Jameson in," Liz said, pulling a book on Treasure Coast shipwrecks off the shelf.

Kate's large, dark brown eyes opened wide. "Who do you think did it? And does this mean we have another murder to solve?"

"There is no 'we' in this scenario, Kate Fields. The less you know, the better off you are."

"That sounds ominous. Are you or anyone from the Indialantic in danger? If you want, you can stay at my place."

"Thanks for the invite, but I'm not leaving a sinking ship. The only one who might be in danger is Birdman or one of the other archeologists. But they'll be leaving tonight. For once I'm listening to Ryan about this."

"Good for you. But if you need anything, just remember how I helped you last January. I can see why Ryan enjoys being a private eye—it's all quite exhilarating. Like when you catch that really rough wave pre-hurricane and you don't know if it's gonna be the ride of your life or a trip to Davy Jones's locker." Kate and her boyfriend were major surfers. When she wasn't scouring garage sales, antique shops, used bookstores, or flea markets, or talking to characters in one of her vintage books (one of Kate's endearing proclivities), she could be found with her handsome professional surfer-dude riding the waves at the Sebastian Inlet Beach.

"I don't think Ryan would call all his PI work exciting. But he sure has been an asset to my father in his law cases."

"How are Fenton and Charlotte? What's the latest?"

"Dad's over the moon, he's so happy. It's only his second time in Europe; the first was with my mother to visit her family in France. I was worried he would be melancholy, but that's not the case. I'm truly happy for him."

"Twenty-three years is a long time to grieve. Your mother must have been something special," Kate said.

"From what I remember and the stories my father has told me, she was. And meeting you at the finger-painting table in kindergarten sure helped me get through it all." Liz felt her eyes water.

Kate reached over and squeezed her hand. "Twenty-three blissful years of friendship."

"Except for the time you made me steal that Victorian bookcase from the curb and Mr. Rottweiler decided I was trespassing and chased me to your van."

"I had the motor idling," Kate said, laughing. "You were in no danger."

"Tell that to my jeans jacket, which I saw him ripping to shreds in the rearview mirror as we pulled away."

"And look at the bookcase now." Kate pointed to the refinished bookcase that held only Victorian-era items. "Back to its old, beautiful self and very thankful for your rescue."

"Don't tell me you're now talking to furniture like you do your books?"

"Hmm, now that you mention it. Wood furniture comes from live trees and so does paper, so maybe I could get a dialogue going."

"Sorry I mentioned it."

"Just kidding. I don't talk to wood or paper, I commune with characters in books—and if it's a memoir, the author. Aunt Amelia agrees with me that the energy people put into their written work stays long after they're gone. She was referring to plays, but I like the thought. So sue me. You know I'm not crazy."

"I do?"

Kate lightly punched Liz on the thigh. "Plus, you're an award-winning fiction writer. If anyone should understand, you should!"

"Alright, alright," Liz said with a grin. "We've had plenty of good times rescuing old junk, and it's okay for you talk to characters in books. It's true. When I'm writing, my characters are as real to me as anyone who is living and breathing."

"To the good times," Kate answered, raising her plastic cup. She tapped it against Liz's imaginary glass, took a sip, then put the cup on the corner of the sales desk, next to a pile of books. *A disaster waiting to happen,* Liz mused—but she was sure one of those books would probably speak up and warn Kate if they were in danger.

"Sadly, no more good times for your Jameson guy," Kate said with a serious expression. "I never met any of the archeologists, except that cute Evan."

"He's not an archeologist, just Dr. Haven Smith-Crawford's intern." Liz locked eyes with her and said, "You and Alex aren't having problems, are you?"

"Evan came into my shop looking for some books on local history. I really don't have that many, because as soon as they come in, they go out. I felt bad—you know how much I love matching people up with my books. So we went over to Deli-casies, and while sipping our lattes, I told him the stories I've heard, most of which Aunt Amelia has told me, about the Indialantic by the Sea's history. Did you know that his grandfather worked as a bellhop at the Indialantic sometime in the fifties? And, no. Alex and I are not having problems. But a girl can look, at least until someone puts a ring on it." She held out her left hand and pointed to her finger. "How about you, when do you think Ryan might pop the question?"

Liz felt her face heat. "It's too soon. But I do think he's *the one*."

"Of course he's the one, buddy."

"I'm floored by the news that Evan's grandfather worked here," Liz said. "I would think he would mention that to Aunt Amelia."

"He kind of let it slip when I told him about all the movie stars and gangsters who supposedly stayed at the hotel. It's so sad that Birdman

Bennett had to be involved in all this. My brother has learned so much from him over the years. He's one of the reasons Sky became a conservationist."

"I didn't know they knew each other," Liz said. Kate's brother had spent almost as much time at the Indialantic as Kate when they were children. What Liz hadn't learned about natural history from Birdman, she'd learned from Skylar, who now ran the Environmental Learning Center on Orchid Island.

Kate laughed. "Where do you think Skylar was escaping to when you and I were playing with Aunt Amelia's Barbie dolls? Speaking of which, wait till you see what I found." She got up, her glossy chestnut ponytail swinging from side to side as she rooted through one of the boxes by the checkout counter. She finally found what she was looking for and pulled out a worn hardcover book titled *Barbie's Easy-As-Pie Cookbook*. "Wouldn't it be great to make some of these recipes for Francie's fashion show? The book's dated 1964, right in her wheelhouse!" She opened the book to the center and looked down. "Even, I, the gastronomically challenged, could make some of these meals."

"Hence the easy-as-pie title," Liz said, laughing. It felt good to be with Kate. She'd forgotten how her uplifting, sunny personality could make even the darkest times brighter. "It's meant to be a cookbook for adolescents, not adults."

"Well, still, you or Ryan could replicate a few of these and give them your own gastronomic spin. Gourmet them up."

"Gourmet them up? Great idea. But first, you better find a midcentury Easy-Bake Oven for us to cook in."

"Wonder if they made a G.I. Joe cookbook?" Kate asked, sitting back down.

Liz looked at her, hoping she was kidding, but Kate was off to the races, communing with Cynthia Lawrence, the author of the Barbie cookbook. "Get this one. Don't separate bacon before putting it in the frying pan; wait until it cooks a little, then separate with a fork." She looked up at Liz. "See, I didn't know that!"

"Since when do you cook bacon? You're a vegetarian, remember?"

Her face crumpled. "Well, how cool would it be if you were wearing the Barbie apron from the What's Cooking set and carrying a rolling pin and this cookbook for the fashion show? Ken, a.k.a. Ryan, could accompany you wearing Ken's Cheerful Chef BBQ set. Remember—the apron that had the cute saying on the front, Chow Time, Come and Get it. It came with those little hot dogs and strips of bacon! Come on, you two would be adorable."

"Rein it in, fashion doll fanatic," Liz said, swiping Kate's iced macchiato from the counter and taking a sip. "As for Ryan, I'll be lucky if he walks down the runway in one outfit, let alone two. And I'm sure Francie will put a modern spin on things like she always does. Plus, why should I be the one with the rolling pin? Time to get rid of female stereotypes. Plus, Ryan's as good a cook as I am. But tell him that I said that and..." Liz smiled, remembering their last cook-off. Ryan had been the chef at the Brooklyn fire station he'd belonged to, and Liz was classically trained by Grand-Pierre. Their cook-offs kept their relationship interesting.

"Great idea. You'll come down the runway with the BBQ accoutrements," Kate said, clapping her hands in glee. "You're right. I guess we're lucky as women in this modern age. Although you and I never used gender stereotypes when we played with Aunt Amelia's Barbies. I seem to recall your Midge wearing Ken's football helmet."

Liz laughed. "I forgot about that. My dad raised me right. Nothing was off-limits because I was a girl. But I think women have a lot further to go. A female president would be nice." Her mind went to the sexist comments Jameson had made to Haven in front of her husband. Could her husband have gotten revenge? The Crawfords weren't lovey-dovey. Now that she thought back to their fight yesterday morning and the way Dr. Crawford talked to Haven like she was a piece of property, she thought he deserved a slot in the misogynist hall of fame right beside Jameson Royce.

Liz reached in her pocket to check the time on her phone. She and Ryan were meeting Suzie from Sunset Realty at three at Squidly's. She glanced down at the screen. It was only two o'clock. When she went to return her phone to her pocket, the pregnancy test in the plastic bag Ryan had given her fell between her and Kate on the sofa.

"OMG! OMG! Elizabeth Amelia Holt. Is there something you want to tell me?" Kate picked up the bag and looked at the plus sign on the test. "Are you pregnant?"

"Of course not. It's not mine."

"Interesting," Kate said, knowing by the look on Liz's face not to ask who it belonged to. "Well, I know all the females at the Indialantic, except you, are postmenopausal, so that leaves the female archeologist you said was on the team. See," she said proudly, "I'm not a bad private investigator."

Liz didn't answer her.

"It's not Charlotte's, is it? Is that why your dad whisked her away for the wedding and honeymoon? I promise I won't tell anyone you're going to have a baby sister."

Liz stood up. "Stop. No. It doesn't belong to Charlotte. The stork isn't dropping a baby half sister on the hotel's dock. And you're not to breathe a word of this to anyone. It is none of our business." Liz had never thought of the fact that Charlotte might want a child. Her father was in his fifties, but Charlotte was in her early forties. As the head of homicide for Brevard County, how would she ever have time for a baby? But hadn't Liz just said there shouldn't be male/female stereotypes? Her father was semiretired because of his heart. But a baby at this late date...

"What you mean to say," Kate said, "is it's none of our business unless it has something to do with that archeologist's death."

Maybe Kate would make a good private eye.

Chapter 17

When Liz and Ryan entered Squidly's, it was easy to locate Suzie. Liz hadn't seen her in over ten years and probably wouldn't have recognized her if not for the fact she was the only person in the entire restaurant sitting at a table. It was three o'clock, never much action between the lunch and dinner hour, but it also could have something to do with the oppressive heat. The regulars, fishermen and fisherwomen and a few retirees, were sitting at the bar under the air-conditioning. In the seating area, Squidly's was open to the elements with only plastic flaps that could be rolled up or down. Seeing as the temperature was a blistering ninety-five, today they were up. Quite cleverly, someone had devised a system much like they have in grocery stores for fresh produce. On the deck that ran along three sides of the waterfront restaurant, huge industrial fans were set up below a water system that drizzled a fine mist, which cooled off patrons who sat at tables near the open windows. For some reason, Suzie was sitting at a table in the middle of the restaurant, not close enough to benefit from the bar's AC or the mist-blowing fans.

As they walked toward her, Suzie jumped up. She wore a tailored navy skirt and white cotton long-sleeved blouse. Liz saw a navy blazer hanging from the back of her chair. *A blazer in August?*

Looking only at Ryan, Suzie said, "So, you must be Ryan." She actually licked her glossy lower lip like she'd found him on Squidly's appetizer menu, right below a dozen raw oysters on the half shell. "You're exactly as Brit described you," she said, smiling—more like gawking—showing off large porcelain-white teeth. It took a few seconds before she could tear her eyes away and address Liz. "I thought perhaps you were going to bring your aunt?" When Suzie's eyes finally found Liz's face, she paused on Liz's right cheek, then quickly looked away, then back again.

"Amelia is my great-aunt. Good to see you, Suzie," Liz said, not letting Suzie see her sweat, which was hard in this heat. Liz planned to find out why Suzie had called Jameson while he lay dead, then get as far away from her as possible. "Any chance we could move over to the bar or one of the tables by the fans?"

Suzie giggled. "Hope you don't think I'm vain, Ryan. I just had my hair blown out, and you know how humid it's been. Plus, a lady doesn't sit at bars." Suzie was the same age as Liz, twenty-eight, but she dressed and applied her makeup much like her bosom buddy, Brittany, and looked more like she was in her late thirties. Liz assumed Brittany dressed the way she did to bring in a more moneyed crowd to her emporium shop, Sirens by the Sea—but what was Suzie's excuse? Liz always dressed the same way in August: sleeveless cotton sundress or shorts and a tank top, sandals, and a pair of gold hoop earrings that had been her mother's. Her unruly, long strawberry-blond hair spent most of the summer trying to escape the huge alligator clip at the back of her head.

Suzie sat down and took the napkin off the table, unfolded it, and put it on her lap, then looked up at them. "Plus, we need to talk quietly. I'm so excited you want to put the Indialantic on the market."

Liz knew she was in the driver's seat with Suzie. "Well, I have to insist," Liz said firmly, "either we sit by the window or at the bar. It's too hot here."

As if it was a Sophie's choice conundrum, Suzie glanced at the bar, then the tables at the windows, needing to choose between her hair or a possible seven-figure real estate listing. Decisions, decisions.

Ryan, gallant guy that he was, suggested, "Why don't we sit by the fans, Suzie, and I'll sit next to you to block the spray."

She beamed. You would have thought he'd decided to father her child, which reminded Liz about Haven and the pregnancy test. Of course, her husband must be the father, maybe she just didn't want him to know. But then again...

"Hello! Earth to Liz. We're moving over there," Ryan said, nodding his head in the direction of a table across the room. He grabbed her elbow and guided her toward the table, muttering under his breath, "You owe me a home-cooked osso buco dinner for this one."

After they were all seated, there was an awkward silence. But it didn't last long. Susie pulled out an entire prospectus on the Indialantic. The large brochure included architectural drawings, details like how much they should charge per square foot, and how, unfortunately, the market had taken a downswing and they'd have to go with the times on pricing. The brochure also included a large gold key with a memory stick at its end. "Just stick that in your laptop and you can preview my staging ideas. You'll see the Indialantic by the Sea as you've never seen it before. I even found old photos from its early years. And if you or your aunt, I mean great-aunt, agree, I can do a video presentation to give out to everyone. I do have connections to many overseas agents and an amazing website and social media presence. And," she said, jutting out her pointy chin, "I've racked up over fifty million in sales this year alone!"

"That is impressive," Ryan couldn't help but say.

Liz forced herself to smile at all of Suzie's self-praise. Things hadn't changed from high school. When Suzie finally got down to business and threw out a ridiculous lowball number, Liz choked and almost spit out her Arnold Palmer. "Sorry, went down the wrong pipe."

After Suzie wound down and finished three-quarters of the fried calamari with Cajun remoulade dipping sauce, which she'd eaten in a very unladylike manner, right down to licking her fingers like she was in a Kentucky Fried Chicken commercial, Liz couldn't take any more of the Suzie Malone Show. She said, "Suzie, I have some concerns about the Bennett property next door. It's in pretty rough shape. I'm afraid *if* my great-aunt ever thinks of selling, it will hurt our chances of getting a good price. You're the expert. What are your thoughts?"

That's all that was needed for Suzie to spill the beans on Jameson's connection to Birdman. And yes, Liz felt guilty for setting Suzie up. Especially so as they were getting up from the table and Liz noticed Suzie's auburn hair glistening with beads of moisture and taking on the shape and Brillo pad texture of fellow redhead Bozo the Clown. (At age six, Liz had run out of the screening room in terror after Aunt Amelia had showed her the old children's show. Since then, clowns, especially Stephen King *It*-like clowns in any shape or form, were to be avoided at all costs.)

After Ryan escorted Suzie to her Mercedes, where Liz spied Suzie slipping her business card into Ryan's pocket, Liz and Ryan walked back to the Indialantic. Usually she felt lucky that one of the top seafood restaurants in the area was only a hop, skip, and jump from the Indialantic. This afternoon, she wished they'd taken Ryan's Jeep.

"Well, that was enlightening," Liz said, as they stepped onto the circular drive in front of the hotel. "I'm going to contact Betty. We'll meet you at eight on the dock, and we'll go out on your boat for a late night boat-ride. Oopsie, I mean we'll have a late-night boat *sit* instead, seeing she doesn't have an engine per se."

Ryan's new/old 1969 Chris-Craft forty-seven-foot Commander that he'd christened *Mermaid's Kiss* had been moored at the Indialantic's dock for three months. He'd gotten the name for the boat from a recently published short story Liz had written for a top literary journal. She'd been surprised and honored when she saw the gold lettering on the stern. He'd even allowed Liz the privilege of breaking the bottle of champagne against her while she called out the boat's name. She hadn't had the heart to tell him boats were usually christened when they set out on their maiden voyage; it would be a good six months or more before *Mermaid's Kiss* was deemed lagoon- and seaworthy and left the Indialantic's dock. She wasn't complaining; she was thrilled that city boy Ryan was embracing island life.

"Yes," Liz said. "Time for a meeting on *Mermaid's Kiss* of the three detectiveteers. Speaking of kisses..." She looked up at him, her blue eyes meeting his deep brown. "Thanks for doing that with Suzie. I think it helps to know what Jameson was up to. Dinner at my place. See you at six."

"Sounds good, but stop talking, bossy pants." Ryan lifted her chin and came in for a satisfying kiss; then they walked to the path leading south to the hotel's lobby entrance. At the intersection that would take him to the lagoon and his cottage, he said, "If you've decided to send the archeologists packing, what's the need for meeting on my boat?"

"Until they're officially gone, gone, gone, I want to make sense of things. Don't want Auntie, Captain Netherton, Greta, Grand-Pierre, or Betty getting murdered in their sleep."

"Uh-huh, I see. So that's how you're spinning it," he said, smiling. "Okay, see you later, alligator."

"Greta and Grand-Pierre are taking over tonight's meal at the hotel. See you at six for dinner, crocodile."

She watched him walk away, admiring the view. When she turned back to the front of the Indialantic she saw Professor Talbot rooting through the bushes by the front veranda.

What the heck?

"Professor? Can I help? Did you drop something?"

He looked flustered. "I, uh, I dropped my cigar from the second-floor terrace, and I was afraid the burning embers might set the Indialantic on fire. Betty wouldn't be too happy with me if that happened."

Nor would anyone else. "Let me help you."

After fidgeting in the hibiscus bushes for a few minutes, he finally stood upright and held up the cigar. "Oh, here it is. Found it! Silly me, I must have just stepped on it. Clumsy oaf," he said in a squeaky cartoon voice.

It looked okay to her except its tip was missing.

"Still good enough to smoke, though." He quickly put it in his pocket and scurried away, calling back at her, "See you at dinner." Before she could say she wouldn't be at dinner, he'd already disappeared through the revolving door. Was it just Liz, or was he acting squirrelly?

Curious, she went to where he'd recovered the cigar, searching the ground until she finally found the cigar's crushed tip. The strange thing was, when she toed the pieces with her sandal, there was no charring, proving the cigar was never lit. The professor was obviously looking for something else that he'd dropped when she'd showed up.

She bent back down to see if she could find the *real* item he'd been looking for. Sweat dripped down from her forehead and into her eyes, but even through the blur she spied the paper band from the cigar with the name Cohiba Spectre. Next to the band was a charred piece of newsprint with an article on it. It had the newspaper's name and a partial date. No year. She deftly picked it up, the burned edges flying in the humid air like a flock of bats. The paper was too fragile to put in her pocket, so she held it gently in her closed fist, then moved toward one of the golf carts parked by the hotel's entrance. As she walked, she felt someone's eyes on her from above.

It was Professor Talbot looking down from the Swaying Palms Suite's veranda. Jameson Royce's suite. He quickly darted away, but she'd recognized his abundant, shocking white hair. They hadn't told the team that Jameson was murdered, unless Agent Bly had already informed them. Plus, she'd locked the suite against Dr. Crawford and had told Greta to keep it locked.

For the first time, she put the kindly old professor in the slot under Nigel as Jameson's killer. A shiver traveled up her spine, around her shoulder, and into the hand holding the burned newsprint.

The good news was that what was left of the team would be leaving tomorrow. Right after Liz had a conversation with her great-aunt. She got in the golf cart and put the piece of newsprint and cigar band in the storage compartment. Her head was about to burst; this is the reason three heads were better than one, and she was looking forward to meeting Betty and Ryan on *Mermaid's Kiss.* She set course for her cozy beach house, needing a nuzzle from Bronte, a cold drink, and a cold shower. In that exact order.

She stopped when she reached the hotel's boardwalk and looked out to the constant sea. Steady, rhythmic, and soothing. The plank boardwalk had at one time followed the shore for the entire width of the Indialantic by the Sea resort, but after decades of hurricanes and storms, the boardwalk had been reduced to a tenth of its original size.

The scene was tranquil; too bad her thoughts weren't. *Who would have the most to gain from Jameson's death?*

If Suzie told Agent Bly what she'd just told her and Ryan, Liz knew for sure that Birdman would rise to the top of Bly's suspect list. And Liz would never let that happen. Maybe it was a bad idea to turn their part of the investigation over to Bly after the archaeologists left the Indialantic. Then she felt her conscience whispering in her ear, *Even though you care about Birdman, you don't know for a fact he didn't kill Jameson.*

She put her foot on the pedal and zoomed toward home. The faster she went, the cooler it felt. Instead of anything having to do with the picture of Jameson Royce's corpse frozen in her mind, she reviewed what ingredients were in her fridge that she could use for dinner: *Sea scallops, oranges, basil, zucchini, and couscous.* A one-bowl meal.

Easy, breezy, and simple.

Too bad the past eleven hours couldn't have gone that way.

Chapter 18

Upon entering her cozy beach house, Liz said, "Thank you, Dad." She was thankful that her father had thought to convert the old beach pavilion into her home. She kicked off her sandals and stepped into the great room. Bronte greeted her by weaving in and out of Liz's legs. "How've you been, my little tiger?" She picked up Bronte, and they rubbed noses for a few seconds, then she placed her on the cushioned window seat. The gray-and-white-striped kitten was the opposite of a tiger, over a year old and still tiny for her age. Kate had nicknamed her Thumbelina after some vintage baby doll, which was funny, because it was Kate who'd rescued her and named her Bronte, because the kitten liked to sleep on top of a stack of the Bronte sisters' books in Kate's shop. As long as Bronte was healthy, which she was according to Dr. Peterson, the Indialantic by the Sea's go-to vet, Liz refused to worry. She loved having a cat the size of a kitten to snuggle with, especially after today.

"It's been a rough one, Bronte. How about a cat treat for you and small glass of Grand-Pierre's sangria for me?"

Bronte meowed her assent.

On the way to the kitchen, Liz passed the long granite counter that separated the great room from the kitchen. The beach house's open floor plan made it easy for Liz to chat with her guests from her dream kitchen. Chef Pierre had helped with the layout of the kitchen, knowing which appliances she would need as a gourmet cook. Bestie Kate and the crew at Home Arts by the Sea had helped with the interior design of the beach house, adding one-of-a-kind items: vintage accents and books from Kate's shop, hand-blown glass bowls and vases, paintings by artists from the collective, and fluffy, lightweight throws made from raw silk yarn in shades of aqua, coral, and cream. For the area behind her white sofa, Minna Presley from Home Arts had gifted her a huge mixed-media mural in soothing colors of sand, sea, and sky. A writer couldn't ask for a more tranquil and inspiring place to create.

In the kitchen she poured a small glass of sangria, then grabbed a couple of cat treats from the white jar on the countertop. Before bringing Bronte her treat, she took a sip of the sangria, her shoulders relaxing. What was she making such a big deal about? *A murder, that's what.* One more day and the archeologists would be gone. Her father and Charlotte would be home soon, and Grand-Pierre and Liz had a wedding brunch to plan. One day. They could survive one day, for gosh sakes. Then she thought of Jameson Royce's face, wishing the group could leave tonight, before something else happened.

Bronte jumped down from the window seat and came into the kitchen to see what the holdup was.

"Here, baby. Maybe if you're a good girl, I'll give you a sea scallop later. Ryan's coming over."

She knew it was probably her imagination, but she swore Bronte's ears twitched. Then she realized why; if Ryan was coming it usually meant Blackbeard was too.

"Sorry, Blackbeard's staying at home tonight. But I promise to bring you to the caretaker's cottage tomorrow. It's Ryan's turn to cook. Now I need a shower; it's been the longest day, and the hottest. Here you go." She leaned down and opened her palm. Bronte accepted her treat, then went back to the window seat and hopped up, barely making it because her legs were so tiny, then she climbed on top of a set of Hemingway books on the lower bookshelf at the foot of the window seat and burrowed in. It was crazy that Bronte would rather sleep on top of books than on the down cushion atop the window seat. But Liz knew one thing: when it came to the pets at the Indialantic, abnormal seemed to be the new normal.

When Ryan arrived at six for dinner, he told her that everything seemed quiet at the hotel. As he'd passed through the dining room on his way to tell Betty about their plan to meet on *Mermaid's Kiss*, he saw Evan and Professor Talbot sitting together, while Dr. Crawford had been sitting alone at a table across the room, his wife noticeably missing.

"Was there a place setting for Haven at the table?" Liz asked, after he kissed her in welcome and rubbed Bronte's back in her favorite spot.

"No," he said. "Must be the pregnancy thing, right?"

"Yes. The pregnancy thing," she said, smiling.

"How about we shelve all talk of murders and pregnancies and instead focus on that smell coming from your kitchen." He kicked off his sneakers and took a seat on the white sofa.

She went to the fridge and took out a bottle of Shark's Net IPA beer and brought it over to him, then went back into the kitchen.

"Wow, I didn't even have to ask," Ryan called over, holding the frosty bottle in the air.

"I hope complacency doesn't lead to boredom in this relationship, Mr. Stone."

"With you? Never."

"What did Grand-Pierre make for our *nonpaying* guests' dinner?"

"Baked salmon with a garlic, Dijon, and lemon glaze, asparagus with lemon butter, and dilled fingerling potatoes."

"Ah-ha! I knew dill was one of the ingredients," she said. He looked at her quizzically, and she pointed to her mouth. "There's a sprig of dill between your two front teeth." She shook her finger at him. "Hope you didn't ruin your appetite by sampling Grand-Pierre's cuisine."

Ryan laughed. "Caught me." He got up and strode to the kitchen. "Do you have a toothpick?"

She gave him a look, like "duh, what cook wouldn't have one," then opened the cupboard to the right of the sink and handed him a few.

"Be right back." He put the bottle of beer that she'd just given him back in the refrigerator.

A couple of minutes later he came back into the kitchen. Glancing down at the small bowls she'd lined up on the counter, he said, "Outdoing yourself again, I see."

She was used to putting her ingredients in recipe order, something she did with Grand-Pierre since he'd begun having memory issues. "Why'd you put your beer back in the fridge?" she asked. "I thought it was your recent favorite."

"I was thinking we might want to have a glass of champagne instead." He grinned, showing off small dimples at the corners of his mouth, the look in his eyes mischievous. Something was up. "But first..."

He left her in the kitchen and went out onto the deck, leaving the door open. The wind chimes that hung off the deck's railing played a manic melody. They'd been a gift from Ryan early in their relationship, giving her hope that someday she might be happy and learn to live and love again after all the heartache she'd gone through with Travis. Fast-forward a year later, and here they were.

Ryan walked back in carrying a large carton. He kicked the door closed behind him and placed the carton on her long wooden farm table. She'd commissioned one of the woodworking artisans from Home Arts to make it, a replica of the one in the hotel's kitchen. The same place she had such fond memories of meals with her family and their live-in residents.

"Something came for you at the hotel. Aunt Amelia asked me to deliver it."

"Oh, boy!" Liz knew what was in the carton, she could tell by its shape. She'd received a similar one when she'd lived in Manhattan. "My books!" She jumped in excitement and ran over to him.

Ryan went to the kitchen, opened a drawer, took out a knife, then came back and handed it to her.

She unsealed the box and looked down at a dozen hardcover copies of *An American in Cornwall.* "Oh my. Oh my. I mean, I've seen the mock-up cover, but this exceeds my wildest dreams. Look how glossy." She took one of the books from the box and held it to her chest. The cover depicted heather-topped cliffs that towered over a sweeping Celtic Sea. Her heroine stood at the top of the cliff, dressed in a US Army nurse's uniform, the wind blowing through sections of her hair that had escaped its French knot. Liz's heroine held tight to her nurse's cap in one hand and used the other to shade her eyes from the sun as she looked down at the beach where a WWII British warplane had crashed onto the rocks. Behind the auburn-haired woman was the silhouette of a castle, the same one Liz had put in the pages of her first Cornwall novel, *Let the Wind Roar.* The castle was the single thread that would tie the trilogy together.

"Now for some champagne," Ryan said. "I'm so proud of you. I don't know how you do it, or when you have time between your wacky but lovable great-aunt, helping Pierre, and doing odd jobs around the hotel and emporium."

She smiled at him. Feeling very lucky, indeed.

"Oh, and how about solving a few murders in your spare time," he added.

"With a lot of help," she answered. "Why don't we save the champagne for later, when we're on *Mermaid's Kiss.* I know there's a bottle in the hotel's fridge. Betty, my proofreader and mentor, deserves a glass of the bubbly too."

"In that case," he said, coming up to her and ruffling the hair on top of her head, "get in that kitchen and make this man of yours some grub."

"Yes, master," she said, bowing. That was another thing she loved about Ryan: he never demanded anything, never took her for granted, and always held his ego in check—if he had one.

"To the kitchen I go. You want that beer?"

"Sure."

"Get it yourself, I have a meal to prepare."

He laughed. "Gladly. But wait, I think you have something stuck between *your* two front teeth."

"I do?"

He took her in his arms, kissed her, then said, "I know I'm not so great at showing my feelings, but I am really proud of you. You're one hell of a woman, Elizabeth Amelia Holt."

She felt her cheeks heat. "And you're one hell of a man, Ryan Stone. Hey, I just realized I don't know your middle name."

"I'm not telling." His cheeks grew crimson under his tan.

"Oh, I'll get it out of you. And if that doesn't work, there's always Pops. I just realized another thing: I don't know what your grandfather's real name is. He's always been Pops to me and Auntie."

"That I can tell you. His name is Paul. Paul Erasmus Stone."

"Oh, no! Don't tell me Erasmus is your middle name."

"Okay. I won't tell you," he said, looking embarrassed.

Bingo!

Chapter 19

After dinner, Ryan left to feed and walk Blackbeard. Liz had tidied the kitchen, then spent a little time on her laptop, trying to find out if Jameson Royce had any family besides the four ex-wives Dr. Crawford had alluded to. All she found was a photo of Jameson breaking ground at nearby Leon de Mar. Giving up, she turned on a few lights, put on some classical music for Bronte, then left for her rendezvous with Betty and Ryan on *Mermaid's Kiss.*

When she entered the hotel's kitchen, Greta was emptying one of the two industrial dishwashers.

"I haven't seen much of you lately," Greta said. "Can you believe Mr. Royce was killed? If I didn't know better, I would think someone put a curse on the guests who come to this hotel. Luckily, this was just an accident. Poor man."

Liz took Greta into her confidence and told her that Jameson had been murdered. Greta was not just the Indialantic's live-in housekeeper, but also part of the extended Holt family. "Can I ask you a question?"

"Uh-oh. I hope you're not getting involved in something dangerous like last time. It wasn't too long ago when you were up in the bell tower..."

Liz smiled on the outside, but inside she cringed just thinking about what had happened. "No worries. Between you and me, I'm having Aunt Amelia kick out our four guests."

"So, you think one of them killed Mr. Royce?"

"Yes."

"That detective guy was here a little while ago. In fact, he left his card." Greta went over to the counter next to a glass dome–covered cake plate displaying what was left of the chef's morning pastry. The single glazed confection seemed to have a neon sign with Liz's name written on it.

Greta handed Liz the business card, and as she thought, Agent Bly had been at the Indialantic, which meant the archeologists knew about the murder. "Yes, I've already met him. Hey, do you want me to take that lonely pastry off your hands, then you can wash the dish for tomorrow morning's fresh-baked assortment?"

Greta smiled, grabbed a napkin from the cupboard, and snared the lemon-filled, glazed beignet from under the dome, handing it to Liz. "You want a plate?"

Half of it was already in Liz's mouth. She mumbled, "No. I'm-m good." After she swallowed the last bite, threw away the napkin, and washed her hands, she asked, "Who did Agent Bly talk to when he was here?"

"The four of them were taken one by one into the library."

"Darn."

"Why darn?" Greta asked.

"Because I wanted to know if you overheard anything."

"I did bring a tray with a pitcher of your auntie's iced tea and five glasses into the library, and I might have overheard the detective questioning that young Evan. Such a handsome young man."

"You and Auntie have the same taste. And..."

Greta smiled. "I didn't hear much, and remember I had no idea Mr. Royce had been murdered. What I overheard was that Evan grew up in Satellite Beach, that's all. Nothing earth-shattering, I'm sure."

Satellite Beach was a small town just north of Melbourne Beach. Both towns shared the same barrier island. Liz already knew Evan had been a Brevard County lifeguard in his summers off during college, but she hadn't known he lived only twelve miles from the Indialantic. That would explain his grandfather working at the Indialantic back in the day. Liz had no idea if it was important. However, she knew from the past that it was the small things added up, one by one, that helped to catch a killer.

"You never know. I guess I don't have to tell you to keep your eyes and ears open. At least Ryan said dinner went well, that's one good thing, I guess." As Liz talked, she went to the wine cooler and grabbed a bottle of Moët.

"Yes," Greta said, eyeing the bottle of champagne. "Congrats, by the way, on your new book. I can't wait for my signed copy."

"Wow. News travels fast around here. Ryan, no doubt."

"He seemed very proud of you. He just stopped by and showed me a copy. It's gorgeous, just like that guy of yours. He's a keeper."

"Agreed. He said you served Dr. Haven her dinner on a tray. How's she feeling?"

"I really don't know. I made her a bland dinner like she asked for, but when I went to her suite, she wasn't there. I left the tray on the table in the sitting room, then an hour later went to check, and the tray was still there, the food untouched. Shouldn't you fill your father in on all this?"

"No. They're due back next week. Hopefully by then things will settle down. Barnacle Bob's being quiet tonight. Usually he throws me a few adorable curses from the butler's pantry." Liz glanced toward the open door of the pantry.

"That's because he's not there. Your auntie is trying to force a relationship between him and Carmen Miranda by keeping both macaws in her sitting room."

"That should make for an interesting night," Liz said, laughing. "Hope Auntie wears earplugs."

"Ha. The birds need earplugs. Have you ever heard Amelia snore? I had to move my bed away from our connecting wall, to the opposite side of the room."

Liz didn't know how to break it to Greta, but Liz had walked by Greta's suite a few times to the sound of a lawnmower running out of gas. "Hand it over, I'll wash it," Liz said, referring to the cake plate.

"No way, missy. You go celebrate your big achievement. Now scoot."

Liz blew her a kiss. "Thanks, Greta. Why don't you go relax, and if you can, maybe check on Aunt Amelia. She seemed to take the news in stride, but you never know."

Liz went into the quiet and serene butler's pantry and got out a Lucite champagne bucket, then went to the back hallway that led to her father's apartment and scooped some ice from the ice machine into the bucket. Back in the kitchen, she put the bottle of champagne in the bucket and headed for the kitchen's outside door. Halfway there, she turned to Greta and said, "One more thing. Anything unusual that you can think of in the archeologists' suites? I know there's a safe in the closet of the Oceana Suite, but how about Jameson Royce's suite, the professor's, and Evan's?"

"I thought you were staying out—never mind. I haven't checked the closet in the Sea Breeze Suite, but if you insist," she said, with a twinkle in her hazel eyes, "I surely will. As for Mr. Royce's suite, I know he didn't have a safe in his room, because last evening after the snake incident he had me tearing apart the Swaying Palms Suite looking for anything slithering around—those were his exact words. All I found was a gecko, which I didn't squeal on. Though there was something interesting under his bed."

Liz walked closer to her, excitement buzzing up her spine. "Yes?"

"At first, I thought it was just a rolled-up towel, though it wasn't one of the Indialantic's. I shined a flashlight under the bed and used my broom handle to lift the fabric up, wanting to make sure there wasn't anything nesting underneath and ready to strike."

"Where was Jameson when you were doing this?"

"Cowering in the sitting room," she said, adding a smile. "For a man of his size and an explorer, he sure was scared of snakes…. That's not how he died, was it?" Greta covered her mouth at the thought.

"No. Not a snake. Please, go on."

"Anyway, I lifted the towel or maybe it was a piece of velvet or suede; whatever it was, something was underneath."

"What was it?"

"It looked like an huge old turtle's shell. I think it was made from some kind of metal."

"Yes!" Liz shouted, then she asked for Greta's master room keys. After Greta handed them to her, Liz passed off the champagne bucket and said, "Can you stick that in the fridge?" Then she ran out of the kitchen.

A few minutes later, she was in Jameson's suite. She got down on the floor, turned on the flashlight from her phone and searched under the bed. Nothing.

Well, at least she knew what Jameson's big discovery was. Or kind of knew, remembering what the professor said they were looking for to prove Ponce de León had landed nearby...a conquistador's breastplate.

She couldn't wait to share the news with Ryan and Betty.

Chapter 20

"It's been an interesting day, for sure," Betty said to Ryan and Liz as they gently bobbed on the lagoon aboard *Mermaid's Kiss*.

The night sky didn't show any promises that tomorrow might be storm-free. In fact, Tropical Storm Odette had suddenly veered toward the Bahamas, not the gulf side of Florida as forecasted after the latest weather update. Liz thought of what Aunt Amelia and Barnacle Bob liked to repeat whenever the prognosticators got it wrong with their promises of fair weather: "It's not nice to fool Mother Nature." The quote came from a margarine commercial from the early seventies. Aunt Amelia had starred as a grocery shopper confronted by a living, breathing Mother Nature, wearing a flowing gown and a crown of flowers on her head, referring to the "oleo," as her great-aunt called it, being so close to the taste of butter you couldn't tell the difference.

After the threesome toasted her book, they got down to business, with Liz filling them in on what Greta had just told her.

"The metal breastplate Greta saw under Jameson Royce's bed has to be related to Ponce de León," Ryan said.

"Liz," Betty asked, "didn't Jameson say his discovery was going to put him in the history books?"

"Yes. It had to be about Ponce de León. Ais relics wouldn't put him in the history books because there have been so many scientific finds already around this area."

"To have this precious object hidden under a towel doesn't sound like he thought it was so special," Ryan added.

"You're right," Liz said. "Not to speak ill of the dead, but I bet it was a fake."

"I don't know about that," Betty said. "He would have known that once he declared his find, it would be taken away, analyzed, and authenticated by a third party."

"True," Liz said. "Well, it isn't there now. So where is it?"

"Fake or real, it would buy him time to claim Birdman's property for himself so he could build another Leon de Mar," Betty said.

"What!" Liz jumped up, and the tray with her champagne glass went sliding as the boat rocked from side to side. They hadn't even told Betty about their conversation with Suzie at Squidly's.

Betty explained how she'd found an interesting document in public records when searching under Jameson Royce's name. Her discovery explained the paper that Birdman had signed and what Jameson's hold had been. Jameson Royce Ltd. had paid all the back taxes on Birdman's property.

Liz was stunned. "Does that mean he had a claim to the land if he found something priceless?" She sat down and leaned against the boat's teak bench, bracing herself for more revelations.

"I didn't get that far," Betty said. "I'll look into it if you want. But as you said, you're getting rid of our suspects. Plus, it gives Birdman Bennett a reason to have killed him."

Liz wanted to protest, but knew Betty was right. She stayed silent, digesting all the different scenarios while Ryan filled Betty in on their meeting with Suzie from Sunset Realty.

Betty looked up at the stars, her mystery brain in high gear. "So, you're saying he contacted the Realtor to see about buying the Bennett property?"

Liz said, "Not exactly. He wanted to know all the restrictions for building on the Bennett property, which makes sense after what you just told us. Also, Jameson had asked Suzie to find out if she could get the owners of the property next to Birdman's to sell to him, and to keep pushing Aunt Amelia to sell the Indialantic. I don't think this has anything to do with Ponce de León, and everything to do with building another Leon de Mar development. Betty, this is like one of those puzzles your heroine in your Sherlock Holmes London Chimney Sweep Mysteries might have an answer for."

"Did this Suzie say if Birdman's other neighbors were interested in selling?" Betty asked.

"That's why she was calling Jameson the morning he was found," Ryan said, putting his arm around Liz. "Apparently, they are willing to sell, but for an astronomical price."

Betty swatted at a mosquito on her wrist. "She was calling him at six in the morning. That's pretty early."

"Oh, you don't know Suzie Malone," Liz said. "She's Brittany's evil twin, only with more energy."

"Betty, why was the professor so adamant about seeing you after lunch? Did you ever catch up with him after Liz gave you the message?" Ryan asked.

"What he wanted to know wasn't anything urgent, and frankly, it was a little embarrassing, but he showed me a map and asked where he should go on his next dig. And..."

"And what?" Liz asked.

"If I would go with him. I told him as politely as I could that I couldn't go with him. He seemed momentarily upset, then quickly asked me what I knew about Birdman. I didn't have much to say, only that he kept to himself and was a close family friend of the Holts. Finally, he got to what I think he was really after, what I knew about Mr. Royce's death. Naturally, I didn't say a word."

"Enough talk of murder. Let's do a quick suspect list, then hand everything over to Agent Bly after the foursome leave," Ryan said, giving Liz a peck on the cheek. "Time to celebrate your book and this awesome night."

"Before we begin, one last thing," Liz said, looking at Betty. "I was told by Evan that it was Jameson who chose to come to Melbourne Beach to dig. Yet I thought you said the professor contacted you?"

"He did. He said when he learned of the location, he remembered that I was a resident at the Indialantic. It's just a coincidence."

"I don't believe in coincidences," Ryan said.

"Then how about this one," Liz said, taking a sip of champagne. "Per Kate, Evan's grandfather worked at the Indialantic in the early fifties. I have no idea how it's related to Jameson's death, but it is worth mentioning."

Betty reached in her huge tote bag and brought out Watson. "I think we should get everything down on pixels, then hand it off, as Ryan suggested."

"Good idea," Liz seconded. "We'll list each suspect and our deceased. Then my private investigator, a.k.a. my main squeeze, can turn it over to his source." Then she told Betty how Ryan played softball with Agent Bly's firefighter daughter-in-law. "Oh, I forgot! I didn't even tell you, Ryan. I'll be right back." She hopped out of the boat and onto the dock. She didn't know if the dock was swaying or it was the champagne, but she walked cautiously until she reached the pavement, then jogged to the garage where the golf carts were stored at night. When she was about a hundred feet from the door, an owl hooted; then she heard footsteps and voices from the direction of Aunt Amelia's garden, which separated the hotel from the emporium. Spooked, she ran behind an orange blossom bush, the branches scraping against her skin when she tried to peer out.

Haven and Evan stepped out under the lamplight. Haven walked two steps ahead of Evan. He called after her, "We've come this far, we have to keep going. I know what he told me. We have a chance to make a killing when we resell them. Think of the baby. You won't have to beg for money from that cheapskate husband of yours. You won't have to stay with him, and we can..." Liz couldn't hear the rest of Evan's words.

Haven stopped short, turned around, and pushed Evan backward. "Stop. Things are different now. And no matter what you say, it's still called stealing." He advanced toward her with his arms outstretched. "No," she said, "go back the other way. We'll discuss this tomorrow. It's a pie-in-the-sky plan anyway. So far everything's been a dead end."

That was all Liz could overhear. The pair separated, and she waited a few minutes before going into the garage to retrieve from the golf cart's console the scrap of newspaper that she'd found on the ground when the professor was searching for his fictitious *lit* cigar.

After she made sure the coast was clear, she jogged back to *Mermaid's Kiss* and, out of breath, told Betty and Ryan about what she'd just witnessed. Then she showed them the piece of newsprint. It was unanimous that Betty would bring it back to her suite and research it.

Finally, around ten, Betty emailed them via Watson the list of everyone involved in Jameson's murder.

Jameson Royce—No accreditation as an archeologist. Developer of all-inclusive luxury community on nearby Orchid Island. Bankrolled the Brazilian expedition and promised to pay for the team's room and board and expenses relating to the Melbourne Beach dig. Scared of snakes (Liz added). Paid all of Birdman's back taxes. Might be the father of Haven's baby. Might have faked a Ponce de León artifact. Chose the dig site at the Bennett property. Had a small key hidden between his phone and cell phone case. Planned to build a new development on Birdman's property.

Dr. Nigel Crawford—Was jealous of the dead man's attention to his wife. Frugal, no money. Had big blowup with his wife; the pair are always sparring. He sleeps separately from his wife. If he's the father of Haven's baby, he doesn't seem to know she's pregnant. Very good with plants and their Latin names. Was meant to lead the dig in the Amazon and Melbourne Beach, but Professor Talbot came out of retirement to lead it. Was trying to take Jameson's laptop from his suite. Jameson was always belittling him and lording his wealth and looks over him, putting him down in front of Haven.

Dr. Haven Smith-Crawford—See above. Hid pregnancy test inside empty toilet paper roll. Beautiful, personable, and friendly, but materialistic when it comes to clothing and accessories. Conspiring with her college intern about stealing something—possibly the artifact Greta saw under Jameson's bed. Father of baby not known. Could be her husband's, Jameson's, or Evan's? Evan knows about pregnancy. She had no problem with Jameson's compliments until the snake incident. What had changed between Jameson and Haven?

Evan Watkins—Lives nearby when not at college. Grandfather used to be a bellhop at the hotel in the 1950s. Seems to have some kind of attachment to Birdman. Was snooping around Birdman's the morning Jameson was found dead. In love with Haven? He was Haven's teaching assistant at University of Florida and is now interning with the team for credit toward graduation. Not a fan of Jameson and his attention to Haven. He wasn't on the trip to Brazil, like the other four. Plans on stealing something.

Professor Walter Talbot—Came out of retirement to go on the Amazon dig and the Melbourne Beach dig. Old-fashioned and goes by the rules. Claimed to have dropped a lit cigar from his balcony and was looking for it. The cigar hadn't been lit and Liz found what remained of a newspaper clipping after it had been burned. Moments later he was seen on Jameson's balcony. Per Evan, had argument with Jameson the night before he was murdered.

Burton "Birdy" Bennett—signed off for Jameson to pay his back taxes. Maybe he found out that he might lose his land. It was his diving spear tipped with poison that killed Jameson, and he was the one who found the body.

After they'd broken up the meeting of the three detectiveteers, Liz had gone home and snuggled with her fuzz-ball kitten Bronte while trying to distract her thoughts from the fact that Birdman now had a motive in killing Jameson Royce.

Jameson was trying to steal Birdman's home.

Chapter 21

The next morning, Liz held back a ten-foot-high elephant-ear leaf at the entrance to Birdman's property, allowing Aunt Amelia and Carmen Miranda, who was riding shotgun on her great-aunt's right shoulder, to pass by. They were on their way to Birdman's cottage to tell him some good news.

"Auntie! Do you really think the mosquito netting under your African pith helmet is necessary?"

"Of course it is, Lizzy. It's the perfect opportunity to wear Lovey Howell's fashionable explorer's hat from the episode 'The Secret of Gilligan's Island.' I think it was 1966 or 1967...." Lost in her memories, Aunt Amelia stopped, looked off in the distance, and mused, "I played a stunt double for Tina Louise, a.k.a. Ginger, in a scene where she saves the castaways from being trapped in a pit where they're looking for an ancient hieroglyphic tablet that will tell them the secret to get off the island."

Liz's mind couldn't help going to another pit. One with Jameson Royce at the bottom of it. "Thanks to all the bats inhabiting Birdman's bat boxes, you don't need the netting. I'm worried the veil will obscure your view and you'll trip and break something." She looked at her great-aunt and smiled. "I know, I know. You have the bones of a thirty-year-old."

"I'll acquiesce to having the bones of a forty-year-old," Aunt Amelia said, grinning. Then she asked Carmen, "How old are you, my pet?"

Carmen didn't answer, but glanced shyly at her new master.

Laughing, Aunt Amelia said to the macaw, "You're right, us girls must keep our age a secret."

"Has she opened up at all?" Liz asked. "Yesterday, BB was singing to her when Ryan and I were in the lobby, and she actually bobbed her head to the beat."

"That's wonderful. We'll have her talking in no time."

"I also noticed Barnacle Bob has lost a few more feathers. Hope he makes friends with her soon, before he becomes completely bald." Carmen ratcheted her head in Liz's direction at the mention of Barnacle Bob. Maybe the feathered Casanova did have a chance in the romance department.

"Dr. Rich said stress is the cause of the loss of BB's noggin feathers, even suggested adding some meds to his water. Barnacle Bob can be a tad high-strung, so it probably couldn't hurt."

"You think?" Liz asked sarcastically.

Aunt Amelia took a step and the toe of her inappropriate heeled footwear caught a low-lying vine. Liz grabbed her elbow and Carmen went surfing across Aunt Amelia's shoulder, her beak getting caught in the helmet's netting.

"Stay still, Auntie." Afraid she might get nipped by Carmen, Liz reached over and gently separated the mesh from Carmen's beak. It seemed the macaw was not only shy, but gentle. "Good girl, Carmen. Barnacle Bob could take a lesson from you. Okay, ma'am, now will you take off that ridiculous contraption? I think I've made my point."

"Okay, okay. You win. But if they start swarming, I'm putting it back on." She took the hat off and stuffed the netting inside, then placed it back on her head, saying, "The actress Natalie Shafer, who played Mrs. Thurston Howell III, thought I did a fantastic job in the scene. So much so, she gifted me the helmet that matched her stunning khaki ensemble. In all honesty," she giggled, turning her head to Carmen Miranda, "I would've rather she'd given me her gold lamé belt. You should have seen the costumes and accessories for the show."

They continued to walk toward Birdman's cottage.

"I've been meaning to ask you about that," Liz said, stopping in front of the ruins of Birdman's old manse. "If, as the theme song from *Gilligan's Island* states—the same little ditty Barnacle Bob repeats ad nauseam"— Carmen turned her pretty blue head again at BB's name—"the castaways only set out for a *three-hour tour*, how could they have had so much clothing?"

"Oh, my dear," Aunt Amelia replied, adding a click of the tongue, "that is easily explained. You see, the Howells were on their way to a Hawaiian resort and had all their luggage on board the S.S. *Minnow*."

"Ah yes, that explains everything. Right, Carmen Miranda? Wink, wink."

The bird looked at Liz. At least she knew her name.

Aunt Amelia turned to her. "Lizzy, you're incorrigible. Good thing I love you so much."

"It certainly is. Back at ya."

Liz recalled the episode of the sixties sitcom *Gilligan's Island* that her great-aunt referenced, especially the scene with a rear view of her great-aunt as she tumbled headfirst into the pit. Aunt Amelia's fiery red hair had been a perfect match for actress Tina Louise's. Back then, Aunt Amelia wasn't as curvy as the Marilyn Monroe knockoff Tina, but it was doubtful anyone noticed except Liz, because it had been only a two-second shot. Now, at eighty, Liz would call her great-aunt full-figured, owing mostly to Chef Pierre's gourmet cooking and baked goods. But she was also a specimen of health because of her active lifestyle that included yoga, Pilates, surfing (yes, surfing), and even kickboxing. Liz smiled at the memory of last year when Aunt Amelia kicked a thick wood plank in half, causing her instructor to fall back onto the mat, dazed and winded.

"What are you smiling about, Lizzy?"

"You, Auntie." She gave her a kiss on her fuchsia cheek.

"I am quite a character, aren't I?" she said.

"You sure are."

"Well, that episode sure put the kibosh on me wanting to be a stunt double. First and last time. Never again. No sirree. Not because stunt doubles don't get any glory, although they certainly are underrated; it was more that I'd skinned my knee during my leap into the pit and had to put off doing a Lustre-Creme shampoo commercial. It was quite an amazing product. I still might have a jar—"

Liz was about to ask why a skinned knee would matter in a shampoo commercial or what kind of shampoo came in cream form, but she knew not to fall into that trap. As a distraction, she said, "Such a shame about the old house." They both looked ahead. Moss hung in thick lacy sheets from old oak trees, the sky was dark and stormy, and there was vegetation growing up from the center of the old mansion. If not for the palm trees, Liz felt like they could be in fictional Collinsport, Maine, on the set of *Dark Shadows* with Aunt Amelia.

"Auntie, do you need to rest for a while?"

"Oh, my dear, I'm sorry, are you winded? Of course, you must rest."

"Not me. You. Aren't you hot in that getup?"

"Oh no, dear. I'm used to island summers."

"Well, that stream of sweat pouring down the side of your face says otherwise," Liz said, steering Aunt Amelia and Carmen to the path leading to Birdman's cottage. "Did you and Birdman ever play together when you were younger? What's your age difference?"

"I think we're around the same age. He might be a couple of years younger."

"You ever have a thing for him?"

"A thing? No, nothing like that. My sights were on leaving the island to find fame and fortune. Kind of like you, leaving Melbourne Beach for Manhattan and your writing career. And look at us now. Both of us back home at the Indialantic and happier than a pearl in an oyster shell."

Liz laughed at her analogy, knowing it took a lot of sand and grit to make a pearl—maybe Aunt Amelia was right.

"Poor Birdy," Aunt Amelia said with a sigh. "Because he had to take care of his mother, he didn't have time for romance."

"Romance was never a problem with you, was it, Auntie?"

"Pshaw, you'll make me blush."

"Did he ever leave the island?" Liz asked as they rounded the bend and Birdman's cottage came in view.

"I don't think so. He never went to college, which is a shame because he has an amazing mind, and quite an artistic talent. When I was in my teens, before I moved to Burbank, he'd let me watch him sketch. I even helped him collect specimens for his drawings. I don't think he minds leading a solitary existence—the land and wildlife seem part of his DNA. I would say he's the only person I know who could talk to a wounded animal or bird, and I swear they would listen to and heed his advice. He was, I mean is, the Dr. Doolittle of our barrier island. Barefoot since a child, always climbing trees or nursing an injured egret or heron, or just sitting on the beach with his legs in the lotus position, absorbing nature through his dark-tanned pores."

"He still does all those things," Liz said, "except perhaps climbing trees. Then again, I wouldn't be surprised if he did climb a tree or two or hide out in the osprey nest by the lagoon. Especially to spy on the archeologists. I'm so glad you agreed to ask them to leave. We'll all sleep better tonight. Including Birdman."

"Firstly, I want to make sure Betty's okay with kicking out the professor," Aunt Amelia said. "Ha ha, the Professor, get it? Like in *Gilligan's Island*."

No, Liz didn't get it, not remembering anyone on the show named the Professor.

"Betty and Professor Talbot were once an item, you know," Aunt Amelia said with a wink.

"Trust me, Auntie. I had a talk with Betty. She's fine with it. I think she's too busy writing to get involved in another murder at the Indialantic." (That was a white lie.)

"On the other hand," Aunt Amelia said, "maybe that's where she gets the ideas to write her tales. Lately, things have been stranger than fiction. What happens if the archeologists want to pay for what they owe us, dear? Should we still kick them out?"

"Yes, Auntie, we should. With Dad and Charlotte away, we really need to keep our noses clean."

"Let's get to Birdy's before my Secret deodorant isn't a secret anymore. I will tell our guests to leave as soon as we get back to the Indialantic."

You mean our suspects, Liz wanted to add. But why worry Aunt Amelia, seeing they would soon be leaving.

"Did I ever tell you that the actor who played Thurston also did the voice for Mr. Magoo? He—"

"Hold that thought," Liz said, feeling the phone in her pocket vibrate. She pulled it out and looked at the screen. *No, impossible.* Had they just jinxed Birdman? "Auntie, let's hurry to the cottage. Ryan just texted me that the sheriff's department is bringing Birdman in for questioning."

They moved as quickly as possible without upsetting Carmen Miranda. At the gravel-and-shell walkway to the cottage, Liz saw that the holes in Birdman's garden had been filled in, the soil leveled and ready for planting. August in Florida wasn't the best time to plant. She promised herself to make a point of pilfering from Grand-Pierre's larder and dropping off items anonymously to Birdman, like she'd done with baked goods in the past. With the archeologists leaving, they would have extra stores of food.

"So, we shouldn't warn him he's going to be questioned, right?" Aunt Amelia asked, panic in her emerald eyes.

"I don't think so. What if he gets scared and bolts before they show up? It would make him look guilty."

Before taking a step, Aunt Amelia looked back at her and said in protective mode, "Pshaw. They won't arrest him. And if they do, it will be up to you, Ryan, and Betty to clear his name. Here." Aunt Amelia reached into the bag slung crosswise against her body. She pulled something out and handed it to Liz. "Hold this crystal. Dorian once gave it to me to ward off bad mojo."

And look what happened to her, Liz wanted to remind her, but held her tongue. She'd give the crystal to Birdman, but only if they got there before the sheriff.

He was the one who needed it.

Chapter 22

Liz was out of breath by the time they approached Birdman's door. Aunt Amelia wasn't winded in the least. However, Carmen Miranda's feathers were in disarray, small tufts of royal-blue pinfeathers making her resemble a peacock instead of a macaw.

"Okay, Auntie, let's make it quick. We need to stay out of it. I'm sure the sheriff only wants to hear Birdman's statement for the record; then they'll let him go. After all, he's the one who found Jameson, then led me to him. A guilty man wouldn't do that. I just want to make sure Birdman knows that the group staying at the Indialantic is no longer welcome. Less stress."

Aunt Amelia added, "And we need to make sure he calls us if anything goes wrong. I wish my nephew were here. He would know what to tell Birdy about his rights."

"Oh no, Auntie. We need to leave Dad out of this. I'm sure it's just routine questioning."

"What if Birdy needs us?"

"Birdman has the pay-as-you-go phone, right? You told me his bills get automatically taken out of his social security check."

"Yes. And he has my number. I know he knows it by heart. I think I'm the only one he calls, but I don't think he can text or if his phone even offers that as a feature."

"Okay, Auntie, time to paste on our smiles and act upbeat."

"I'm always upbeat, darling."

It was true, she was, but Liz knew if someone crossed her or hurt anyone she cared about, Aunt Amelia could be fierce and frankly, a tad dangerous.

"Birdy's so innocent as to how these things work. Too bad you can't go with him, Lizzy. Think of all your recent experience with the authorities."

She gave her great-aunt a sideways glance to see if she was being sarcastic. She wasn't. Unfortunately, what Aunt Amelia said was true—in the recent past, Liz'd had more than her fair share of interrogation rooms.

They stood at the screen door and looked in. Birdman was sitting at his kitchen table, his head in his hands.

Aunt Amelia knocked on the worn frame. "Birdy, we've come to introduce you to Carmen Miranda. I'm here with Lizzy. We need you to see if you can find out why Carmen isn't talking."

"Come in," he said, his voice soft, sounding defeated.

The screen door creaked as Liz opened it, then followed Aunt Amelia inside. The doorframe was so low, Carmen Miranda had to bow her head.

Liz gasped when she saw that the bookcase on the north wall of the cottage had been toppled over. Piles of books and sketchbooks were trapped under its weight, some splayed open and forever ruined. "Birdman, what happened?"

He looked up at them with soulful eyes. "I was out checking the lagoon nests. When I came back, I found this." He nodded his head in the direction of the bookcase. "And the sketchbook I've been working in has been damaged. Someone was quite rough with it. Why would someone care about my doodling?"

They took a seat at the table. Aunt Amelia sat next to Birdman and Liz sat on an unsteady caned-seat chair across from them. A fan blew in their direction from the Formica counter in the kitchen, but the small space was still hot and sticky. Liz knew Birdman had a small window AC in his bedroom, because she could hear it rattling. Birdman never bothered or couldn't afford to have one in the cottage's main room.

"This is lunacy," Aunt Amelia said, lightly pounding the scarred wood table. "Birdy, why would someone do this?"

And why would someone dig holes in his garden, Liz thought. She hadn't told her great-aunt about that, or the fact that the diving spear belonged to Birdman. Liz said, "For one thing, your sketches aren't doodling, they're exquisite nature studies. And for the other, you should call and report this."

"I don't think a toppled bookcase and a harmed sketchbook is cause for alarm. But there is one missing that has great sentimental value to me, and some of my mother's classical poetry books have been damaged. Poetry was her refuge from my father's indiscretions. The sketchbook taken was one of my earlier ones, and it included drawings of my mother. I guess it was more like a visual diary. I don't have any photos of her, and I often look at it. Why would anyone want to steal it and leave all the others?" Liz saw tears welling. Birdman quickly rubbed his eyes, then got up and wearily shuffled over to a stack of sketchbooks piled next to his desk/ drawing table. The top of the desk was a mess, and the drawer was pulled out as if someone had been searching for something. He picked up one of the sketchbooks from the floor and brought it back with him and sat down.

Liz couldn't fathom why someone would do something so strange. Was it related to Jameson's murder? Or just some kids, bored on summer break? No. The fact that the diving spear sticking up to the heavens like a trident in the garden had been the weapon used in Jameson's death squashed that theory.

Liz held out her hand and Birdman handed over the sketchbook. She skipped to the last page, where he'd drawn a close-up of a sea turtle nest in the sand. One of the eggs in the picture showed a fissure, a baby ready to hatch and see the world. He hadn't had a chance to add watercolor to it. But even in pen and ink, his artistic prowess was extraordinary.

"Do you remember the date on the one that was stolen?" Liz asked, afraid to meet his sad gaze.

"Nineteen fifty-one," he replied. "I date all my sketchbooks."

"Hopefully, it was just some kids," Aunt Amelia said, stating out loud what Liz had thought earlier. Making a tsk, tsk sound, she said, "Birdy, if it was one of our archeologists, you'll be happy to know that we're kicking them out as soon as we get back to the hotel. One less thing for you to worry about." Aunt Amelia patted his hand, and Liz saw a weak smile on his chapped, sunburned lips.

"I don't want to take a chance." Birdman got up again, went to the corner of the room, and got down on his bony knees under the single window. They watched him take a folding knife from his pocket, then he pried up two oak floorboards. Reaching inside the open space, he began removing sketchbooks and a small book or diary. He replaced the boards and came back over to them, placing the stack on the table. "Berry Girl, you take them and keep them safe. These are from when my mother was alive. They were the only things that made her happy when she'd look at them. My father never made her smile, that's for sure. I put them away after her death and occasionally take out one at a time, like I did with the one that's missing. A couple of my books have images of my father in them. He always said I was a ne'er-do-well. Maybe he's right."

"Stop that talk this instant, Burton Bennett!" Aunt Amelia said, her eyes watery.

"I would rather you keep them safe, Berry Girl. There's also my mother's diary. I don't believe it was children who did this. I've lived here going on seventy years and have never been bothered before. Only by real estate developers and tax men. I know you might think I'm a crazy old man, but I've been feeling that I'm being watched ever since they showed up. To me, these hold value." He laid his long-fingered artist's hand on top of the stack. "I doubt they do to anyone else."

He didn't need to clarify who *they* were, but Liz asked anyway. "How long have you felt you were being spied on?" Then she answered her own question, "A week, right?"

He nodded his head.

"Have any of the team been inside your cottage?" Liz asked.

Birdman looked up at the ceiling, "Just Mr. Royce." His face clouded, then he added, "And young Evan."

"Did you show either of them your sketchbooks?"

"I showed Evan a couple of the most recent ones. I'm embarrassed to say, he brought me a bottle of Jack Daniel's and things got a little hazy."

She knew it! Evan had just moved to the top of Liz's suspect list. She couldn't wait to have a word with him for lying to her. The only problem was, if Evan killed Jameson, what was his motive? He continued, "I'm not a drinker, nothing like my father. My father would drink, disappear, then bring back presents for my mother. Probably things he stole. She never wanted things, she just wanted him at home and out of trouble. She came from a wealthy family, but when she married Father they disowned her. Even though your mother, Amelia, invited her to the Indialantic often, she was too embarrassed about what happened at the party. I didn't know anything about the accusations of my father stealing from the Pieces of Eight 1715 salvaging operation. An aunt I'd never met before told me about it at my mother's funeral. 'She should have never married that low-life scoundrel,' she said."

A pall hung in the air for a while, until Aunt Amelia said, "Well, I know my mother and your mother met quite a few times at the orchid house. I was told your mother had quite a green thumb."

Liz was thankful the subject had changed.

"Mother always wore an orchid in her hair," he said wistfully, "but she never told me that she met your mother, Amelia. I sketched her many times with a flower in her hair and she always had a flower on her bedside table. That's why I want you to keep those older books safe. They're all I have of her."

"All your drawings have value, Birdman." Liz locked eyes on his. "Isn't that what I've been telling you? I will guard these with my life. Right, Auntie?"

"Birdy, after the hotel's guests leave, I insist you come stay at the Indialantic until this thing is cleared up. I'll keep you far away from Barnacle Bob," Aunt Amelia added.

Birdman smiled.

Aunt Amelia brought her fist to her heart. "I feel so bad that I asked you to have them on your property. I will never forgive myself. I thought because you have so much pride in your land and because of your knowledge of the rich history of our little island, that it would be exciting for you if they found anything of significance. And now a murder on your property."

"Murder. So, it's official," he mumbled, not seeming surprised.

"I'm afraid it's true," Liz added, trying to get his attention so he didn't tell her great-aunt about the diving spear. Liz should have known he wouldn't bring up something so brutal to Aunt Amelia.

He put his hand on Aunt Amelia's shoulder. "It is not your fault, Amelia. I'm to blame for things too."

Liz glanced at Birdman's frowning lips, waiting for him to tell them what he could be to blame for, then remembered that he'd allowed Jameson to pay the back taxes on his property. She prayed no one else, including Agent Bly, found out about that. Last night, Betty had said she'd do some more digging on what would happen to the land if Jameson had called in the payback card. What if Jameson was the one spying on Birdman, and he wanted to kill Birdman with the spear tipped with some of the poison dart frog venom he'd brought back from the Amazon? They'd fought and instead of Jameson killing Birdman, Birdman had killed Jameson in self-defense. If Birdman was dead, would the land automatically go to Jameson? Or what if Jameson's motive to get rid of Birdman had to do with the Spanish breastplate? With Birdman dead, Jameson would have been able to own all the rights to the artifact, cutting out Birdman and the remaining archeologists, not to mention the state of Florida, from reaping any of the rewards. Her head was spinning from all the scenarios. She needed to talk things over with Ryan. His cool demeanor was always the perfect salve to her wild imaginings.

Liz looked at her watch. "Auntie, we'd better get back and deliver the news to our guests."

Aunt Amelia glanced at Birdman's troubled face and realized (not her usual MO) that it was time to leave, before the sheriff's department showed up. "You're right, dear."

"Wait," Birdman said, then he made a cooing sound, held out his hand, and looked at Carmen Miranda, who hadn't made a peep during their whole conversation. She happily left Aunt Amelia's shoulder and hopped onto Birdman's arm. Using two fingers on his right hand, he stroked her back gently. "She'll talk when she's ready. No need to rush it. It's there. Be patient." Then he said, "Go back to Mother, little beauty."

Carmen hopped back onto her mother's shoulder, and Aunt Amelia beamed at Birdman's endearment. "Thank you, Birdy. That's all we needed to hear. Right, Carmen?"

Liz and Aunt Amelia stood, and Liz gathered up the sketchbooks. There would be plenty of time to ask Birdman questions later, especially about Evan Watkins's boozy visit. She knew something wasn't right about Evan's interest in Birdman. And what had Evan been doing before he'd showed up at Birdman's shed yesterday morning? If there was one thing she'd learned from spending time with Birdman, he'd never told her a lie. He would tell her the true story; she only had to ask.

But that would have to happen when Aunt Amelia wasn't around.

Chapter 23

"Well, that didn't go as we'd planned, Lizzy," Aunt Amelia said as they took the path leading them back to the Indialantic.

"Wait!" Liz said.

Aunt Amelia stopped. "Oh my, what now!"

From her great-aunt's shoulder, shielded by the pith helmet, they both heard Carmen Miranda say, "Oh my, what now! Oh my, what now!"

"She spoke!" Aunt Amelia said, clapping her hands. Liz couldn't clap her hands because she was holding Birdman's sketchbooks.

"Oh, Birdy, you do know how to perform miracles!" Aunt Amelia said, then she blew a kiss to Carmen and stroked her royal-blue back feathers with two fingers like Birdman had done.

Liz wanted to pet Carmen too, but was distracted by the sound of not one but two vehicles advancing through the brush behind them, heading toward Birdman's cottage. It seemed that they'd left just in time. The sheriff had arrived. Luckily for Liz, Aunt Amelia's hearing wasn't quite the same as when Liz had left for Columbia University eleven years ago.

"Auntie, I think I left my phone at Birdman's." She pretended to pat down one of her pockets, knowing the other pocket held her phone. "I hope it didn't fall out on the way here. I'll need to retrace my steps."

"I'll come back with you."

"No. You and Carmen need a cool drink and some air-conditioning. Now might be a good time to put Carmen's cage next to Barnacle Bob's. Maybe they'll strike up a conversation. Do you think you can handle carrying these sketchbooks and diary?"

"Of course I can. You know I can lift—"

"Great!" Liz stuffed them into her arms, then took her by the shoulders, turned her around, and aimed her the short distance toward the Indialantic's property line.

When Amelia was out of sight, Liz went back the way they'd just come, but not to retrieve her phone. Her phone was safely in her pocket. What she needed to do was find out why it took two patrol cars to pick up one eighty-year-old man for questioning.

When she was near the direct path to Birdman's cottage, Liz heard voices. Two to be exact, and neither was Birdman's. She veered right and took an alternate route that she hoped would lead her to the rear of the cottage, near the shed. It wasn't the safest way to get there, because she would have to walk through the center of the crumbling mansion.

Due to all the vegetation, the going was rough. She had on sneakers but wished she'd worn boots. Even though the snake placed in Jameson's armoire drawer had been nonvenomous, she knew the island also had its share of poisonous reptiles, including rattlesnakes and the scarlet king snake's look-alike, the coral snake. Usually in this situation, she would clap her hands loudly to scare them away, but she didn't want to draw attention to her approach. She looked at the murky sky and sent up a silent request for her safety.

When she reached the center of the old mansion, she stopped and twirled around. It was like she was in some child's story: *The Secret Garden*, or even *The Jungle Book*. Decades ago, the roof and second floor of the mansion had been blown away and probably could be found at the bottom of the Indian River Lagoon. Unlike antebellum mansions that were built pre–Civil War, the Bennett mansion had been built with brick, then plastered with stucco. Only the north and south walls remained, crumbling to the ground brick by brick. In some places the walls were seven feet high, in others only three. Liz picked up a thick, pointed tree branch from the ground and used it as a makeshift machete. The only way she knew she was getting closer to the cottage was when the voices, which she assumed belonged the sheriff's deputies, got louder and louder. Where the mansion's rear wall used to be, Liz saw a small area where it appeared that someone had been digging. She knew it wasn't one of the locations the archeologists had set up. There was a small mound of dirt and unearthed weeds in front of a group of mangroves. Promising herself she would check it out on her way back to the Indialantic, she hurried toward the voices.

Finally, she reached the path between the cottage and the shed. As she lifted her foot to step onto it, she froze when she heard Agent Bly say,

"Morrison, come with me. I want you to read Mr. Bennett his rights. It will be a good learning experience for you."

They were going to arrest Birdman! She was torn between staying hidden and marching up to Agent Bly and giving him an earful. She decided to cool her jets. The best way to win this war was with a good defense. If only she could think of one. She slunk down and followed a line of hibiscus bushes until she was facing the front of the cottage.

Bly had beat her there. She almost choked when she parted a giant fern and saw, of all people, Dr. Crawford standing outside Birdman's cottage. *What the heck.*

She heard Agent Bly say, "Thank you for bringing us to Mr. Bennett's house. I don't think we could have found it without you. I've been here before, but I came from the crime scene with Ms. Holt and Mr. Stone. It's like the Lost World from *Jurassic Park* around here."

Dr. Crawford appeared flustered. "I didn't know you were going to arrest the guy. I've only known him for a week. Knows his plants and the animal kingdom. I suppose you're here because I told you about the snake and Jameson; I mean because Jameson, Mr. Royce, accused the guy of putting it in his room."

Bly shook his head. "I can't discuss the case with you. Like I said, I needed one of you to show me how to get here from the road."

"Oh, okay." He seemed truly relieved. Liz wondered if it was an act, or had Dr. Crawford shifted the blame onto Birdman to keep the authorities from looking into his personal life, rather, his wife's personal life? Did Dr. Crawford know about his wife's pregnancy? In Liz's eyes, that was motive enough for killing Jameson. Plus, unlike Birdman, Dr. Crawford had recently been to the Amazon. As soon as she got back to the Indialantic, Liz was going to round up Ryan and Betty to talk about the latest events. Another thought hit her: there was no way they could kick the team out of the Indialantic now. If Birdman didn't kill Jameson, and she knew he didn't, then that meant one of the remaining four did. Come hell or hurricane, Liz was determined to prove which one it was in order to prove Birdman's innocence.

Bly put his hand on the door handle to the cottage. Before opening it, he glanced back at Dr. Crawford, who was watching him, looking like he wanted to stay to see Birdman's arrest. "Doctor," Agent Bly said, "do you want one of my deputies to drive you back to the hotel?"

"No. No. I hope I can find my way back. Usually I travel via a golf cart."

"It's no problem, Doctor. But I'll have to ask you to wait in the second squad car."

"I'll be fine. After all, I made it through the Amazon without being harmed. That is, except for a nasty infection from a palm tree thorn."

Agent Bly turned and walked back to him. "You were in the Amazon?"

"Why yes, the whole team was."

"Can you be more specific? Who was in your team?"

"Myself, my wife, and Professor Talbot."

"Jameson Royce?"

Nigel's cheeks pinked, and it wasn't from the heat. "Why, yes. Jameson was there."

Bly's face didn't show any emotion. "Thank you, Doctor. I must get inside." Bly opened the screen door and stepped into Birdman's cottage.

Liz watched Dr. Crawford turn toward where she was standing. Panicked he would see her, she scurried back toward the mansion's ruins, twigs and branches snapping as she went. Near a row of palmettos, at least a dozen startled white ibis flew up from the ground. Uprooted from their feeding grounds, they emitted an eerie nasal honk as they hightailed it into the dark sky. Liz felt like she'd walked onto the set of a Hitchcockian thriller.

Near the center of the mansion, she stopped to catch her breath. Her lungs were on fire and so were her thoughts. Was it possible to take Dr. Crawford off the suspect list? Would he mention the trip to the Amazon if he was the one who used the poison dart frog venom to kill Jameson? It seemed unlikely. Then again, there were three other people on the trip with him. Never underestimate a killer's wiles (like she'd done one too many times).

When she reached the lime tree next to the single-armed statue in the mansion's center courtyard, she paused and looked down at her bloody, scratched ankles, knowing Grand-Pierre would have her patched up in no time with his natural salves. She took a step toward home, then another. Then she remembered she'd wanted to check out where someone had been digging beyond the rear wall of the mansion. She turned back, wishing she'd left breadcrumbs or some kind of marker to designate the spot. Finally, she spotted the area. She took a step and instead of terra firma, she felt only air. Her left foot disappeared into a narrow hole and her body catapulted forward, her arms outstretched. Her chin came to rest on a prickly bed of pine nettles, the sharp point of an agave leaf grazing her unscarred cheek.

Holy cow!

What next?

Chapter 24

Thankfully, she didn't feel any pain. Just a tightness and a burning sensation at the top of her foot where it was trapped by what felt like a large rock.

Getting up on her elbows, she glanced straight ahead. "Fancy meeting you here, Earl."

The snake looked back at her in fright, then slithered away. She hadn't needed to repeat the rhyme to realize it was Earl or one of his king snake brothers, not a coral snake. At the thought of a deadly coral snake, she realized it wasn't the time to be patting herself on the back just yet. Corals weren't the only poisonous reptiles on the island. And what better place to roam than the woodsy, marshy terrain surrounding her.

She stood on shaky legs and tried to free her foot by twisting it left to right, hopefully making the top of the hole larger. *Yes!* She succeeded. Well, maybe not. As the top of hole widened, small rocks and pebbles broke free and buried her foot even more. "Ouch," she yelped. A second later, she heard twigs and branches snapping.

Someone was coming toward her.

Not having time to think about if it was a friend or foe, she called out, "Hello? Hello. I could use a hand over here."

No one answered.

Through a gap in the bushes, she spied a pair of work boots and slim, tanned legs. Haven! Why wasn't she answering? And why was she traipsing through the ruins of the old mansion? Was she the one digging holes like the one she'd just stepped in? "Haven, it's Liz. Can you please help out?"

More silence.

Liz let out one more plea for help and held her breath, exhaling when she saw Haven turn and move toward her.

After a game of hot potato, with Liz calling out hot and cold clues, Haven finally reached her.

"Looks like you're in quite a pickle. Can't you just pull your foot out?" Haven asked.

"Karma seems be playing a little joke on me," Liz answered, wincing as she tried to wiggle her buried foot. "I just need you to help dig it out."

After taking a collapsible shovel from her backpack, Haven got down on her knees, then looked up at her. "Your cheek's bleeding." Her dark, luminous eyes held concern.

"Just a scratch." *I hope.*

"Well, let's get you out of here."

"Are you sure you can do this in..." Liz wanted to say, *in your condition.*

"Of course."

Within seconds, her foot was freed.

"Now see if you can walk," Haven said.

Liz placed her left foot on the ground, took a tentative step, then winced. "As long as my foot is still attached, I think I'm okay." Liz flexed her foot. No problem with her ankle, except for a little stiffness. She bent and loosened the ties on her sneaker, then gingerly pressed on the top of her foot. Other than a pulsing sensation and a slight swelling, it felt fine. "Looks like I'm good to go," she said to Haven.

"You better clean that scratch on your cheek. You don't want it to get infected." Haven looked cool and collected in white shorts and a white sleeveless blouse. Not a trace of sweat dripped down the side of her face. Liz was drenched.

"I will. Thank you."

Haven reached in her backpack and pulled out a package of hand-sanitizing wipes, withdrew one, and dabbed at the scratch on Liz's cheek. "Looks like you're lucky. The wound is very shallow."

"I do feel lucky. Lucky you came along, but I don't think this is a good place for you to be walking around, as I can attest to." Now that Liz was free, her mind wandered back to why Haven was creeping around Birdman's property. Plus, she knew Agent Bly had left strict instructions for the team to leave their equipment where it was for now, and not to trespass, especially beachside, where Jameson's body had been found. She glanced over at Haven. Her formfitting blouse showed a flat stomach, confirming that her pregnancy was in its early stages. Haven's face was pale, but other than that, she seemed to have conquered her morning sickness. It wasn't morning, so maybe that's how it got its name.

Liz decided to go for it. "Why are you here? You know it isn't safe. Auntie gave your team carte blanche to use the golf carts. Do you have any idea who is digging around here?"

Haven didn't answer. "Where were you headed?" Liz asked.

"Can't be that dangerous, if you're here," Haven replied, with a slight edge to her voice.

Touché.

"Birdman, Mr. Bennett, is a friend of the family," Liz explained, making it up as she went. "He's noticeably upset about Jameson Royce's death. I don't suppose you have any theories as to who killed Jameson? I know you were in the room with him when Mr. Royce found the snake." Liz was thankful Ryan or Betty wasn't here to chastise her. Ryan would have to give her a lesson on more tactful ways to extract a confession. But Liz was living in the moment, knowing Birdman would go insane being caged in a cell.

"I have no theories on who killed Jameson," Haven spat. "But now that you mention it, he did seem to think that it was Mr. Bennett who put that snake in his armoire drawer, and I know for a fact your family friend has been spying on Jameson, on not just one, but two occasions. Strange, don't you think?" she asked in a snarky tone.

Where has Ms. Calm, Cool, and Collected gone?

"Well, do you need my help getting back to the hotel?" Haven asked impatiently.

Liz took a couple of steps. Careful steps. "No. I'm fine. Just a little embarrassed. I'm sure you're an expert at walking through jungles and climbing mountains. Professor Talbot said you just came back from the rain forest in Brazil. How does that terrain compare to this? I bet it's more dangerous in Brazil, but exceptionally beautiful at the same time."

Haven wasn't going for Liz's attempt at girly chitchat. "Yes. Beautiful. Are you okay on your own, Ms. Holt?" Before Liz could answer, Haven collected her shovel, folded it, put it in her backpack, then slung the backpack across her back. Abandoning her original trajectory, Haven turned toward the Indialantic and started to walk away; then she changed her mind, turned, and came back, then offered her arm. "I'm sorry for being so short with you. I'm taking out my anger at someone else on you." She smiled a dazzling smile, and Liz forgave her at once.

"I'm sure we're all on edge, no apologies necessary." Liz was dying to know who it was she was angry at. If she had to guess, she would pick

Evan, based on last night's scene. "Did you know Evan's grandfather worked at our hotel years ago?"

Haven turned her head away so Liz couldn't see her expression and mumbled, "That's interesting." Liz's spider sense set off warning bells. Haven was evading the question. But why?

Liz held out her arm and let Haven support her. She didn't feel much pain, but she exaggerated her limp to play on Haven's heartstrings. "I can't believe the sheriff's department thinks Mr. Royce was murdered."

"Why can't you believe it?" Haven asked, looking at her. "He was a vile man. Not that he deserved to be killed," she added, a little too late for it to sound sincere.

"Do you think it was over whatever he found? Did Mr. Royce ever tell you what it was?"

"No. He didn't. Jameson only told me that his find was related to Ponce de León," Haven said, her voice calmer than earlier.

Liz took advantage of the change and asked, "I don't mean to be nosey, but on Monday during the snake incident, you seemed pretty happy about how upset he was. And in return, Mr. Royce seemed pretty angry at you. I thought you were friends?"

Haven stopped next to the summerhouse. "His anger had nothing to do with me, it had to do with Nigel. I wasn't about to throw my husband under the bus, or myself either, so that Jameson could take credit for whatever he'd found. We are a team, and we did all the painstaking work, while Jameson just rented machines to do his part. When Nigel told Jameson that someone contacted the state of Florida, spilling the beans that Jameson wasn't an accredited archeologist, he blew his top. Threatening to ruin Nigel's and Professor Talbot's reputations, saying he'd even make up lies. The one thing my husband and the professor prize above all else is their reputation in the scientific community. I'm in it more for the excitement of discovery, getting field experience, and passing on my knowledge to my students."

"Is there money to be made with a discovery of this kind?" Liz asked as they started toward the hotel.

"Oh, my dear. Money isn't even in the equation when it comes to archeology, or for that matter, professorships. Even with tenure, we barely make ends meet."

Liz glanced at the white belt around Haven's trim waist decorated with the *G* for Gucci insignias. Was Jameson buying her off with expensive presents? If so, what had she had to do in return?

As they passed the fountain at the hotel's main entrance, Haven said, "Here we are. Do you need help inside?"

"No, I'm fine. In fact, I'm going to take one of these golf carts home and soak my foot. Thanks for helping me out. I'm forever indebted."

"No problem. I think I might go rest myself." Then Haven looked toward the ocean and said, "A storm is coming. I guess it's par for the course. Professor Talbot says we are heading out the day after tomorrow, as soon as they let us collect our gear. We just don't have the money to continue the dig. The professor has been trying all morning to get funding from the state, but with a murder investigation at the dig site, it seems an impossibility. My heart's not in it, anyway."

There was one last question Liz wanted to ask: *Then what were you doing creeping around the Bennett property?* Instead she said, "Okay. Take care. I'll see you at dinner."

If they planned on leaving the day after tomorrow, it was time to kick things into high gear and find Jameson's real killer, because it wasn't Birdman. The first thing Liz planned on doing was going down to the sheriff's station to see Birdman and make sure they let him out on bail. If her father were here, he'd defend Birdman. But he wasn't. She hated to admit it, but it might be time to call him, if only for advice. On second thought, she would bounce things off Ryan and Betty, and she'd bring one of them with her when she went to the sheriff's station.

After Haven disappeared inside the hotel, Liz got in one of the golf carts and looked down at her left foot. It was double its normal size. Grand-Pierre would know what to do for it. She put her foot on the gas and followed the drive south. At the huge magnolia tree, she turned right toward the hotel's kitchen entrance. It was then that she felt the phone in her pocket vibrate. She stopped the cart, reached in her pocket, and pulled it out.

It was a text from Ryan. **All hell's broken loose. Come to the lobby ASAP.**

That didn't sound good.

Chapter 25

Ryan was waiting for her just inside the revolving door. The first thing he said was, "What happened to your foot?"

Liz had taken her sneaker off, so she had one shoe on and one shoe off.

"And how did you get that scratch on your face?"

"It's a long story. What's going on? You said it's urgent. There hasn't been another murder, has there?"

"No. Something else has happened, but first, we have a visitor."

Suzie Malone stepped from behind a potted palm. "Murder! Are you saying Mr. Royce was murdered? I read this morning there was an accident. But murder! I'm sorry to say,"—she looked around to make sure no one was in hearing distance, then whispered—"this will bring down the price per square foot. I know he was killed next door, but he was staying here, and with all your other recent troubles that Brit has been telling me about—"

Liz had had it. "Get out!"

"What?" Suzie said, looking to her left, then right. "Are you talking to me?"

"Yes. Please leave. My aunt is not selling the Indialantic."

"Is this because of what happened at senior prom? It was Brittany's idea, not mine."

Ryan stepped up to Suzie and said, "Ms. Malone, you had better listen to Liz. As you can see, she's been in an accident and needs medical attention. And it is true, Amelia will not be selling. If she changes her mind, I will be the first to tell you."

"Why, thank you, Ryan. That is all I'm asking." She turned to Liz. "Just one more thing, Lizzy. You wouldn't know who Mr. Royce's next of kin is, would you?"

Liz bit the inside of her lower lip just to keep from running over, grabbing Suzie by her hair, then dragging her to the revolving door and shoving her inside. Ryan must have seen that in her expression, because he took Suzie's elbow and led her to the door. "Maybe you'd have better luck asking the sheriff's department for that information. We'll be in touch."

Liz waited until she was out of sight before saying, "Thank you. I was just at my limit with her. Was that the reason all hell was breaking loose? You seemed to handle her very well."

"Well, no. It's another matter."

"I better sit down for this one."

"Don't you want Pierre to look you over? Tell me what happened. Our next little problem isn't going anywhere."

"Well, I was cutting through the old Bennett mansion when I fell into a freshly dug hole. I'm fine. It doesn't even hurt. Haven rescued me."

"Haven?"

"I'll tell you more later, but now you. What's so urgent?"

"I was overseeing the workers trying to secure that retaining wall in the basement, and, well, you'll have to see it to believe it. But first you need to get that looked at," he said, pointing at her foot.

"Can't you just tell me?"

He wouldn't meet her eyes. "We've uncovered something in the basement. A secret room and..."

"And?"

"A skeleton."

"Oh my god! Whose?"

"That I don't know. Dr. Crawford is down there now. He has a doctorate in anthropology; as he was coming in, he overheard one of the workers who was leaving the hotel talking about it."

"Talking about what?"

"It's better if I show you. I didn't want to call in anyone an official capacity, especially with all the other stuff that's going on, until we know what we're dealing with."

She was stunned. "Can you please run out and get my other sneaker? It's in the white golf cart. I have to see this right away."

"Thought you might."

"Oh, by the way," she said to his retreating back, "Birdman was arrested for Jameson's murder."

"The hits just keep coming," he said as he went out the revolving door to get her sneaker.

Chapter 26

Beyond the rubble of the collapsed wall, Liz saw Dr. Crawford leaning over a skeleton wearing tattered clothing covered in white dust, looking like the perfect prop for one of Aunt Amelia's favorite Vincent Price movies.

Stepping into the small room, she glanced around. There were wine racks with vintage bottles that were covered in what looked like a thick white powder. A couple of wooden chairs on either side of an old oak barrel stood in the corner of the small room.

Dr. Crawford said, "Pretty sure he's male. I did an internship back in the eighties with a forensic anthropologist. You can tell by the jaw and shape of the skull, but it doesn't mean it couldn't be a large female. What remains of the clothing looks male. I'd guess he's been here for decades."

"I knew nothing about this room," Liz said, looking at Ryan.

"There's something interesting over here," Ryan said. Taking her hand, he led her to where an old whiskey crate stood. He picked something up and said, "Open your hand." She did and he placed a three-inch tarnished silver pin in the palm of her hand.

She felt Dr. Crawford behind her, his warm breath on her neck. He said, "It's an AAF senior pilot's wing pin from WWII. I know because my father had the same one with that shield."

"So, this guy's been down here since WWII?" Ryan asked.

"It's possible," Dr. Crawford said. "However, oftentimes my father would put on his dress uniform for special holidays or reunions."

Liz got out her phone and turned on the flashlight function, then swept the room with light. "Hey, what's that?" She walked to the wooden barrel and shined her light at its base. Bending, she picked up a rolled piece of fabric she thought might have been a duffel bag, but when she unrolled it, she saw it was a military uniform jacket adorned with numerous sewn-on patches.

"It's an air force sergeant's dress jacket," Dr. Crawford said. "See the patch on the sleeve with the wings and pierced star in the center and the three stripes?"

She held the jacket up by the shoulders, sneezing twice from the chalklike dust floating in the air and drifting down to the stone cellar floor.

"Check the pockets," Ryan said.

"You check them," she answered.

"Sissy," he said with a smile.

That's all she needed to hear to make her immediately put her hand in one of the pockets. Never dare a Holt or call them a sissy. Something clattered to the floor, and a cloud of white powder shot up. The fabric lining had disintegrated, and her fingers were poking through the hole in the pocket.

Ryan bent down, sifted through the dust, and came up with a pair of military dog tags on a long chain. Brushing away the powder, he read, "'Leggett, John A.,' and then there's some numbers below."

"Why does that name seem familiar?" Liz racked her brain for the answer, but none came.

"Maybe a long-lost relative?" Dr. Crawford suggested.

She'd forgotten he was there. "No, I don't think there are any Leggetts in the family that I know of. I guess after we tell Aunt Amelia about this, we better call in Agent Bly. Now I'm starting to wish we had called my father and Charlotte." She didn't go further, knowing that Dr. Crawford was still a suspect in Jameson's murder.

"I guess we should leave things as they are for Agent Bly and his forensic team." Ryan placed the dog tags on top of the uniform jacket that Liz had laid on top of the barrel.

"I think we all will need a shower before dinner," Dr. Crawford said. "I don't think Sergeant Leggett is going anywhere."

Leggett, Leggett, Liz repeated in her head. Where had she heard that name?

Ryan took her hand and led her to the stone staircase. "You need to see Pierre for some of his natural remedies for that foot of yours. I think it's grown double in size since I saw you in the lobby."

She smiled at his concern. "It is starting to bother me."

"I could carry you up," Ryan said, as she placed her good foot on the first step.

"I'll hobble up, using only my right foot, but we should let Dr. Crawford go ahead; this might take a while."

She stepped back so Dr. Crawford could pass. "That foot doesn't look good at all. Look what happened to me in Brazil, and that was just from a thorn piercing the bottom of my foot. It got infected and there was a time I thought they might have to amputate; the pain was unbearable. The natives at the site gave me some potent natural medicine that's been used as a painkiller in Brazil for centuries. However, there is a caveat: it has the potential to kill a man in the wrong dose. I have a vial up in my suite that I can get for you. Only, I must be the one to administer the dosage in the proper way, or you might end up like Sergeant Leggett back there," he said, adding a chuckle.

Liz and Ryan didn't return his laugh. Liz held her breath as Ryan asked the million-dollar question. "Doctor, you say it's natural. Where does this magic pain reliever come from? A plant?"

"Oh no, actually, it's quite amazing. The venom comes from a Dendrobates tinctorius azureus. Commonly called the poison dart frog. Would you like me to run up and get it?"

"Definitely," Liz said with a fake grimace. "I'll try anything at this point."

"Will do. And by the way, please don't tell my wife about this. She would have my hide if she knew I brought the stuff into the country."

"Promise," Liz said.

"I'll meet you in the lobby, then?" Dr. Crawford asked as he ascended the staircase.

"Yes, we'll be there," Ryan answered.

They waited until Dr. Crawford disappeared from the top of the staircase and they heard his retreating footsteps. "And Agent Bly will also be waiting," Ryan added, then he punched a three-digit number into his phone.

Nine one one.

"Could things get more bizarre?" he asked Liz before talking to the dispatcher.

Liz didn't answer because they both knew.

Of course they could.

Chapter 27

"It's not there," Dr. Crawford said as he descended the spiral staircase in the lobby. "You don't understand how lethal this stuff is. I need to talk to your house..." He stopped on the second step from the bottom when he saw Agent Bly and one of his deputies staring straight at him.

Bly advanced toward him with a solemn expression and said, "Oh, I think we do know how lethal the stuff is, Dr. Crawford."

While Liz had been getting a quick checkup from Grand-Pierre, who'd told her that nothing was fractured, then administered one of his magical poultices to the top of her swollen foot and the scratch on her cheek, Ryan had waited in the lobby for Agent Bly. He'd told Bly about what was behind door number one, the person with the poison dart frog venom, but told Liz he'd wait to tell Bly what was behind door number two, i.e., a possibly seventy-year-old skeleton by the name of Sgt. John A. Leggett.

"What's going on?" Dr. Crawford asked Agent Bly, looking confused. Then Liz saw by his change in expression that it must have dawned on him that Jameson had been killed with poison dart frog venom. "I don't know what you're insinuating, but I had nothing to do with Jameson's death. Someone must have stolen it from my room." He looked toward Aunt Amelia, who, after they'd told her about the skeleton, had put on a full-length black mourning gown from one of her plays at the Melbourne Beach Theatre Company. Liz was guessing *Macbeth,* but she could have been wrong. The good news was Aunt Amelia decided not to wear the matching black veil after Liz had told her it might be a tad too much.

"Shall I take him into the library?" Agent Bly asked Aunt Amelia.

"Yes, Sam, the library does seem to be the best place for these kinds of things, don't you agree, Lizzy?"

"Yes. May I show you the way?" Liz asked, stunned that Aunt Amelia was calling Agent Bly by his first name. *What was that about?*

"No need, I already know the way."

Dr. Crawford came down one step, then froze.

"Let's go, Doctor. No monkeying around."

As Bly, Dr. Crawford, and the deputy passed the brass elevator, Barnacle Bob called out, "Hey, hey, we're the Monkees, and people say ..." Then, surprise of all surprises, Carmen Miranda, who was in the cage next to BB, joined in. Barnacle Bob must have taught her the song from the old sitcom. If they hadn't just found a skeleton in the basement, and the owner of the poison that killed Jameson Royce, Liz might have gone straight over to Carmen's cage and moved it as far away from Barnacle Bob as she could, maybe even bringing it to her beach house. That's all they needed—two obnoxious macaws. But she was too exhausted, physically and mentally, to consider moving anything.

Ryan said, "Agent Bly, when you're done, maybe you can come back to the lobby. There's something else that needs your attention."

Agent Bly stopped and said, "Will do. A pair of agents will be arriving shortly; please direct them to the library."

"One thing at a time, Ryan dear, Sam's got his hands full," Aunt Amelia said as she collapsed into the wicker peacock armchair near the registration counter, then went to town tracing a never-ending circle on her knee while humming the tune to "You'll Never Walk Alone" from the musical *Carousel*.

"No problem, Amelia," Bly said with a smile; then the smile disappeared when he said, "Let's go, Doctor; you know the way."

Dr. Crawford started to walk, then turned around, his eyes beseeching Liz's. "Please tell Haven about this."

There was the swish of the revolving door and Haven and Evan came into the lobby's foyer.

"Thank God," Dr. Crawford said when he saw his wife. "Haven, you might have to find me a lawyer."

"Oh, Nigel, what have you done?" she asked, looking concerned.

"I need you to tell them about the poison dart frog venom. How it helped with the pain."

She strode over to him. "Don't tell me you brought that into the country? You promised." She glanced at Agent Bly and the deputy. "That's how Jameson was killed, wasn't it? My husband didn't kill him," she said, directing her gaze at Agent Bly.

"Then, Dr. Smith-Crawford, do you know who did?"

"No-o-o, why would I? As soon as I call a lawyer for my husband, I will be there beside him. Don't say a word, Nigel."

Liz didn't think Haven had it in her—it was like a mama bear protecting her cub.

Evan grabbed Haven's wrist. "Maybe it's best if you don't get involved."

Haven gave Evan a look that made him shrink back against the bamboo paneling; then she walked to a private alcove on the other side of lobby and pulled out her phone from her Hermès handbag.

Evan looked at them, smiled his winsome smile, and said, "Think I'll just go up to our suite and tell the professor what's going on."

Ryan, who'd been quiet, said, "Not a good idea, Mr. Watkins. How about going into the kitchen and asking the chef for one of his pastries? I think the sheriff's department plans to search all the suites."

"I'm not a little boy who needs a treat. I am a grown man, who has every right to go up to my suite if I want to. And who are you anyway?"

Something had Evan's dander up. Liz said, "Evan, you better do what he said. I'm sure Agent Bly will want to talk to you, too. So it's better if you stay on the main floor."

With a forced smile and a shrug of his shoulders, Evan said, "Tell Dr. Haven if she needs me, I'll be in the kitchen." Then he dragged his feet as he took baby steps toward the hallway, no doubt waiting to hear Haven call his name. But that didn't happen.

After Evan left the lobby, Haven came up to Liz, looking defeated. "I can't get a lawyer. They all want a retainer, and I just don't have it. Our stipend for the last dig hasn't come through yet." She looked at Liz, Ryan, and Aunt Amelia as if one of them would loan her the money.

Liz immediately went and sat in a chair next to Aunt Amelia, shooting her a penetrating stare, but it was too late.

"Oh, I'm so sorry, Dr. Smith-Crawford. If only my nephew was here. I'm sure he would help out, he used to be Brevard County's top public defender. But he's on his honeymoon with Charlotte, who happens to be the lead homicide detective for the sheriff's department."

Haven's face flushed. "Oh, too bad, Amelia. When are they expected back?"

"Next week. Maybe I can..."

Liz reached over and grabbed her great-aunt's hand, giving it a gentle squeeze. Thankfully, Aunt Amelia didn't finish what she was going to say. "But I'm sure Sam—Agent Bly—will be fair. After all, he's a good friend of my nephew's; they went to high school together."

"They did?" Liz said.

"Oh yes, Lizzy. They've been friends for years. You didn't know that?"

"No."

"Sam. Sam who your dad plays pickleball with? You never heard him talk about him?"

"Pickleball Sam is Agent Bly?"

"Yes," Aunt Amelia said. "See, we will get this all sorted out in no time."

Haven looked panicked. Could it have something to do with whatever she and Evan were talking about stealing? Or did she really care about her husband's welfare? "Oh, well, thank you anyway. I'm going to call my sister, maybe she'll help. Is it okay if I use the dining room to make the call? I might have to do some begging," she said, adding a nervous laugh.

"Of course, dear," Aunt Amelia said. "I'm sure everything will be fine."

After Haven left the lobby, Ryan sat next to Liz. "So, what do you think?"

"I think it's time to turn everything over to Pickleball Sam. I can't believe all this time he was a friend of Dad's. And I think Dad should give him a call and tell him to release Birdman, especially now that we know he had nothing to do with the poison."

Aunt Amelia, always the upbeat one, said, "I think we should let Sam do his job. I'm going to the Enlightenment Parlor and rest before dinner. It's been quite a day. Plus, I have to do my lesson plan for class tomorrow. Oh," she said, turning to Liz. "Do you think under the circumstances, I should cancel the class?"

"I wouldn't," Liz said. "It will be a good way for you to keep busy. I'm sure the hotel will be swarming with agents from the sheriff's department tomorrow, so the emporium's a better place to be. Especially because of the other thing in the basement. If someone needs you, I'll come and get you. But I'm sure Ryan and I can handle things. Right, Ryan?"

"Of course. It's all under control."

Not even Liz believed that one. "Auntie, do you know anyone with the name Leggett? John Leggett?"

Aunt Amelia glanced up at the lobby's twenty-foot ceiling. "You know, the name does seem familiar, but I can't place it. But I will. I never forget a name or a face. As soon as I remember I'll let you know. And by the way, Lizzy, I took one of the golf carts earlier and dropped off Birdy's sketchbooks at your place. I didn't feel it was safe leaving them here after his break-in."

"Break-in?" Ryan asked. "What break-in?"

"Auntie, I'll let you know when you can go up to your suite. And I'll tell Greta to bring you some tea. Which Island Bliss blend do you want?"

"Oh, let me think. I think a pot of Relaxing Rose Hips mixed with Jasmine Garden would be sublime. Thank you, darling."

Ryan extended his hand and helped Aunt Amelia from the chair. For the first time that Liz could remember, her great-aunt looked her full eighty years. "Love you, Auntie."

"Love you back double, Lizzy."

After Aunt Amelia left the lobby, Liz explained about her and Aunt Amelia's visit to Birdman's and the missing sketchbooks, then told him more details about her accident and Haven's rescue.

"I think if Agent Bly is a friend of your father's, we should round up Betty and turn over everything we know about the case," he said.

"Which case?" she said with a weak smile.

"Funny. The case that's going to free your Birdman."

"I'm all for that," she said. "I'm going to go home, make tea and toast for dinner, and look through those sketchbooks. Even if we tell Bly everything we know, I feel we're still in the dark. And do you think Dr. Crawford killed Jameson? 'Cause I don't. Why would he tell us about the venom if it was what he used to kill Jameson? He had no idea I would hurt my foot and he'd be in the position to offer it as a pain reliever."

"I agree. So now we've narrowed it down to three."

"Thought we were giving everything to Agent Pickleball Sam Bly?"

Ryan grinned. "Doesn't mean we can't work on things until they release Mr. Bennett. Plus, I thought maybe we could make a deal with Bly to share information. Remember the key in Jameson's cell phone case? I would love to know if it's to a safety deposit box and if so, what was in it?"

"Wow, has it only been two days since this all started? We will need a vacation after this."

"Sounds good to me. I think Maine might be our coolest choice for August. My uncle has a cabin."

"Sounds perfect. Except..."

"Except what?"

"Francie's fashion show."

"Ugh, why'd you remind me?"

"We'll go after that. How about Brooklyn? September's a great time of year for New York."

"After what you went through with your ex and the press when you lived in Manhattan, I didn't think you'd ever want to return."

"With you by my side, I can conquer anything. I wouldn't mind taking you to some of my favorite Soho restaurants."

"And I wouldn't mind taking you to some of my favorite Brooklyn restaurants."

Liz stood and extended her hand. "Okay, let's shake on it. New York in September."

Ryan pulled her to him. "I don't do handshakes, only this..." He took her in his arms and kissed her.

Afterward, she murmured in his ear, "You sure know how to seal a deal, Mr. Stone."

Chapter 28

It was the pile of sketchbooks on Liz's kitchen counter that triggered her memory of where she'd heard the name Leggett. She hobbled to the rattan trunk in front of her sofa and opened it. Nestled inside were the things that belonged to Cissy, the maid who supposedly killed herself in the Indialantic's pool after she'd set fire to the center section of the resort back in 1945. 1945! V-E Day. The time period at the end of WWII. Liz got down on her knees, not an easy task with her swollen foot, and dug around until she found a stack of letters, tied with a faded teal ribbon, that had been addressed to Cissy Bollinger care of the Indialantic by the Sea Hotel from a J. Leggett, who Liz now knew was Air Force Sergeant John A. Leggett.

After looking through a few of the letters, many of which she'd read before, she put in a call to Betty and told her about Dr. Crawford and the skeleton in the basement.

"We were right! Cissy never started the hotel fire, and her death was no suicide!" Betty shouted.

Liz had found Cissy's small suitcase in the hotel's luggage room when she was ten, around the same time Betty had moved into the Indialantic. Since then they'd been trying to prove Cissy's innocence. Now that they'd found Cissy's fiancé rotted away in the hotel's basement, Liz knew they'd been right. It seemed the hotel had a few more murders to add to its list, Cissy's and John's. If ever there was a cold case, this would be it. Even if they never solved who'd killed the pair, Liz was happy that the young girl's name could be cleared. Maybe, after things got back to normal—if that was possible—Liz and Betty could try to track down Cissy's family and tell them the good news.

After Liz filled Betty in on Birdman's arrest, her fall and rescue by Haven, and the missing poison dart frog venom, Betty said, "Well, I've had quite a day myself, though not quite as exciting as yours. I'm at a rest area near Daytona Beach, after a trip to St. Augustine."

"Wait! You're driving? You don't have a license."

"Not a problem. Clyde is with me."

"Does this have something to do with Jameson Royce's murder?" Liz asked.

"It might."

"Let's regroup in the morning," Liz said. "We'll find out then if Dr. Crawford was arrested and Birdman released. If he hasn't been released, I plan on going to the sheriff's station and talking to Pickleball Sam."

"Who? I think you're breaking up."

Then Liz explained about Agent Bly and her father being friends. Betty said, "Wish we'd known that a couple of days ago."

"Just tell me quickly, does what you found have to do with Dr. Crawford?"

"No."

"Okay, that's good, because I don't believe Dr. Crawford is guilty. But Haven and Evan as a team, I wouldn't rule out." Liz had purposely not added the professor's name with Haven's and Evan's. She still didn't know what exactly Betty's feelings were for her old boyfriend. However, Betty had been willing to kick the four guests out of the hotel, and she did have the captain. Hopefully, all would be clear when she met with Betty in the morning.

After Liz hung up the phone, she sat down at the dining room table and propped her foot up on a chair, then began to look through Birdman's sketchbooks, starting with the oldest. Even at the age of seven, Birdman had been an amazing artist. Not only did he draw what he saw in nature, he also included some interior sketches of the mansion before it fell into disrepair prior to Birdman and his mother moving into the cottage. There were many in situ studies of his mother, who, like Birdman, also resembled a bird, but a more fragile creature like a hummingbird or painted bunting. She didn't see any photos of his father in the sketchbook, and she didn't know if that was on purpose or if Birdman's father, Roy—no Rory—had been serving time in prison like Aunt Amelia had told her. One thing you could tell was how beautiful Birdman's mother must have been. Liz thought of her own mother. She had photos and even a video that she looked at often. Suddenly, feeling overwhelmed by the past couple of days, she turned the AC way down, then went to the window seat and lay next to Bronte, pulled up a hand-knitted cashmere throw, and fell into a deep sleep.

She woke in darkness to the sound of a fierce wind, her wind chimes clashing against the wooden supports to the beach house in an angry cacophony, not the least bit soothing as they usually were. When she looked toward the south, the sky out the bow window was pitch black. She sat up with a start, realizing she must have been asleep for hours, then remembered a strange dream that involved Evan pouring whiskey down Birdman's throat as he was sleeping on his sofa, then turning to Liz, who really was Haven, and saying, "Who loves you, baby? Now get a lawyer—a divorce lawyer."

Liz anchored herself in reality by looking over at Bronte, whose nose was pressed against the window. "You poor baby, I think we both missed dinner. Let me remedy that."

After feeding Bronte and herself, taking a quick shower, then changing into an oversize Columbia T-shirt and shorts, she went into her small office with a cup of Aunt Amelia's Island Bliss chamomile tea. There was no chance she could go back to sleep to the sound of the howling wind that made the branches of her hibiscus bushes claw at her windows like demons wanting to get inside.

It wasn't until she was sitting in her desk chair that she realized that her left foot didn't hurt at all, the swelling had gone down, and her foot looked almost normal. *Thank you, Grand-Pierre! Who needs poison dart frog venom when I've got you?*

She opened her laptop, which sat on the French Empire—style desk that had once belonged to her mother, and turned it on. Of all their suspects, it was Professor Talbot that she knew the least about. Even his old friend Betty had lost touch with him for decades. Liz recalled that Evan said Jameson and the professor had argued the night before his murder. Could it be that Jameson threatened to pull the professor off the team? They certainly weren't besties. But that wouldn't explain yesterday at lunch when Professor Talbot didn't seem to care one bit if Dr. Crawford took over as head of the team.

What else would make the professor want to kill Jameson Royce?

Thirty minutes later, after putting "Professor Walter Talbot" in the search bar, she hadn't found anything disparaging or sinister that the professor had been involved in, only accolades about past digs, rave reviews about his book *Tales from the Pits*, and prestigious awards given to him from the scientific community. There were only a couple of mentions of their trip to Brazil, and she got the impression that they hadn't found anything of importance (except for poison dart frog venom). At 2:00 a.m., she shut down the laptop and went into the great room, then continued to the French doors leading outside. Opening one door, she stepped out onto the deck and could barely close the door, the wind pushing her back two steps for every three she took forward. Just before she reached the deck's railing, she saw a flicker of a flashlight and a figure with sloped shoulders moving slowly toward the Bennett beach.

Was he a mirage? Or was Professor Talbot, the man she'd just been looking into on her laptop, creeping around the beach? Without thinking she ran down the wooden steps to the shore. The tide was in and the waves were huge. Maybe if she'd thought before following the figure, she would have brought a flashlight, or at least her phone. But she'd done none of that. Because the man was moving so slowly, she soon caught up with him at the steps leading up to Birdman's property.

Throwing caution to a merciless wind, her mouth filled with sandy grit, she shouted, "Hello there, this is private property! You'll have to go back the way you came."

The figure turned toward her. "Liz, is that you? It's me, Professor Tal..." His words got lost in the sound of the surf.

She stepped closer. "Professor, what are you doing out here in the middle of the night, especially in this weather?"

"I know, I'm an old fool."

That line didn't work when her great-aunt said it, and it didn't work when Professor Talbot said it. He wasn't a fool; far from it, judging by all his stellar credentials.

"I have a bad case of insomnia. I'm usually up this time of night. It's when I do my best thinking. I thought it would be better to come out here and take a walk on the beach, instead of tossing and turning."

In this weather?

"Well, as you can see," she said, putting her mouth near his ear so he could hear her, "it's high tide and I think this is the beginning of the tropical storm they forecasted. If you want, Professor, you can sit on my deck. It's much safer."

"Oh, no. I'll head back. I think I underestimated the elements, my dear."

They both turned around and headed north, the professor's flashlight leading the way. As they walked, he said, "Why aren't you sleeping, my dear? Stupid question—I think I can guess. Right before Nigel and Haven turned in, Nigel told me about your skeleton in the basement."

That answered one question she'd wanted to know. Dr. Nigel Crawford hadn't been arrested, which meant Birdman was still locked up. She wanted to ask the professor more, including why he was going to the scene of the crime, but the wind and the waves made it too hard. They parted at her porch steps. If he was Jameson's killer, he now knew where she lived. She'd be sure to turn on the alarm her father had put in last fall. Sad, because before then, they'd never needed alarms or motion detectors in their quaint island town.

"Goodbye, Professor. Sleep tight."

"You too, Liz. I want you to know I'm sorry for this whole thing with Jameson. Hope we see each other again in better circumstances."

So that was it. They were leaving.

As far as Liz was concerned, unless one of them stayed behind in the Brevard County lockup charged with murder, that wouldn't happen.

She just didn't know how she'd pull it off.

Later, before getting into bed, she shot off a text to Ryan. **Please send me the photos you took of the crime scene. I'll explain in the morning.**

Ryan answered, **This is the morning. Three-thirty!!? What's going on?**

Plz, just do it. I'm fine, she responded, then she added a smiley cat face.

After scooping Bronte up from the window seat, she went into the bedroom and got under the covers. Good boyfriend that he was, she heard the ding that she'd received mail. She'd leave perusing the photos until the morning. But she knew one thing; Professor Talbot was planning to go to the crime scene, but for what, she hadn't a clue. However, it wouldn't hurt to look at the photos. And if she did see something, try to get to it before he did.

Thankfully, she immediately drifted off to sleep; the wind had calmed, and the only sound was Bronte's gentle purring.

Chapter 29

Liz was up at sunrise, but there was no sun to be found. The sky was murky at best, but at least it wasn't raining. After looking through the photos Ryan had sent her, she'd grabbed her raincoat and went out into the miasma. The tropical storm was not meant to hit until midnight, but the stormy skies and a fierce wind warned of its approach. She hurried down the steps leading to her beach, then turned south, like she'd done last night when she'd followed Professor Talbot. The pounding waves crashed to the theme of *Jaws*. Ignoring the warning, she continued to the beach dig site, knowing exactly what she was looking for and praying it would still be there.

At the steps to Birdman's place, she looked to the top of the cliff and saw crime scene tape crisscrossing the banister in front of the gate to the landing. The tape being intact hopefully meant the professor hadn't doubled back after they'd said good night.

She glanced to the left and right to make sure she was alone on the beach, then jogged up the steps. After ripping the tape from the railing and leaving caution *tape* to the wind (a joke only Betty would appreciate), she continued to the encampment. It looked the same as when she and Ryan had been there yesterday. Peeking around the tent's flap to make sure it was empty, she entered.

By comparing the photo Ryan had sent her to her surroundings, she was able to find what she was looking for. The bad news was, she'd have to climb down the ladder to pick it up. She took a minute to think if she should call Pickleball Sam first or just take the notebook, then later the three detectiveteers could look at it together. She chose to do a combination of both. She'd thought ahead and brought gloves. She took them from her pocket and put them on, then went down the shaky ladder. Or was she the one who was shaking?

At the bottom, she grabbed a small notebook that was half-buried in the sand and soil, and quickly went back to the ladder. A vision of a three-pronged diving spear coming toward her propelled her up the ladder in record time. At the top, she bent at the knees and thought, *Good going, Nancy Drew.* Then she revised her not-well-thought-out plan: If she took the notebook, it would be considered tampering with evidence. Plus, it needed to be next to where Jameson was killed. Realizing her impulsive ways might jeopardize the investigation, she took out her phone and alternated between taking photos of the pages and peering out the tent to make sure no one was approaching. She could fit two pages per photo because the notebook was so small, but it still took twenty minutes. When she finished, she climbed down the ladder and left the notebook in the exact spot she'd found it. Now she had to pray the professor wouldn't come back to get it.

After she left the tent, she started to question herself. Was the notebook what the professor had been looking for last night? Even if it wasn't, and he'd taken an innocent stroll, when flipping through the notebook she'd noticed each entry was dated. It would be an interesting diary of the team's past week.

A light drizzle started, just enough to turn her hair into strawberry-blond cotton candy. Instead of heading to the Indialantic the smart way, via the beach where a golf cart was waiting at her beach house, she followed the trail west to Birdman's property, because it was a shortcut to the summerhouse, where she was meeting Betty to go over the fruits of Betty's trip to St. Augustine. Then Liz planned to go have a talk with Agent Sam Bly—he had some explaining to do for not mentioning he was her father's buddy. That's when it hit her: her father and Charlotte must know everything that was going on with Jameson Royce. She felt relief, knowing that even though they were thousands of miles away, they had everyone's back at the Indialantic by the Sea.

As she walked, she chose the main path, which was sheltered by overhead branches and vines that shielded her from the rain and wind. At Birdman's cottage, all was quiet. She peeked in the front window, hoping she would see him inside at his sketching table. But the cottage was dark and empty.

When she reached the turnoff that led to the ruins of the mansion, she kept walking. Suddenly, the laces on her left sneaker got caught on a low-lying vine. She pitched forward but was able to steady herself by hanging on to the trunk of a small palm tree. Her foot, for the most part, was healed;

she'd only had to loosen her shoelaces slightly, but obviously she hadn't tied them into the double bow Aunt Amelia had taught her at age six.

Liz bent over, freed the laces on her left shoe, then retied them a little more snugly. When she stood up, she was face-to-face with someone wearing a black hooded raincoat

"What are you doing here?" she asked.

Chapter 30

It was a scowling Evan. He looked about as happy to see Liz as she was him. "I've come to check on Mr. Bennett," he said by way of a greeting.

Either he didn't know Birdman was in jail, or he was here for other reasons, like stealing more of Birdman's sketchbooks or digging holes that people could fall into, namely Liz. She said, "That's a nice, friendly thing to do. But he's not here, I just checked. By the way, I heard from Professor Talbot that you all plan to leave tomorrow. Is that true? I'm sure you'll be happy not share the suite with Professor Talbot anymore. He told me he was an insomniac—that must be a pain, seeing as you sleep in the sitting room. He must keep you awake." The transition from Birdman to the professor wasn't her best, but Evan didn't seem to notice. He kept glancing behind him as if waiting for someone. Someone named Haven?

"The professor has insomnia. That's a laugh. He sleeps more than a newborn baby, and he snores so loudly, I wear earplugs. No way he has insomnia, he even takes naps. Although he did go out last night. Maybe he's upset about Mr. Royce's death, not that they had a great friendship. Far from it."

Liz tried to sound casual when she said, "Hey, my friend Kate from Books & Browsery at the emporium told me that your grandfather used to work at the Indialantic in the 1950s. I'm surprised you didn't tell my great-aunt about that when you checked in."

"Hmm, pretty sure I mentioned it." He pushed off his hood, then used his right hand to make furrows through his hair.

A nervous tic?

"Between you and me," he said, "Miss Amelia is the most amazing elderly woman I know for her age, but she probably forgot that I told her about Grandfather."

Liz knew for a fact that Aunt Amelia didn't forget much. She could memorize her lines in half the time the younger actors took. "Well, I suppose that's possible." *Not.* "What's your grandfather's name? I'll be sure to ask her about him. My great-aunt would have been about nine or ten then; she might even have some fond memories of him."

"I doubt it. He was a sixteen-year-old bellhop who only worked one season."

"I'll make sure to ask her, just tell me his name," Liz pressed.

"Tommy," he said reluctantly.

"Watkins?"

Evan nodded his head, then shrugged his shoulders, looking nervous.

The skeleton in the basement was dead way before Evan's grandfather worked at the hotel, so why would he lie that Aunt Amelia knew about his grandfather?

"Does he live in the area? Bet Auntie would love to visit him."

"Yes. Hey, I've to get going. Anyway, Grandpa's not completely together in the head anymore. He's in a nursing home."

"Maybe Auntie could go see him."

"Not a good idea. What's with the third degree, anyway? You know these old people. Even you have to admit, Miss Amelia is a bit on the ditzy side. She might upset him."

No one was allowed to call Aunt Amelia names. Liz stepped closer, anger bubbling up. "I don't agree that my great-aunt is ditzy." She took a deep breath, then let it out. That didn't help so she forged ahead. "Why did you go to Birdman's cottage and get him drunk on Jack Daniel's the other night? What's your agenda? You told me you barely knew him. Did you steal his sketchbooks? What are you looking for? Are you the one digging holes inside the old mansion and in his garden?"

Evan clenched his jaw and formed a fist with his right hand.

Oops. She realized she had no backup. She hadn't told Ryan or Betty about her plan to go to the crime scene.

Instead of raising his fist and punching her in the face, he took a step backward, like she might punch him. "Whoa, relax, little lady."

That did it. "What did you call me? I don't like you hanging around here. This is private property, and until the murder is solved, it's off-limits. I'm meeting with Agent Bly in a few minutes and I have a lot to tell him. So outta my way."

She pushed past him, walking at a fast pace, holding back from breaking into a run like she wanted to do. The crunch of his work boots and snapping twigs told her he was walking slowly, taking measured steps. In no rush. Never let them see you sweat, Aunt Amelia always said, kind of impossible during a Florida August with a potential killer following you. Only once did she look back. Evan stopped walking and waved, even smiled like they were besties out on a nature walk—instead of Liz just having told him that she planned to turn him in to the sheriff's department.

She returned his wave, then jogged toward the summerhouse. Through the glass she saw Betty's petite form, her head bent over Watson and her finger scrolling away.

Liz's fight-or-flight response evaporated at the sight.

Chapter 31

Betty offered Liz half of her pastry, then said, "Wow, what a story—and quite a morning you've had. Let me fill you in on yesterday; then we can look over your photos of Walter's notebook."

"Hopefully, we can go over the pages where there's air-conditioning, because there are a lot of them," Liz said.

"While you're in with Agent Bly, I'll look through them."

"Good idea," Liz said. "It's not like we can tell Bly about the notebook anyway. But if it has incriminating evidence against the professor, we'll have to somehow get Bly to search the crime scene again. Maybe I should have kept it and said I found it on my beach."

"One thing at a time. All you have to do is tell him about Walter's suspicious stroll toward the crime scene last night. If Agent Bly's a halfway decent cop, he'll go check and find the notebook. You've done good, Elizabeth," Betty said, patting Liz's hand.

"Learned from the best. Are you sure you can be objective when it comes to Professor Talbot? After all..."

"If that was the case, then I wouldn't have gone all the way to St. Augustine to track down the origin of that half-burned newspaper article that Walter was scrambling for in the bushes. The article came from the *St. Augustine Record*. It was a notice about an auction by a private collector who claimed to be selling his collection of Florida artifacts dating all the way back to the early 1500s. The auction was six months ago."

"Was there a Spanish conquistador's breastplate mentioned? Or even a photo that Greta could look at and identify as the one she saw under Jameson's bed?"

"That's where we need to do more digging," Betty said. "I got in touch with the auction house; they were very adamant about client confidentiality on both the seller's and the buyer's sides. I've done some research, and it seems the auction house is very reputable."

"Meaning, if they have such a good reputation, they would've made sure the items that went up on the auction block were authentic, right?"

"It seems likely. I did get out of them that they have surveillance cameras, and the auction was videotaped. Plus, bidding over the phone wasn't allowed, which means whoever attended the auction will be on the video, whether it's Walter, Mr. Royce, or one of the others. I'm good on the internet, but I'm not good enough to get a copy of the video."

"Well, I'm ready to turn everything over to the authorities, especially knowing my father and Agent Bly are friends. If you don't mind sending me what you have, then I'll show him. Bly could surely get a copy of the video, but if he doesn't move quickly enough, then I'm going to have to break down and call Father and Charlotte to intercede. Birdman must be going crazy. He's used to the open sky, not a cage. Do you know that he once suggested Aunt Amelia let Barnacle Bob go free?"

"Didn't you tell me that the only time Birdman came to the Indialantic, he slept next to BB's cage?"

Liz laughed. "You have a point."

"I've updated our suspect list with my new information. Now let me go back to my rooms and add what you've just told me," Betty said, standing up. "Then I'll print a copy for you to give to Agent Bly."

"Can you do one more thing? Can you find which nursing home a Tommy or Thomas Watkins is in. Evan said he was nearby. I would check Satellite Beach first, then maybe Melbourne. After I talk to Bly, we can take a little road trip."

"Evan Watkins's grandfather, right? The one who worked at the Indialantic."

"Right," Liz said.

"Are you going to invite Ryan along?"

"No, he's tied up with the crime scene in the basement. Auntie has her acting class to teach. Speaking of which, I want to catch her before it starts and ask her about Evan's grandfather. See if she remembers anything from that time period. I have no idea if it's important, but as you always say, knowledge is power."

Betty laughed. "Thomas Jefferson said it first."

Liz stood and looked back toward Birdman's property. "If Evan left Birdman's property as I told him to do, we would have seen him by now.

I'm tempted to go back and drag him away from there." Liz knew Betty wouldn't stop her if that was what Liz wanted to do. It was one of the things she loved about Betty; she wasn't a coddler. She didn't say, "Oh, do be careful of the Big Bad Wolf, dearie." Or "It isn't safe going alone." Maybe because Betty had such an adventurous spirit herself, she'd passed it on to Liz.

"Hopefully," Betty said, "we can find out what Evan and Dr. Haven are up to after we talk to Evan's grandfather. That's if Watson can find him. Ugh... Now you have me calling my iPad Watson. I think maybe Sherlock would be more fitting; he's more analytical than Watson. Watson has a heart."

"I think you're a combination of them both, Betty, with a little Miss Marple and Nancy Drew mixed in. Are you ever going to tell me which Nancy Drews you ghostwrote? I think you can trust me by now."

She smiled. "I'll throw you a bone, but that's it. Once, you mentioned a book that took place in nearby Cocoa Beach. It's possible I penned that one. But I will never break my promise to the Stratemeyer Syndicate. I don't think even supersleuth Nancy would want that."

"It doesn't matter anyway, because you're our supersleuth, and now you have a new alter ego in your Sherlock Holmes London Chimney Sweep Mysteries."

"Enough compliments, I'll get a swelled head," Betty said as they started to walk toward the hotel. "We'd better get to it. If, as you told me, the team is leaving tomorrow, this is our only chance to nab our man or woman."

Next to the fountain in front of the lobby entrance, Liz pointed. "Oh my, look toward the emporium parking lot!"

Walking in single file was Aunt Amelia dressed in a nun's habit, her acting students following in line behind her like baby ducks following their mother (superior). All but one of the girls wore navy dresses with white Peter Pan collars and straw hats with a navy band and ribbon. The tall blond prima donna who Liz recognized from her great-aunt's first acting class was, naturally, the only one not in costume.

Betty gasped. "I think I've seen everything when it comes to Amelia, but she always seems to surprise me."

"True. I better run and catch Auntie before she tries to fly away."

Betty laughed. "No. Don't tell me. She wasn't. Was she?"

"Okay. I won't tell you that in an episode of *The Flying Nun*, Aunt Amelia played the part of a novice. I recognize the habit. Her Spanish-American accent wasn't too shabby."

"Can't say I ever watched that show. But knowing Amelia, that's probably the video she plans to show them right now."

"I wouldn't bet against it."

Betty advanced toward the revolving door and Liz called out, "I'll pick you up here in thirty."

"See you then," Betty replied; then she disappeared inside.

Chapter 32

"I'm glad I caught you, Auntie," Liz said as Aunt Amelia exited her classroom and stepped into the emporium's hallway.

"I thought I'd grab some smoothies for the girls; they've been so excited about the play. I had no idea they all grew up reading the *Madeline* books. My mother, your great-grandmother, read *Madeline* to me."

"And you read them to me. I remember I even had the dolls and a carrying case."

"I forgot about that. Some children's stories are timeless, like..."

"Is that why you have them dressed as little Madelines? To act out a scene from the books?"

"Oh no, darling," she said, waving her hands in the air, "we've decided that instead of *Cat on a Hot Tin Roof*, we're going to do *Madeline in Melbourne Beach* for our next theater production. It took a while for me to convince Ziggy, but I promised him you would help with the script, make it more adult friendly. You do know *Madeline* was once a play on Broadway."

Liz had to cut her off because time was a-tickin'. "Auntie, I have to ask you something that could be important. Did you know that Evan's grandfather used to work at the Indialantic as a bellhop?"

"Why, no, I didn't know that. But it explains why he's always asking me to tell him stories about the Indialantic and our island's history. Strange he wouldn't mention it."

"His grandfather's name is Tommy Watkins," Liz prompted. "He would have been sixteen in the early fifties."

Aunt Amelia thought for a moment. "I would have been around eight or nine. As a matter of fact, I do remember him. He was a handsome boy, looked a little like Evan, except his eyes were brown."

"Wow, you remember his eye color. Why do you think Evan didn't mention it to you?"

"Well, I don't know, dear. It does seem strange."

"Auntie, if you can think of anything that might help tie up why Evan didn't mention his grandfather to you, but told me he did, and at the same time is grilling you about the Indialantic, please text or call me."

"I wouldn't say he's been grilling me, but we have shared a few glasses of brandy in my sitting room."

Here Evan was again, plying the elderly with alcohol. "Well, think back to any specific questions he's asked you. Or anything having to do with Birdman."

"I'll put my thinking cap on, dear."

"Looks like you already have it on, Auntie. Or is that your flying hat?" Liz said with a grin.

"Isn't it perfect for the play? So, you'll help with writing the adaptation." She clapped her hands. "You're the best, Lizzy."

Instead of saying she would or wouldn't, Liz smiled, then said, "Have to run. Remember what I said. Let me know if you think of something. Maybe some event from the time Evan's grandfather was here."

Liz started to walk away, and Aunt Amelia called after her, "Give my love to Birdman."

"I will." Aunt Amelia was more intuitive than Liz gave her credit for.

Thirty minutes later, Liz pulled up to the lobby entrance in her father's Jeep. Betty was waiting outside, dressed in a white, sleeveless, linen tunic-length shirt over navy capris and red ballet flats. Her white hair was in a chignon, and she was holding a tote bag that was almost as big as she was. She had a huge grin on her face as she came around the car, opened the door, and hopped into the passenger seat. After closing the door, she said, "Found him!"

"Where?"

"Satellite Beach."

"Fabulous."

Betty dug in her bag and came out with a folder. "Three copies. One for you and Ryan along with one for Agent Bly."

Liz put the car in drive and pulled out onto A1A, then headed north. Betty was busy on Watson and Liz was busy thinking about how everything was connected. Evan and Haven. The professor. How did it all tie into Jameson's murder? She realized she'd left Nigel off the list, and the skeleton in the basement. Nigel brought the poison dart frog venom into the country, but she didn't believe he killed Jameson with it. If only they could find it.

"Did you find out why your great-aunt was dressed as a nun?"

"Are you sure you want to know? Looks like Ziggy caved," Liz said, "like he always does. No, the costumes have nothing to do with The Amelia Eden Holt School of Acting. *Madeline in Melbourne Beach* is going to be the next play at the Melbourne Beach Theatre. One thing you can say for Auntie, she's a sharp businesswoman; the theater won't have to pay the girls to perform, yet they can add stage experience to their resumes. Just hope they can act."

Betty added, "And dead bodies don't start showing up like in the past. Speaking of dead bodies, I guess I'm to blame for bringing the team to the Indialantic."

"And my fault about last New Year's Eve, in a roundabout way."

"I guess when it comes to murder, the blame should go only to the one who does the murdering."

Glancing ahead to her right at the entrance to Juan Ponce de Leon Landing Park, Liz spied the huge statue of Ponce de León holding up the Spanish cross in one hand and a rolled document in the other. How did such an inspiring quest to find additional proof of Ponce de León's first steps in Florida turn into something so sinister and deadly?

By the time they reached the sheriff's station, it had begun to rain.

Liz and Betty got out of the car and ran inside. After going through the metal detectors, Liz left Betty in the small waiting room, and was led to an office whose door sported a placard that read Agent Charlotte Pearson. When she entered, Agent Bly was sitting at Charlotte's desk, his face hidden by an open laptop. He closed it and stood, reaching out his hand. "Liz, I've been waiting for you to show up. Frankly, your father and I thought you'd be here sooner with your theories about Mr. Royce's death."

Liz extended her right hand, holding the folder in the other. "Pickleball Sam," she said with a smile. "Well, here I am. Doing exactly that." She handed him the folder and said, "I demand you release Mr. Bennett immediately; he didn't murder anyone. And if you've been in touch with my father, he should have told you the same thing."

"Murder?" Agent Bly said. "Who said he was arrested for murder?"

Liz collapsed into the nearest chair. "He wasn't? But..."

"It was your father's idea. Mr. Bennett had missed a court date having to do with some past financial issues and had an outstanding bench warrant."

"So you arrested him and put him in jail?"

"Again, your new stepmother, Agent Pearson, thought it would be for the best, at least until they returned home. For his own safety. When your father returns, he plans to represent him if need be. I sent Agent Pearson the evidence against him, and we both agreed it wasn't enough to charge him with murder."

Stepmother? "Wow, that's a relief. It would have been nice if I'd been given a heads-up."

"Your father thought it best this way. Not because he was worried that you and your PI boyfriend would screw things up—actually the opposite. He told me, if you thought Mr. Bennett was arrested for murder, you guys would have more incentive to find out who the real killer was, then compare your sleuthing to my investigation." He laughed. "I don't think he had any idea an old skeleton would show up in the Indialantic's basement, but even that he seemed to take it in stride."

Liz smiled, not at Sergeant Leggett's death, but the calm manner in which her father handled everything that came his way. That's what made him a great lawyer of the people, and a great father.

"So, this is it, is it? The fruits of your digging." He opened the folder and Liz remained silent while he read through it.

"I also texted you some info on an auction that might have some bearing on Mr. Royce's murder."

After five minutes passed, he closed the folder. "Good work. I can see you've given me a lot to look into. Some, we already know about."

That was when Liz said, "Oh, and something strange happened last night." She went on to tell him about Professor Talbot being on the beach, just as she and Betty had rehearsed in the car, and ended with, "I think they plan to leave tomorrow. Is there any way you can keep them there longer?"

"That might be impossible. But I promise to keep tabs on them all."

"Now, can I see Mr. Bennett? He must be going crazy being locked up."

"I think you will find Mr. Bennett is just fine."

Chapter 33

"And I found Birdman with a pair of virtual reality glasses on, watching live drone footage from Everglades National Park," Liz told Betty as she pulled out of the sheriff's station parking lot. "He wasn't in a cell but in a conference room with windows looking toward the lagoon. They'd even set up a portable bed for him and sketching supplies. I could barely get him to talk to me. I'm going to kill my dad for this subterfuge. I've been worried sick."

Betty put her hand on Liz's wrist. "Look at it this way. If you didn't think Birdman had been arrested for murder, would you have tried so hard to catch the real killer?"

Liz turned her head and met Betty's gaze. "That was what my father and Charlotte were thinking. But still, I don't really know how close we are to catching Jameson's murderer."

"Between Agent Bly, your father and Charlotte, and the three detectiveteers..."

"Don't forget Watson," Liz added.

"We will find him. I think we're close."

"I did ask Birdman one question, and it seemed a reasonable answer. I asked him to explain why he was on the Indialantic's property the day before Jameson was murdered. His explanation made sense. He said, when he had gone into his shed, he'd noticed the diving spear was missing; he knew, or thought he knew, that it was Jameson who took it. Too afraid of getting caught, he claims to have chickened out about entering the hotel. And I believe him. How'd you do with the photos of the professor's notebook? Find anything?"

Betty looked away.

"What?" Liz asked. "Don't tell me there was nothing of substance in them."

"It seems I forgot to charge Watson. And there was no wi-fi in the station to open the photos on my iPhone."

"Don't be so hard on yourself. Let's go see Tommy Watkins, then zoom back to the Indialantic and look at them together."

They fist-bumped to cement the plan.

Five minutes later, just north of the Satellite Beach city limits, she saw the sign for Sunrise Coast Manor and made a right into the parking lot.

After parking and turning off the engine, she asked Betty, "By the way, how exactly are we going to get inside to visit Mr. Watkins?"

"Just follow my lead." Betty pulled out a pastry box from Deli-casies tied with string and a rolled-up piece of floral cotton fabric from her tote bag. "Wasn't it nice of my great-nephew Evan to send along a box of goodies from the Indialantic by the Sea to bring to his grandfather?"

"Sure was," Liz answered. "But who am I?"

"My health aide, of course."

"Wow, that's a stretch. You look the furthest from needing a health aide of anyone I know."

"Not today, I won't." Then Betty unrolled the fabric to reveal a dress, or housecoat as Aunt Amelia called them, and slipped it over her blouse. After pulling random sections of hair from her chignon, she hunched her shoulders, and said in a cackling voice that reminded Liz of the Wicked Witch of the West from *The Wizard of Oz*, "Well, dearie, let's go."

"You look like Granny Clampett from *The Beverly Hillbillies*. What about the red shoes? They look too upscale for the look you're going for."

"Thanks for reminding me." She dug into her bag and came out with a pair of rubber-soled house slippers. "Voilà!"

A half hour later they were back in the Jeep. Betty's plan had worked brilliantly, with one hitch. Evan's grandfather's memory was worse than they'd bargained for. He hadn't been able to remember what he had for breakfast, let alone what had gone on in the early 1950s when he was a bellhop at the Indialantic. Liz felt for him, and had to wipe away more than a few tears as she walked out of the room, knowing that Grand-Pierre's memory problems might someday lead to the same thing. The only bright spot was that Tommy generally seemed happy. She guessed that's all you could ask for in life, to be happy in the moment, with no past or future weighing on you. Tommy did perk up at Evan's name, grinning and pointing to a photo on his dresser of Evan when he was around ten.

At the end of the visit, Claudia, Tommy's nursing assistant, who had stayed in the room with them, had walked them back to the lobby. "Some days Tommy's memory about the past is spot on. Today wasn't a good day, but he sure seemed happy to have visitors, whether he recognized them or not."

Betty had asked in her old lady voice, "Has my great-nephew been in recently to visit him?"

"Not this week, but he was here a couple of weeks ago. If you see him, tell him his grandfather would love a visit. Evan always makes him smile," Claudia said.

They had said they would, then Liz had handed Claudia her business card. "If Mr. Watkins has a good day, maybe you could give me a call. I'm sure Betty would love to have a chat when he's more clearheaded. Day or night."

Claudia looked down at the card. "You're an author and a health aide?" she asked. "Your name sounds familiar."

Liz laughed. "Authors don't make much money."

"Neither do healthcare workers," Claudia said. "I'll call you, if I can."

"That's all we ask, dearie," Betty had said, then grabbed Liz's wrist and pulled her through the atrium's open sliding doors with the strength of a professional wrestler.

After they got in the car, Liz started the Jeep, then pulled out of the lot and headed south toward the Indialantic. While they'd been inside, the weather had taken a turn for the worse. Both Betty's and Liz's phones got text banners notifying them they were under a tropical storm warning: Tropical Storm Odette was heading their way and due to brush by the Melbourne Beach coastline around midnight. No direct hit was forecasted, but all the same, they would definitely feel it.

"Why do storms and hurricanes always seem to come in the middle of the night?" Liz asked Betty, as they drove through quaint Melbourne Beach with its T-shirt shops, open-air restaurants, and shorts and flip-flopped crowd.

"I know. You can't even take a sleeping pill in case you have to move inland," Betty said, pulling the dress over her head and tossing it in the back seat. "The price for paradise."

"Well, that was a bust," Liz said, changing subjects. "At least we didn't have to go that far to see Tommy. And we know that Birdman is okay."

"And your father, Charlotte, and Agent Bly have things in hand. I would say our first order of business is to quietly let the team leave tomorrow, then we'll follow up on our end. Although I don't think there is any threat of anyone being murdered by whoever did this. One thing I think you should do is maybe confess to your father, not Agent Bly, about the key you found between Mr. Royce's cell phone and the case. Before they leave tomorrow, Bly should check Mr. Royce's banking records."

"Good idea. After I fill Ryan in on Birdman, I'll have Ryan call my father."

"Chicken," Betty said, looking in the visor mirror while fixing her hair. "Well, I'm gonna look through the pages of Walter's notebook. Maybe that's another thing you should have Ryan tell your father about."

"I did tell Sam, Agent Bly, about Walter's strange behavior on my beach. For the professor's sake, I think we only squeal if the notebook holds something incriminating. Why muddy the professor's name?"

"I agree," Betty said.

"And while you're looking through the notebook, I plan on looking through Birdman's sketchbooks to see what Evan is up to. I'll hunker down with the storm and make sure I have an electric lantern ready in case the power goes out. And you, Betty Lawson, better charge all your electronics, just in case we lose wi-fi."

"I won't need wi-fi once I load the photos onto my iPad, and I bought a cordless battery power pack after the last storm—so we're good to go."

Liz pulled into the back of the Indialantic and parked the Jeep in her father's spot. After she turned off the ignition she turned to Betty and said, "Knowing Birdman is safe, I think this is the first time I'll be happy to let all the suspects go on their way, whether they're guilty or not."

"I tend to agree with you on this one. However, there's one thing you're forgetting. Even though the authorities don't think Birdman killed Mr. Royce, someone framed him. Wouldn't you like to find out who that someone was?"

"Ugh," was all that Liz could come up with.

Chapter 34

The power went out around nine, way before the storm hit. Liz and Bronte were on the window seat; the wind and rain battering the windows reminded Liz of when she was small and her father would take her to the car wash—it was fun and frightening at the same time.

She'd started with Birdman's sketchbook dated May 1950; the book that had been stolen was also around that year. Most of the drawings were of plants and landscapes, but there were a few of Birdman's mother, Millie. He'd not only drawn her looking happy, but also melancholy. It was after a boom of thunder that rattled the windows that Liz saw it. One of the drawings showed Millie asleep on a chaise in what must have been the courtyard of the old Bennett mansion. On her thin wrist was a bracelet. It hadn't been secured around her wrist, more like draped across, like someone had put it there while she was sleeping. Birdman had colored every other stone in the bracelet a faded grass green, but Liz knew what the stones were meant to represent.

"Yes!" Liz shouted, causing Bronte to twitch her ears and open her eyes wide.

Birdman's mother was wearing Great-Grandmother Maeve's missing diamond-and-emerald bracelet!

Some of the pieces fell into place. Evan's grandfather was probably the bellhop on the night of the party when the jewelry had been stolen. He would have passed on the story to Evan. It wouldn't take much digging to also learn about Birdman's father Rory stealing treasure from the Pieces of Eight Company. It explained the holes on the Bennett property, getting Birdman drunk, and stealing his sketchbook. Was she crazy? Even if she wasn't, it still didn't tell her why Evan would kill Jameson Royce. She jumped up and grabbed her phone from the kitchen counter to call Ryan about her theory. She put her thumb on the screen, but nothing happened. For all her warnings to Betty about making sure to charge her phone, Liz had forgotten to charge hers. She'd called Ryan earlier and they'd spent almost an hour going over everything. She'd been so *charged* up she'd forgotten to put it on the charger.

The hotel had a generator; she stuck the phone in her pocket and moved toward the front closet for her rain slicker.

It was then that she saw them.

Two faces. One on either side of the French doors.

Chapter 35

Evan pounded on the glass. "Let us in, Haven's been injured. We need help."

Was this a ploy like in a slasher movie? Liz didn't think it was, judging by the look on Haven's pale face pressed against the pane of glass. A smart heroine would grab some kind of weapon before opening the door. No, that wasn't smart, because her father had warned her since she was a teen that a weapon could be used against you in a struggle if the other person was stronger. And Evan was definitely stronger. A few kicks or a knee to the right place would be more efficient, though 911 was out of the question because of her dead phone.

Liz took her time advancing toward the door. Evan kept pounding against the doorframe and shouting, "Hurry! Open the damn door!"

So she did.

Evan grabbed Haven from the back, a hand on each shoulder, then either him or the wind propelled her into Liz's arms. Haven's nose and right cheek were scraped, showing pinpricks of blood. Liz led her to the upholstered chair nearest the door, and Haven sank into it.

"What happened?" Liz asked her.

Her clothing was muddy, and both knees were also scraped. "I tripped and fell. I'm fine. Minor injuries only," Haven said.

Evan pushed Liz out the way and got down on his knees. "Call an ambulance."

Liz stuttered, "My phone's dead."

Haven regained her composure and sat straighter in the chair. "No need for an ambulance. I'm fine."

"But..." Evan said, "you had a nasty fall. What about—"

"I'm fine," she said sternly. "Now, tell Liz why we're here. Either you tell her, or I will."

Instead of telling her why they showed up in the middle of a storm, he took a step toward Liz and said, "Why'd you go visit my grandfather?"

Liz took a step back, reaching behind her for the top of the dining room chair in case she had to bash him over the head with it.

"Never mind about that," Haven said in a weak voice. "Tell her, because she's going to hear about it anyway."

"I don't see why we have to," he said. "No one needs to know."

"Does this have anything to do with my great-grandmother's stolen bracelet?"

"See," Haven said, "she knows." She looked up at Liz with tears in her eyes. "Evan broke into your great-aunt's rooms and I found him tearing the place apart looking for the jewels from the portrait over the library's fireplace. I stopped him. This has gone too far. I want no part of this anymore."

"She doesn't keep my great-grandmother's jewels at the Indialantic. They're safe in a bank vault." Liz was angry at the thought of Aunt Amelia possibly being hurt by Evan.

"I had no idea what he was up to," Haven choked out.

"That's not true," Liz said, recalling when she saw them in the Indialantic's parking lot. "I overheard you both talking about stealing something. What part did you play, Haven?"

"I never did anything illegal. Neither one of us did," she answered.

"I'd call breaking into my great-aunt's suite illegal, and ransacking Birdman's cottage, and stealing his property illegal."

"I didn't do that," Haven whimpered. "He did."

"Haven, why are you throwing me under the bus? It's not like I killed a guy."

Haven gave Evan a searching look.

"You don't believe I killed Mr. Royce, do you? How could you?"

Haven didn't answer and instead said, "Tell her everything. I didn't say you killed him. Then we can leave, and hope Miss Amelia doesn't press charges."

Even though Liz was dying to hear, she said, "Wait. Let me get my first aid kit. One of those wounds needs a bandage and some antibiotic cream."

Liz left them and went into the bathroom where a candle was burning. She could tell Haven's wounds were superficial, but she revised her earlier thinking when she saw Evan glancing at the stack of sketchbooks on her dining room table. She swiped a pair of nail scissors from the medicine cabinet, then she took out the first aid kit from under the sink, knowing there was a roll of gauze inside that would give her an alibi for using the scissors. Just in case...

When she came back into the great room, Haven said, "Evan's going to give you an explanation."

A few minutes later, after he was done explaining, she realized his story wasn't far off the mark of what she'd suspected. Evan had told his grandfather that he would be staying at the Indialantic, and in a lucid moment, his grandfather told him about the night of the party in 1950 and the stolen bracelet and jewelry that had never been recovered. Later, Evan researched on his own about Rory Bennett stealing treasure from the Pieces of Eight Company. Fast-forward to last week, when Evan met Birdman, who was Rory's son. After showing Haven old newspaper articles about both thefts, and taking into account the fact that some seventy years later, nothing had been recovered, Evan convinced Haven to join him in looking for the treasure. It was Evan who dug the holes in the garden looking for the jewels and treasure, and it was him who put the diving spear in Birdman's garden to scare Birdman. Liz thought back to the day Evan found her in the shed. He knew where the light switch was because that was where he'd gotten the spear. And of course, it was Evan who trashed Birdman's cottage after Birdman, in a drunken stupor, told him about his father, the good, bad, and the ugly, then showed him one of his early sketchbooks, which was like a log of the time period in pictures.

When Evan finished his explanation, Liz asked, "What made you think Birdman's father buried the jewels and 1715 coins on the Bennett property?"

"It wasn't Birdman's father who buried them, it was his mother. A week ago when I got Birdman drunk, he started crying about his father's treatment of his mother. Telling me that his father was always presenting his mother with gifts after one of his indiscretions and how she would then bury them, not wanting to disgrace the family if the police came calling and searched the mansion."

"Who put the snake in Jameson's drawer?" Liz asked the pair.

"It was Nigel," Haven answered. "I didn't know my husband had it in him. In fact, I was quite impressed," she said, placing her hand on her stomach.

"Haven, what was your part in all this?" Liz asked. If Liz thought Haven looked pale through the window, in the candlelight she looked twice as bad.

"My part is simple and foolish," Haven said, taking deep breaths through her nose, then exhaling through her mouth. "If we could find the missing jewelry and the treasure from the Pieces of Eight Company, I wouldn't have to worry about money. The day you fell in that hole Evan dug, I was going to meet him and tell him I wanted out. Things had changed."

Liz knew what had changed; she was pregnant.

"What are you saying, Haven? You love me." Evan's whiny voice showed his age.

Haven gave him a dirty look. "I never promised that," she said, then clasped her stomach. "Something's wrong," she moaned. "I feel cramping. I need to go to a hospital."

Liz panicked. "I don't have a car. Only a golf cart."

Haven moaned again.

"Give me the keys," Evan said, rushing to Haven's side.

Liz grabbed her handbag from the counter. "No. I'll take her. The storm is getting worse and you don't know the way to the hotel. I do. Help me get her into the golf cart."

"I'll follow by foot," he said.

Liz draped one of her raincoats around Haven, then she and Evan helped her to the door. Liz pushed it open against the wind and it came back at her, walloping her shoulder. "Evan, I could use some help," she shouted over the wind, but he was too busy looking at the table with the sketchbooks. She saw where his loyalty lay. The same place Haven's did.

Show me the money!

Chapter 36

Dr. Crawford happened to be in the lobby when Liz came in with Haven. He took one look at Haven and dialed 911. While he sat with her, waiting for the ambulance, Liz heard her say, "Nigel, we're having a baby. At least I hope we are," she added, her voice strained, her eyes wide.

With tears in his eyes, he dropped to his knees and cradled his wife in his arms.

Well, that answers the question of who the father is.

Liz didn't want to interrupt the touching scene, but after she plugged her phone into the nearest outlet, she said, "While you wait for the ambulance, do you want me to go find Ryan? He used to be a first responder."

"No. Not necessary," Haven said, looking to her husband. "I feel better already, just knowing everything is out in the open."

Dr. Crawford looked confused for a moment, then smiled, no doubt realizing this wasn't the time or place for questions. He said, "Well, you're going to the hospital. No matter what." Then he took her hand and kissed it, just as Evan walked in looking like he was returning from the battlefield, twigs and palm fronds stuck in his dirty-blond hair. He took one look at the poignant scene, then stomped up the stairs. When he got halfway up, he called down. "You just wanted me for the money."

"What money?" Dr. Crawford asked.

"Exactly," Haven said, loud enough for her voice to carry up the staircase.

Evan said, "I'm leaving. Nothing to keep me here."

Liz went to the outlet she'd plugged her phone into and sent a text to Agent Bly. She knew the ambulance would come with a sheriff's car, but this was a different matter. Evan could still be Jameson's killer. After she put the phone down, she shouted, "Get your butt down here, Evan. You're not going anywhere. I contacted Agent Bly."

After the shock on Evan's face passed, he meekly came down the staircase, then sat as far away from Haven and her husband as possible. Liz felt like she was in an episode of *Peyton Place*. She didn't have time to analyze which one of the guests was more duplicitous than the other because Betty had appeared at the second-floor railing that overlooked the lobby. She called down, "Liz, you better send one of the EMTs up to the Sea Breeze Suite when they arrive. Although it's probably too late."

Then she motioned for Liz to come upstairs.

Chapter 37

"I've called Ryan. He's on his way," Betty said, waiting at the open outer door to Evan's and the professor's suite. "Hurry." She held her iPad in her arms, and her face was tearstained.

Liz rushed to Betty's side and followed her through the sitting room and into the bedroom where Professor Talbot was on the bed. A small, empty glass bottle laid on its side on the nightstand next to him. There was no skull and crossbones on a label, in fact there was no label at all, but Liz knew what had been in the bottle—poison dart frog venom.

"He's paralyzed," Betty whispered.

Professor Talbot was on his back with his hands folded over his chest in a coffin-like pose. A single tear trailed down his right cheek. He had a smile on his lips, frozen there, like a mortician had rigged his mouth with a wire.

"Isn't there anything we can do?" Liz asked.

Betty shook her head.

"Did someone do this to him? Evan?"

"No. He did this to himself. I have it all right here." Betty held up her iPad, then went to the bed, pulled over a chair, and sat. She smoothed her hand over his forehead. "It's okay, Walter," she lied. "Help is on the way. Hang on." Then she glanced back at Liz, who was watching the professor's eyes dart left then right, then up at the ceiling—frozen.

Liz remembered what Ryan had read to her about poison dart frog venom. There was no chance for recovery and no antidote.

Chapter 38

The storm came and two bodies left. One alive (Haven) and one dead (Professor Talbot).

Liz, Ryan, Betty, and Aunt Amelia were in the screening room, all quiet and trying to absorb Professor Talbot's confession to Betty that she'd recorded on Watson.

"The gist of it was," Betty said, "Walter found the breastplate when he was snooping around Jameson's suite last week."

"Just like Greta," Ryan said.

"Yes," Betty answered. "It didn't take a genius for Walter to guess what Jameson planned, especially after he remembered something about an auction this past spring in St. Augustine. After finding the newspaper notice of the auction, he printed it out and confronted Jameson. Jameson told him that when he'd won the Spanish breastplate at the auction, he'd registered his paddle in Professor Walter Talbot's name. If Walter didn't go along with what Jameson had planned, they would both go down together."

"But you found out that the auction was videotaped," Liz said. "The professor would have proof that it was Jameson using an alias. Did you tell him that before he took the poison?"

Betty shook her head. "No. We were in my rooms at the time. I had no idea he would do what he did. I didn't tell him about the video because I wanted to hear the rest of his story. It never pays to show your hand too early. But now I regret it; he might not have taken the poison if I had told him."

"Betty, why did he confess?" Liz asked.

"Because of what I found in his notebook."

Ryan said, "You did the right thing, Betty. He wouldn't have confessed to the murder if you'd told him about the videotaping of the auction."

"I suppose you're right," Betty said, "but I know I'm in for more than a few sleepless nights after this."

"We all are," Aunt Amelia said. It was the first time she'd spoken since they came into the screening room. Not like her at all, but understandable.

Betty continued, "Jameson told the professor about his plan to get the state to foreclose on Birdman's land after Birdman defaulted on paying his end-of-the-year property taxes. Jameson planned on building a development similar to Leon de Mar, only it would be even more spectacular because it would be built on the actual site Ponce de León's breastplate was found. Walter told me that Jameson had said, 'That's where the real treasure lies, in the land, my boy, in the land.'"

"How did Professor Talbot get ahold of the poison and the diving spear?" Ryan asked, leaning forward in his stadium seat, Aunt Amelia doing the same.

"Dr. Crawford had confided to him on the plane from Brazil that he'd brought the venom home with him. Even suggesting a minute amount might help with Walter's heart problems. The rest was easy. When Walter heard from Evan about the diving spear in Birdman's garden, he broke into Birdman's shed, stole it, and added the drops of venom from the bottle he'd taken from the Crawfords' suite to the three tines of the spear. All he had to do was wait for Jameson to show up at the dig site with the breastplate.

"When Jameson arrived, Walter suggested that he could take pictures of the breastplate from down in the pit. He already had the diving spear waiting at the bottom. As Jameson stepped down from the ladder, then turned for his photo op, Walter stabbed him with the forked diving spear. Then, as Jameson lay paralyzed, he got a shovel and started digging until one side of the wall collapsed. He grabbed the Spanish conquistador breastplate, took it up with him, then threw it into the sea."

"Wow. That's quite a story," Ryan said. "I'm surprised he'd throw away something so rare."

"His reputation was everything to him. Walter knew the breastplate would be linked to the auction," Betty explained.

"Liz," Ryan said. "I forgot to tell you that Agent Bly cleared up what that key we found in Mr. Royce's cell phone case belonged to. A safety deposit box that had architectural drawings for a new housing development that included the Bennett property, the Indialantic by the Sea, and the neighboring land to the south, but no treasure, artifacts, or cash."

"So, Jameson didn't care about proving anything about Ponce de León's landing...just about land." Liz turned to Betty, who was holding Aunt Amelia's hand, one macaw perched on each of her great-aunt's shoulders.

Both birds were being eerily quiet. "What was in the notebook that made the professor confess?"

Betty showed them the photo of the page from the notebook. *Located newspaper clipping of auction. Called. They confirmed it was I who bought it. Even had my social security number on file. I won't let J bring me down with him. If this gets out, I'm ruined. J doesn't understand the scientific community, and how rare the object is. Soon it will be traced to the auction. I can't let it happen.*

It seemed it wasn't as complicated as most of the murders Liz and company had been involved in recently; it was simply a question of the professor's reputation being more important than his life. Three dead bodies (or bones, in one case) in less than three weeks. A new record. It was time to ban any outside guests from checking into the Indialantic.

"I let him leave my suite to get his raincoat," Betty said. "I waited a few minutes, then went down to his suite. But he'd already taken the poison. He told me he didn't want Birdman to be prosecuted for his crime, saying he only had a short time to live anyway, because of his heart. That's why he came out of retirement. He knew he didn't have long to live."

"I'm sorry," Liz said to Betty.

"Don't be sorry. He murdered someone. It was premeditated, and you don't get a hall pass for that."

"I suppose not," Liz said.

Chapter 39

When Ryan dropped Liz off at her beach house around one in the morning, she tried to sleep but couldn't. The storm was raging, and the pounding of the wind matched her heartbeat as she tossed and turned. Giving up on sleep, she left Bronte under the covers, then padded into the great room. The power had returned while she'd been at the Indialantic, but she wouldn't be surprised if she lost it again.

She made a cup of Aunt Amelia's Slumber Sonata tea and sat at the dining room table, still piled with Birdman's sketchbooks and his mother's diary. She opened the diary and thumbed through it. On most of the pages, Millie would add a few lines about her day, nothing earth-shattering, and usually about Birdman, whom she called Bertie. Occasionally, she would add a few lines or a complete poem from a classical poet that related to her day. In the middle of the diary, Liz saw an entry that referred to Liz's great-grandmother, mentioning how grateful Millie was to be spending time with her in the orchid house. Millie's time in the orchid house was just as Aunt Amelia had told Liz and Birdman the other day: the orchid house was an escape from when her husband Rory was home from his philandering, trying to buy her love with trinkets that Millie would dispose of as soon as he left again, knowing they were stolen.

Bronte came into the room and rubbed against her ankle, almost like she was saying, "Come back to bed." Liz felt drowsy from the tea and melancholy about the professor's death. "Only one more entry," she told Bronte, "then to bed." She flipped to the last entry in the diary, which was dated August 12, 1958.

He's gone. They found his body on the beach. Was it only last week that the police were here asking about his latest theft? I covered for him as I always do. For Bertie's sake, I'm getting rid of all of it before they come calling again. Can't take a chance. My pineapple goddess will be their tomb.

How cryptic, Liz thought. She wondered if Birdman had read this and what he thought of it.

Below the entry were a few lines of poetry:

> *This little lime-tree bower, have I not marked*
> *Much that has soothed me. Pale beneath the blaze*
> *Hung the transparent foliage; and I watched*
> *Some broad and sunny leaf, and loved to see*
> *The shadow of the leaf and stem above.*
> *—S. Coleridge*

Later, as Liz lay in bed, the words "pineapple goddess" kept repeating in her head, which she supposed was better than a vision of Professor Talbot's unblinking eyes staring up at the ceiling.

Sometime around three in the morning she must have drifted off to sleep.

When Bronte nudged her awake, Liz shot up in her bed like she'd been zapped with an electrical current. "Hurry with me to the kitchen, Bronte. Mommy has something she has to do before Birdman comes home."

After feeding Bronte, not even brushing her teeth or grabbing a cup of coffee, she hurriedly dressed, remembered to wear hiking boots, not sneakers, then flew out the door and down the steps to the beach. The sun was shining, and if not for all the seaweed and debris the ocean had kicked up during the storm, she would never have known that last night they'd had a brush with Tropical Storm Odette.

At the beach dig site, she grabbed a shovel, then hurried to the crumbling mansion.

She had a hunch where to find the jewelry from her great-grandmother's party and the Pieces of Eight Company's treasure.

When she reached the lime tree in what used to be the center courtyard of the mansion, she looked over at the statue holding the basket of pineapples— Millie's pineapple goddess—and started to dig.

Chapter 40

Liz and Ryan were standing backstage at the Melbourne Beach Theatre Company. The theater was packed. Liz could tell from the applause and cheers after every outfit inspired by midcentury Barbie fashions made it down the runway that Francie's clothing line was a huge hit.

"I can't believe Dad and Charlotte aren't here on time. I know their plane arrived in Orlando this morning. I bet they're both being cowards about being in the fashion show."

"Can you blame them?" Ryan asked. He was holding a shaving kit and was dressed in a pale blue terry cloth robe with a monogrammed *F* on the pocket, and wore matching terry cloth slippers. A towel was draped over his right arm that said *His*.

They had walked down the runway together. Liz's coordinating sleepwear looked like something Doris Day might have worn in the movie *Pillow Talk*—two-piece baby-blue satin pajamas under a long dark blue velvet robe with satin lapels, pink plastic mules with light blue pom-poms, and pink curlers in her hair.

"Your father was supposed to wear this outfit, hence the *F* for Fenton on the pocket," Ryan said. "I already paid my penance with that last outfit I had to wear."

"Listen, let's just be happy that it's almost over. Maybe it would be nice to get away earlier than we planned? Although I'm enjoying how quiet everything is around here, after Evan Watkins and the Crawfords vacated the Indialantic, and I'm thrilled that Birdman is home and back to his sketching."

Ryan added, "And Aunt Amelia has her mother's bracelet and the Pieces of Eight Company their coins. You know, you didn't have to give the reward from them to Birdman."

"Of course I did," she said. "He needed to pay off the tax lien on his property, and anyway, my agent in New York is trying to get him a publishing contract with one of the big three for his sketchbooks so there won't be any worry about future bills."

"So proud of you, my little sleuth. Maybe you should get a PI's license?"

"Oh, no. I'm busy enough with my next book, *A Walk on the Moors*. It's going to be tricky because I've decided to try to tie in the last two books with the third. I've realized how intricately mixed the past is with the present. It's like a thread that shouldn't be broken. And I also have to keep Aunt Amelia in line; *Madeline in Melbourne Beach* goes into production in two weeks. God save us all."

"Speaking of which," Ryan said, looking behind Liz's head.

Aunt Amelia waddled up to them in a black strapless sequined dress that clung to her every curve and ended at her ankles in a profusion of black tulle. Barnacle Bob was on her left shoulder and Carmen Miranda on her right. Her great-aunt was modeling Francie's interpretation of Barbie's Solo in the Spotlight ensemble, which Aunt Amelia had insisted on wearing because it came with full-length black gloves, a pink organza hankie, and an old-school standing microphone that she'd carried down the runway at the start of the fashion show to thunderous applause. Liz had to wonder if it was the macaws that they were applauding. Either way, she'd made quite an impression.

"Lizzy, Ryan, what are we going to do? Fenton and Charlotte were supposed to wear the tuxedo and wedding dress! And they're not here. It's the end of the show!"

Ryan backed up and Liz went with him. Liz said, "What's that look in your eye, Auntie?"

"Come on, dears. It's for charity, and a chance to get Francie contracts with all the department store buyers in the audience. There's press and everything. We can't let her down." Without waiting for their answer, she grabbed each of them by the arm and dragged them to her dressing room. Then she pulled their outfits from the rolling rack and said, "Here! Get dressed! No dillydallying. I'm meant to announce these last fashions while Francie gets in line to walk behind you for the finale." With that, Aunt Amelia turned and left them alone in the dressing room.

They both did as they were told and put on the clothes tagged with her father's and Charlotte's names.

Ryan struggled with his tie and Liz came over to help.

"Wow!" Ryan said, adding a whistle. "Don't you look stunning in that wedding dress! Although I think you should take the curlers out of your hair."

Liz laughed and adjusted his tie. "All this reminds me of when I did some modeling in New York. Can't say I miss it, but I'm willing to do anything to make Francie's launch a huge success."

Assistant hotel manager Susannah Shay burst into the dressing room and announced in her no-nonsense military fashion, "Chop chop. Get in line. You're up!"

After Liz fixed her hair and makeup in Aunt Amelia's lighted dressing-table mirror, they hurried backstage. Through the gap in the curtain they could see the stage had been set up by the theater's prop department to be a replica of Liz's cardboard Barbie Fashion Salon from 1965.

Suddenly, the lights in the theater dimmed and a smoke machine fogged the stage.

"Okay, go!" Susannah said, placing a hand on each of their shoulders and pushing them onto the stage and into the dense mist.

Liz was disorientated for a moment, but when Ryan grabbed her hand, she got her bearings. Ryan must have been nervous, because his hand was damp with perspiration.

In front of them, through the fog on the opposite side of the stage, Liz saw Aunt Amelia's hazy outline standing behind a podium. Liz knew this was supposed to be the big finale where Aunt Amelia announced her father and Charlotte as Mr. and Mrs. Holt, husband and wife.

Liz and Ryan stopped in the center of the stage facing a runway that had been built down the main aisle of the theater. The lights brightened, and Liz saw her father and Charlotte sitting in the front row. *What are they doing here?* They must have just arrived. Should she stop the show and have them put on the wedding attire? Or at least pull them up onstage? She didn't have to decide because Aunt Amelia announced, "Would our wedding couple please stay where they are for a moment." *Both* macaws and Aunt Amelia broke into song, singing, "Here comes the bride, all dressed in white...."

Liz glanced at Ryan and he gave her a goofy look. Then he got down on one knee, reached in his pocket, and pulled out a ring box. He opened it, and with a nervous grin said, "Elizabeth Amelia Holt, will you do me the honor of becoming my wife?"

Balloons and confetti dropped from the ceiling.

Because of the cheers and whistles coming from the audience, Liz didn't know if anyone but Ryan heard her immediate answer.

Of course, this was all your idea, Auntie, Liz thought, glancing over at her great-aunt as Ryan stood and slipped her great-grandmother's emerald-and-diamond ring on her finger. It fit perfectly.

"Is this part of the fashion show?" she stuttered.

"No," he said, "this is for real. Forever and ever."

Then he took her in his arms.

Recipes from Fenton and Charlotte's Wedding Brunch Celebration

Smoked Salmon Triangles

Ingredients:

    1 container of whipped cream cheese
    1 loaf of cocktail rye bread
    Thin sliced nova lox smoked salmon
    Capers to taste
    Snipped fresh dill

Directions:

Spread cream cheese on bread. Add a thin slice of salmon. Sprinkle with capers and fresh dill.

Pear, Caramelized Onion, and Brie Flatbread

Ingredients:

1 whole ripe pear, peeled, cored, and sliced
1/2 pound pizza dough (you can find fresh pound loaves of dough at your local bakery or grocery store and freeze the other half)
4 ounces brie cheese, sliced, but not too thin
1 medium onion (or sweet Vidalia onion) halved and thinly sliced
Olive oil
Salt and pepper to taste

Directions:

Preheat oven to 450.

Heat a generous drizzle of oil in a medium skillet set over medium-high heat and sauté the onion for 5 minutes, or until soft and turning golden.

Divide the dough in half and roll or stretch out one half into a 9-inch circle or oval.

Place on a parchment-lined or floured baking sheet. Top with brie, caramelized onions, and pear slices.

Sprinkle with salt and pepper and drizzle with olive oil.

Bake for 15–20 minutes, until golden.

Let rest on a cooling rack for 2–3 minutes and serve.

Chef Pierre's French Toast

Ingredients:

    1 day-old French baguette, sliced 3/4" to 1" thick
Vegetable cooking spray
1 tablespoon melted butter
Maple syrup, berries with whipped cream, or powdered sugar (optional)

    Custard:

    3 whole eggs
3 egg yolks
3/4 cup heavy cream
3/4 cup half-and-half
1 tablespoon vanilla extract
1/4 cup Cointreau or Grand Marnier (can use orange juice concentrate as substitute)
1/4 teaspoon cinnamon

Directions:

In a large baking dish, place sliced bread in a single layer. Add custard ingredients to a large bowl and whip with a wire whisk until frothy. Pour custard evenly over the bread. Let the bread soak up the custard for about an hour, flipping the bread every 15 minutes (depending how dry the bread is).

Heat a griddle to medium heat or 375.

Spray vegetable cooking spray on the griddle.

Put melted butter on the griddle and immediately place your bread in a single layer. (You will do this more than once to finish all the bread.)

Brown on one side and flip over, cooking until brown on second side.

Place on a warmed serving dish and cover with foil to keep warm while the balance is completed.

Serve with maple syrup, berries with whipped cream, or powdered sugar. Or as Liz likes it, all three!

Sweet and Spicy Candied Bacon

Ingredients:

Bacon
Crushed red pepper
Cayenne pepper
Black pepper
Brown sugar

Directions:

Preheat oven to 350.
Place a wire rack on top of a foil-lined baking sheet.
Arrange the bacon on the wire rack and sprinkle lightly with crushed red pepper, cayenne pepper, and black pepper. Lightly pat the brown sugar on top of the bacon slices to create a thin layer.
Place the baking sheet in the oven and bake for 30–40 minutes or until the bacon is crisp and the brown sugar has melted. Remove from the oven and allow to cool for 10 minutes.
Using tongs, transfer the bacon to a parchment-lined baking sheet and let cool until it reaches room temperature.
Can be stored at room temperature in an airtight container for up to 3 days.

Roasted Tomato Caprese Salad

Ingredients:

    12 plum tomatoes, halved, with seeds removed
    1/4 cup olive oil, plus extra for drizzling
    1 1/2 tablespoons balsamic vinegar
    2 large garlic cloves, minced
    2 teaspoons sugar
    1 1/2 teaspoons salt
    1 1/2 teaspoons pepper
    16 ounces fresh salted mozzarella
    12 fresh basil leaves, julienned
    Salt and pepper to taste

Directions:

Preheat oven to 450.

Arrange tomatoes in a single layer on a sheet pan with the cut sides up.

Drizzle with 1/4 cup of olive oil, and balsamic vinegar. Sprinkle with garlic, salt, and pepper. Roast for 25 minutes or until tomatoes begin to caramelize. Allow to cool.

Cut the mozzarella into slices thinner than ½″. Layer the tomatoes alternately with the mozzarella on a serving platter and scatter the basil on top. Sprinkle lightly with salt and pepper and drizzle lightly with olive oil.

Watermelon-Cucumber Salad

Ingredients:

      6 cups watermelon, diced
      3 Persian cucumbers, thinly sliced
      3 tablespoons olive oil
      3 tablespoons red wine vinegar
      1 teaspoon sea salt
      1 teaspoon pepper
      1/4 cup crumbled feta cheese
      1/4 cup mint leaves

Directions:

In a large bowl add watermelon, cucumbers, olive oil, red wine vinegar, salt, and pepper. Toss gently to combine. Divide onto chilled salad plates; then garnish with feta cheese and mint leaves. Or use one large serving bowl and garnish with feta and mint. Makes 6 servings.

Berry Spritzers

Ingredients:

      1/2 pound mixed berries
      1/2 cup fresh basil
      3 tablespoons fresh orange juice
      3 tablespoons sugar
      2 tablespoons fresh lemon juice
      Club soda

Directions:

Add berries, basil, orange juice, sugar, and lemon juice to a large glass pitcher. Stir until sugar is dissolved and some berries have broken down. Let stand for 10 minutes.

Fill individual glasses with crushed ice. Pour berry mixture over ice; then top with club soda.

About the Author

Kathleen Bridge is the author of the By the Sea Mystery series and the Hamptons Home and Garden Mystery series, published by Berkley. She started her writing career working at the Michigan State University News in East Lansing, Michigan. A member of Sisters in Crime and Mystery Writers of America, she is also the author and photographer of an antiques reference guide, *Lithographed Paper Toys, Books, and Games*. She teaches creative writing in addition to working as an antiques and vintage dealer in Melbourne, Florida. Kathleen blissfully lives on a barrier island.

Readers can visit her on the web at www.kathleenbridge.com.

Keep reading for a special excerpt!

Liz Holt is bewitched, bothered, and bewildered when a wicked killer objects to a wiccan wedding . . .

Island life can get pretty weird. Wiccan weddings, psychic brides, mermaid parades, eccentric parrots . . . Novelist Liz Holt has gotten used to it since moving back to the barrier island of Melbourne Beach, Florida, and once again working in her family's hotel and emporium, the Indialantic by the Sea. But one thing she'll never get used to is murder.

Groom-to-be and leader of the Sunshine Wiccan Society, white warlock Julian Rhodes is poisoned at his rehearsal dinner on the hotel's sightseeing cruiser. His psychic bride, Dorian Starwood, never saw it coming. An old friend of Liz's great-aunt Amelia, the celebrity psychic engages Liz to find out who intended to kill her intended. With her macaw, Barnacle Bob, squawking "Pop Goes the Weasel" at Dorian's pet ferret, and the streets teeming with mermaids in tails, Liz has got to wade through the weirdness and cast a wide net for the killer—before she's the next one to sleep with the fishes . . .

Don't miss Evil by the Sea, on sale now!

Printed in the United States
by Baker & Taylor Publisher Services